Triple Crown Publications Presents

A Project Chick

Compilation and Introduction copyright © 2004 by
Triple Crown Publications
4449 Easton Way, 2nd Floor
Columbus, Ohio 43219
www.TripleCrownPublications.com

Library of Congress Control Number: 2004100381
ISBN # 0-9702472-6-5
ISBN 13 # 978-0-9702472-6-1
Cover Design/Graphics: www.MarionDesigns.com
Author: Nikki Turner
Editor: Clifford Benton
Consulting: Vickie M. Stringer

First Trade Paperback Edition Printing February 2004
10

Printed in the United States of America

Dedication

This book is dedicated to:
Mrs. Margaret L. Scott

My grandmother, friend, backbone, shopping partner and a true diva, I could not have gotten here without your unconditional love, blessings, prayers and the positive influence you've had over my life.

AND

To every single mother left to fin for herself!
Your struggle is not in vain!
This is for you!

-1-
Another One Bites the Dust

Tressa weaved in and out of the slow moving traffic, swiftly trying to make her way up the Powhite Parkway. She watched the clock on the Pioneer tape deck like a hawk every minute on the minute. She was fully aware time was not on her side. She looked ahead and noticed all the red brake lights in front of her. Traffic ahead had come to a screeching halt, due to the construction of trying to add one more lane to the highway. Frustration was setting in as her twin boys both started to cry at the top of their lungs. Meanwhile, nothing was moving ahead of her. *Lord, if I can just make it up to the Glenside Drive exit, I can hop off and take the scenic route home.*

While sitting in the same spot for three minutes, almost one quarter of a mile away from an alternate exit, and after splitting one little Huggie juice evenly between the twins to try to quiet them down, Tressa never thought twice about hopping onto the median strip to get to the exit. The unpaved median strip was very uneven because of the construction. Tressa hit bump after bump. When she came to the end of the exit, she was unsure about which way to turn, left or right. *I guess I'll go right because if I get on the main road, there will be plenty of traffic from the people who are avoiding the construction on the highway. Plus, there will be less lights.*

A quarter mile away from the main road, Tressa could feel the bump, bump, bump, while going on a heavy shake and then heard a loud roaring noise on top of the twins crying, coming from her late model BMW station

1

wagon. The car was slowing down as she steered to the side of the road. *Shit!!!!!* She opened up the door and walked around the car. The back passenger tire had a flat. "FUCK!!!! A fucking flat!" She screamed.

When Tressa screamed, she startled the babies and they automatically stopped crying. She shook her head and stomped around to the driver's side to get her cell phone so she could call her extremely, possessive, domineering, controlling, obsessive, deranged, jealous, boyfriend and childrens' father, Khalil, only to realize that as of yesterday, she didn't have a cell phone. Why? Because psycho Khalil broke it because she missed one of his calls when she was trying to put both of the twins in the car. It didn't matter that she would call him right back. Not to mention that this was the second phone in the past month he'd broken and had to replace. Just last week, he broke her other cell phone while arguing with her about one of his "other" women that she found out about.

Now ain't this some shit? This is some motherfucking shit!!!!

Now, Tressa was no "Soccer Mom", and if she had to be judged as one, she'd be considered the prissiest one the Soccer field would ever encounter. She had smooth, unblemished mahogany skin with a beauty mole over top of the right side of her lip. Her shoulder length black hair was always covered up with some type of flawless weave, in which the color, length and style, at any given time, were subject to change at least once a week. Wearing hair weaves was a skill she had mastered. Though she mostly dealt with hair on the track, she somehow learned how to run her fingers through her hair as if it was her natural hair. Tressa was 5'7", with long firm legs and a very shapely frame. Although she had just given birth to twins only twenty months before, childbirth had no bearing on her body. She possessed not one stretch mark, cellulite, roll or piece of flab on her entire body. It actually improved the size of her already firm B cup breast, and took her to a well-desired D cup. With that in mind, she purposely wore shirts that showed off her cleavage. Tressa naturally had a voluminous butt, which could stop traffic on any given day. With the combination of the way her hips fit right in with her small 27-inch waist, which actually enhanced her butt, she was declared a "brick house" at the early age of fourteen. Though Tressa was simply beautiful in the face and could have plainly pursued a career in modeling, her trademarks were her brick house shape and her lip-gloss, which gave her the sexiest lips in Richmond.

Tressa didn't work, but she dressed everyday as if she was going to a job, heels and all, while pushing the baby carriage.   She never left the house without being picture perfect.   Her hair and makeup were on point, and whether the outfit was casual or formal, her appearance was put together as if she was a contestant in a beauty pageant.

Motherhood was a natural for Tressa.   She handled those two chubby boys like they weighed 2 pounds each. Though she was only twenty years old, she was very responsible for her children.   She took them everywhere she went, mainly because she didn't have a choice.   Psycho Khalil was not standing for anyone looking after his children except their mother.   It was another one of Khalil's ulterior motives.   He felt if he stuck her with two young babies, gave her a station wagon to drive, an extravagant lifestyle and a phat engagement ring for her left ring finger, no one would want her.   He thought, "What man in their right mind is going to want to even try to touch this ready-made family?"   However, his role as husband and "daddy dearest" only applied when he was in the privacy of their home.   Other than that, she was a single mother dressed up to look like a wife.   That was one of the things in her life that she had no problem with, being a mother to HER kids.

Tressa wanted to be everything to her boys that her mother was to her, before being taken away from her.   She could remember the last time she laid eyes on her mother. She was fifteen years old.   It is a scene she tries to block out of her mind, but she recalls it when she needs to draw strength in order to be strong for her twins.

Tressa popped the trunk to get the spare out to change the tire.   She hoped that she had some sneakers, by chance in the trunk to change into, but in all actuality she knew she didn't.   *Shit, I knew I should have bought those Hurriache Nikes I seen in the damn mall.   Nope, instead, I bought those Via Spiegel sandals.   I just had to have those, didn't I?*

3

She tore the trunk up looking for the spare tire only to remember that Khalil had removed the spare tire, because he felt she didn't need another guy to change the tire. That's what he'd do. Tressa was sweating after taking all her bags, plus that heavy double stroller, out of the car. She was mad, frustrated, pissed off and had gotten dirt on her clothes from the flat tire. To top it off, her weave was sweating and getting out of place.

This nigga is so damn stupid. Now look at his kids and me, out here on the side of the fucking road with a damn flat in this prejudice white-ass neighborhood! I have no spare, no cell phone, and plus it's getting dark. Now what kind of SHIT is this?

She shook her head first, sighed, took a deep breath and grabbed the stroller and started to assemble it. Once it was assembled, she pushed it around to the passenger side of the car and grabbed Lil Hadji out of the car, strapped him into the stroller and did the same thing with Lil Ali.

Ali, the more outgoing one asked. "Mommeee were we going?"

Hadji looked to his mother to answer his brother. Tressa kneeled down, and explained. "Baby, our car broke down and we have to go get help. So, mommy's going to need you to be really good, and when we get to the store, I'll get you a snack, OK?" Both boys agreed by shaking their heads and smiling.

Tressa grabbed the Gucci bag that she used for a diaper bag and her Gucci pocketbook to match. But before she put the pocketbook across her shoulders, she reached into it, grabbed her switchblade and put it in her pocket, and started out on her quest to the gas station. She kept telling herself that it wouldn't be long before they got there. She began singing the Barney Song "I Love You, You Love Me" to the kids to make them feel more relaxed and to make the time go by. The kids began to sing with her.

She continued to sing as she thought to herself, *God, please give me the strength to leave this simple man. God, you know I don't know how much more of this I can take. Lord, please get this nigga out of my life. I don't care if you make him get locked up, or make him just flee.. Pleeeaasse just let him find someone who can suck his dick so good and make him forget about us. I don't even care*

4

*about the money no more. I know this ain't what you want
for me Lord. Please Lord.*

Her thoughts were broken within minutes when a
few passerbys slowed up to ask her if she needed a ride.
The first was two white men, they were a little too pressed
to help. Her first thought was, *could they be the KKK in
disguise? Shoot, they were driving a white S-10 pick-up
truck.* The next was a man who looked like he could be
either one of two things, cracked out or schizophrenic.

"Hey yo, you need a ride?"

"No, thank you, I am just going to this house just
right up ahead." Tressa said calmly, while grabbing her
switchblade.

The third car, a spanking, brand new Range Rover
with thirty-day tags on it, drove pass and pulled over up
ahead of her. He parked on the side of the road, cut his car
off and she saw him step out. He was a sharply dressed
brother, if she must say so herself. He was wearing a
chocolate brown silk suit with some light brown Ostrich
skin shoes, with the belt to match. Without a doubt, he
was dressed as clean as the board of health! By no means
could his appearance be taken lightly. She looked down at
her boys and Hadji had fallen asleep, and just as she gazed
at Ali, he asked. "Who dat, mommy?"

"Baby, I don't know, but listen to mommy very
carefully, if he tries to touch you, your brother or mommy,
you bite him as hard as you can. OK?"

"OK mommy." Lil Ali responded to his mother, in
complete obedience.

As the guy approached, he asked. "Ma'am you need
some help changing your tire back there." He said in a
sincere tone.

"No, I'm fine."

"Listen Ma'am, I am not going to hurt you. Listen, I
have a sister, a pregnant girlfriend and a mother who I
would want someone, just like myself, to help her if she got
a flat." He was just as earnest as he could be.

"I really appreciate the gesture, but we'll be fine."
Tressa said, trying to assure the man. As bad as she
wanted to take the help, she just couldn't accept a ride from
a strange man.

5

"Look, I understand why you wouldn't want to accept help, but you and your kids shouldn't be out here."

As he got closer, she looked like a familiar face. He recognized her.

"Hey, aren't you Taj's little sister, ummm Tressa?" She smiled in relief, but hesitated to speak. If anyone had seen her, they have seen Taj. They were the spitting image of each other.

"I am Peako, me and Taj used to hustle together before he fell and caught his last case." He cheerfully said.

Tressa was glad to hear his name. Her brother always had positive things to say about Peako, so she knew that God had sent her an angel in disguise to rescue her from this dark road.

Peako spoke out. "Now that you know I am practically like family, get in the truck and I will take you back to your car to change the spare."

Tressa embarrassingly said. "There is no spare. I only need to make a phone call."

He handed her the cell phone and went to get little Ali, and he bit him as hard as he could. "Ouch!" Peako yelled. Tressa sort of chuckled a bit to herself about how much spunk her not yet 2 year-old son had.

She tried calling Khalil to let him know the situation, but his voice mail came on after the first ring, which let her know his phone was powered off. She tried three more times and left him messages and Peako's phone number.

"Hey Baby, it's me. The kids and me caught a flat tire on Horsepen Road. There was no spare in the trunk. Luckily one of my brother's friends passed by and is giving us a ride. If you get this message, please call us back at this number." She looked over to Peako to ask him for his number.

Peako called it out. "307-7777."

She brought the message to an end. "Love you, bye."

They hopped in his truck and went back to the station wagon and retrieved the children's car seats. Peako practiced strapping the seats in and boasted on his expecting girlfriend. They laughed and mostly talked about her big brother Taj.

6

Peako could see the disappointment in her facial expression when he mentioned Taj's name. "I'm going to drop you off at home, and I have a friend who can just come and tow your car for you, so it won't be left out here as an abandoned car."

"Thanks, I appreciate it." She graciously said.

"So, have you heard from your brother?"

"Yeah." Tressa said, distracted as she wondered why Khalil's phone was powered off.

"Yeah, I haven't heard from him since he fell a few years ago, but I always drop him a few dollars, when I can. Taj was a good nigga, and as long as I got it, he got it. I wrote him a few times, but you know how he is, he don't write back. I don't trip on that tho, cause I know how he looked out for me when he was out here getting money."

There was a brief silence between them. Tressa's mind was set on trying to figure out what in the world was so important that he didn't have his phone on. *He tells me the only reason why he leaves us, is because he has to feed us. There is money to be made. Now, he works off of his phone, and if his phone is off, how is he making any money?*

To snap out of her negative thoughts, Tressa tried to make small talk with Peako. Shoot, it was the least she could do, he had came to her rescue when Khalil was nowhere to be found.

"So, you mentioned that your girlfriend is expecting a baby?" She asked, while removing her black roller wrapped weave out of her face and placed it behind her ear.

"Yes, in three more months, actually in 87 more days. We are going to the doctor's in the morning to find out if it's a boy or a girl."

"Oooh, that's so sweet! What do you want?"

While trying to keep his eyes on the road but glancing at Tressa with a big Joker smile all across his face, "I don't care, as long as it's healthy. Boy or girl, I am going to love it the same."

Just as they approached the stoplight, Hadji woke up whining. Tressa and Peako both turned around to give their attention to Hadji, when out of nowhere they heard a loud noise. "Boom, Boom, Boom, Boom, Boom, Boom, Boom!"

Tressa felt this brief warm shower of fluid spread all over her and everything else became a blur. In a split second she took a look to realize that the fluid was really blood; she wasn't sure if it was hers or her children. Then the loud noise again. "Boom, Boom, Boom, Boom!"

All she could see was brains and meat scattered over the windshield. She couldn't even see Peako's head attached to his body anymore. All she saw was his shoulders and she could no longer hear her babies and the car was rolling fast until it hit a pole.

"Oh my fucking God!!! God please no! Lord, please don't let my babies be dead." Still in shock, she had no idea if she was hit or not. She opened up the door and before she could get out of the truck to grab the children, she felt someone jerking her out of the jeep. All she could see was a glimpse of a tattoo with some dice and the name Lucky through a banner.

"Look what the fuck you made me do? Your stupid ass, wanna be creeping with some player ass nigga with my fucking kids. Are you crazy or what? Now see how I love you." Khalil said calmly in a mellow tone as he pushed her out of the way while grabbing Hadji's whole baby seat.

"Now, grab Ali and put him in my car and you get in my damn car too." Still in shock, she did as she was told without any questions or back talk. She went over to his car that still sat in the turning lane, with the signal light on which had he made the turn, the only place the road lead to is the Wyndham hotel.

He sat Hadji's car seat on the ground with the baby in it and took his white towel from around his neck and started wiping the passenger side of the car down in a brisk manner. He ran over to his car and placed Hadji in the back seat, and as he looked, he saw the girl that was in the car with him fleeing down the street praying for a successful getaway. But Khalil ran up behind her.

"Boom!" First one shot to the right leg causing her to stumble, but she was still trying to get away. There was no way he was going to let her escape.

"Boom, Boom!" The next shots were to the back of her head. He speed-walked back to the car, hopped in and drove off calmly. He never stopped until he reached the

8

garage of their baby mansion, a $280,000 house on the James River.

The entire ride was silent until he cut on a mixed CD and Tupac's song, a remake of an old song was playing. Khalil began to sing the words to "What You Won't Do For Love." He played it over and over again until they got home. He cut the engine off in the car and grabbed her under the chin and twisted so that she would face him.

"Look at me." He said in a relaxed tone.

Tressa could not even stand to look at him in his face, but she knew she had to. She didn't know what he had in store for her and the kids. She looked at him in his eyes.

"Think about it before you decide you wanna creep out on a brother, because every time I catch you, it's gonna cost you. I'm gonna make sho' you watch me kill the nigga, because that's what you made me do. Now, the next time you wanna be entertaining a nigga, think about how much it's gonna cost him. His life and that shit will be all your fault! Believe it, and I mean that from the heart." He raised his voice. "This Shit is Not A Fucking Joke!"

Khalil searched Tressa's face, looking for some sort of fear, but there was none that he could see.

"Now go in the house and give my sons a bath, and clean up yo self."

She reached in and grabbed Ali, he picked up Hadji and they took both children in the house. She put Hadji down and lit the fireplace to take the chill off the downstairs part of the house.

"Hurry up and take those clothes off you and the kids and give em' to me." She didn't say a word, just did what she was told. After changing her clothes, she proceeded to put both kids in the bathtub. As she kneeled down to wash sprinkles of blood off of the boys, she could hear Khalil come in the bathroom, but she never acknowledged him.

"Now where is your car?"

"Still on Route 280 with a flat I guess, unless the police towed it."

"With a flat?" He asked baffled.

"Yes, didn't you check your messages?" She asked, still keeping her back turned to him and concentrating on washing the boys' hair.

"Nope, I sure didn't."

"Yeah, well I left you a few messages, telling you that we had a flat. I had no cell phone because you broke it. Remember? Then, not to mention, you took the spare out of the car, which meant I had no spare either. So, that dude was nice enough to give us a ride home while you out creeping on the late night, on your way to the Wyndham hotel. What you do with your Number One Hooker in the car? You ride up just like The Sho-Gun Bandit and you, once again, go into a jealous rage and take two innocent lives! Why; all because you wanna be a hoe? But, I bet while you were planning your little rendezvous, I was the last person you was anticipating on seeing, huh? Remember baby, this isn't New York, this is Richmond."

He was quiet for a minute as he listened. Then he tried to make a joke. "Oh, well. Shit, another one bites the dust. That nigga should've been kilt. He gonna pay all that damn money for a Range Rover, and too cheap to pay the few extra thousand to get the 4.6. All he got is a 4.0. He ain't no real player anyway." Khalil said, while laughing.

Tressa stared at him for a long minute and just shook her head. When Khalil saw that she wasn't laughing, he took a more serious approach.

"Baby, I am sooo sorry. I apologize, please forgive me. I'll do whatever I need to do to make it right." He stood in the bathroom doorway, begging for her forgiveness.

"Make it right?" She asks as she got the boys out of the tub and dried them off with their towels. She sent them to their room. As she followed them to their room, Khalil grabbed her hand.

"I really am sorry, baby."

Yeah, I know you are sorry, a sorry ass nigga, she said to herself, but wouldn't dare say it out loud to him. She was pretty sure she was out of the clear with him because he realized that he was indeed in the wrong, not her. As he watched her tuck the kids into bed, she handed him a book.

"Read them a story while I take a shower, please."
He did as he was asked. But as he was close to finishing,
both boys were fast asleep.

As she got out of the shower, he stuck his head into
the bathroom.

"I've got to go get your car, don't try nothing stupid
while I'm gone either." She nodded and he kissed her on
the forehead.

After she heard him make a phone call and tell the
person he needed him to go with him to change the tire, he
exited the house. Usually she'd put up a fuss when he left
back out after dark, but not this night. She was glad he
was gone. She hurried and put her bathrobe on and stood
to the side of the window, so he wouldn't see her shadow.
Once she heard the bottom of his bumper scrape the end of
the driveway, she ran to the door to see what car he took so
she could find the keys for the other car, only to find he had
locked her in the house. The cunning fella had put the top
lock on the door and taken the key with him. *Asshole!*

There was no other way out and she knew it. The
house was built like a fortress to withstand the toughest
storm. In Khalil's eyes, the toughest storm wouldn't be a
hurricane or tornado, it would be the DEA, feds, vice or the
narcotics kick-in squad. The bottom of the house was
made of concrete and reinforced steel. The front and back
doors were also made of steel, but trimmed in wood, all of
which was camouflaged and intelligently disguised with
decorations. No intruder would ever be aware of the
physical strength of the house, making it so there was no
way to break in or break out.

"SHIT!!!!!!" She screamed, and then just broke down
crying. This was the cry that had been waiting to explode
all night long.

Tressa did not know what to do. What would or
should her next move be? She wished her brother, Taj, who
had always bailed her out of every other jam she had in her
life, was here to rescue her. But, that was impossible,
because Taj was in prison doing a twenty-year bid. There
would be no time cuts, sentence reductions or anything.
See, Taj was true to the game. He wasn't anybody's rat,
coward or snitch. He was a conscious player in the game,
and was fully aware of all the consequences of the game,

11

and was prepared to sleep in the bed he made when the heat came. It hurts Tressa to her heart that her brother has to be away from her for so long. She fully respects the rules and principles of the game that he molded into her.

-2-
A Sister's Love

T ressa wondered to herself how did she ever let the situation get this out of control. It only seemed like yesterday that it was her eighteenth birthday. Instead of having a slamming birthday party, Tressa stood on the other side of the glass at the Richmond City Jail listening to her brother, Taj, over the phone, trying to be strong for him as he had always been for her. This was the first time she had ever seen the look of defeat all over her brother's face.

Taj had caught his case and got locked up only a month before. He desperately needed money for his lawyer, because the police had confiscated all of his as evidence during the raids on all four of his houses. Everyone had seen the news report, and all of the footage of the special task force getting special badges of recognition for bringing down the "Pow-Wow Squad." Taj's crew was named the Pow-Wow Squad because of the banging rush that their cocaine gave the fiends back in the early 90's, was unlike any other cocaine sold in the town of Richmond. So, the rock cocaine was nicknamed Pow-Wow.

Taj instructed Tressa to make the necessary calls to go collect his money. However, all the people who owed Taj money gave Tressa the run around. The workers knew that Taj would be locked away for a long time and wouldn't have any means of revenge to assure he got his money. Of course, when Tressa called them on three-way call and Taj

13

spoke directly to them demanding his money, they all played the humble role. They simply stated. "Man I gotcha. You want me to pay the lawyer or give it to who, your lil' sister or your girl?"

"Hell no! Don't give that bitch Wiggles shit of mine, I'm gonna send my lil' sister to get that."

"A'ight." The workers would respond, in a tone like they intended to give Tressa every cent.

When Tressa would call the workers to say she was on the way, they'd tell her it was OK. But when she showed up, they were nowhere to be found. A couple of times as soon as she bent the corner, she would see a dude run and hide in someone's house and when she knocked on the door, she'd hear a dude say. "Tell her I ain't here."

In the past month or so, a couple of situations heavily impacted on the ultimate decision Tressa made. Although, to this very day, she has never completely figured out which reason had more influence on her decision. Was it that she got tired of hearing her brother complain about how he was going to kill his girlfriend, Wiggles, for taking his money and not holding him down like she should? She knew her brother meant every word of his threat. Or was it that her big brother who was so strong and manly, who always seemed to have everything figured out down to the last detail, appeared so weak at this given moment.

He was the only person who loved her when nobody else did. Though he was only five years older than she was, he took on the role as brother and father. Then, when it came time that Tressa needed a woman around, he saw to it that there were plenty of women in his life to nurture his sister, mainly his girlfriend, Wiggles, at the time. This was the brother who threw away his own college dreams to throw bricks at the penitentiary to keep food in her mouth and clothes on her back. This was the brother who had always made a way out of no way for her when their mother was stripped away from them.

Tressa continued to ponder that she may have been moved into action when the other workers told Taj that his girlfriend, Wiggles, already been through to collect and obviously kept the money? Or was it the look of hurt that she saw written all over Taj's face on visiting days when Wiggles never showed up to visit him? The straw that broke

14

the camel's back, was when Taj called Tressa with the sound of defeat in his warrior voice, when he said the court appointed lawyer was trying to make him take a plea bargain for sixty years. After receiving this phone call and hearing the phrase "plea bargain", all she could think of was, this was the same expression that caused her mother to be removed from her life when she was only fourteen.

Taj and Tressa's mother, Cyn, was hauled off to prison for killing her stepfather, who had been beating her over the course of ten years. Their mother always put up with it, because this was the man that moved them out of the projects when their dope-sniffing father left them with nothing. Cyn was a schoolteacher, who loved her children more than life itself, so she tolerated the endless whippings from her husband in exchange for the better life he provided for her and her children. Taj and Tressa had no idea that their stepfather was abusive to their mother, until the day he gave her a bruise that stared them right in the face. He gave their mother two black eyes, which she promptly lied and said she received from falling. Then, the next time he fought her, he beat her with an extension cord. With intentions of only scaring him, she loaded the gun with the bullets that took him to his grave. She was facing forty years when she accepted a "plea bargain", which meant she had to plead guilty in order to receive a lesser sentence. She was sentenced to serve a ten-year sentence at the Virginia State Prison System. The judge never even considered self-defense, although she had been taking the beatings for years.

Ironically, Cyn had endured the countless years of whippings from her husband. But being thrown in prison, and separated from her two children, put a beating on her that she couldn't bare. On July 3, 1987, when Tressa was only fifteen years old, Cyn was found dead in her cell. An autopsy was never performed, the prison officials ruled it a suicide, but everybody else knew that Cyn was poisoned.

With the weight of the world on her back, Tressa had to take matters into her own hands. By no means was she going to let her brother fall victim to another "plea bargain", She could not understand how a person could get so much time for selling drugs. There are murderers, child

15

molesters and rapists who get less jail time, and they are taking lives that can't be brought back.

Then she thought about how ironic the judicial system is set up. The "white man's candy" or "drug of choice" is usually powder cocaine, and the sentencing guidelines are set up to give less prison time than a person caught with crack. Obviously, more minorities sell and use crack. If a person gets caught with the same amount, or less, of crack cocaine than powder cocaine, the book is thrown at them. Tressa's feelings were strong that the whole system was just a conspiracy against minorities. She knew that there was really no escape for her brother, but she wasn't letting him go down without a fight. And to fight the war, her brother needed a damn good attorney to brawl through the legal system with and for him.

At that moment, she made a life changing decision. Since Tressa graduated a year early from high school, and with one year of Virginia Commonwealth College (VCU) already under her belt, she decided to sit out two semesters from college to work full time to help pay for her brother's lawyer. She didn't care if she had to work two jobs on the weekdays and pick up a part time job on the weekend. One thing she was certain of was, that she wasn't going to beg or depend on anybody to give her money that was owed to her brother.

Every Saturday, Tressa worked at the Rite Aid Pharmacy, as a pharmacy technician. Sundays was her free day, and she went to visit her brother. She found a part-time clerical job at a pediatrician's office in the morning. Then she took on a job in the afternoons as a cashier at the University of Richmond, in the cafeteria. Tressa felt like a member of the Caribbean family, the Hedley's, from the hilarious show, "In Living Color". Everytime she went to a different job, she'd say to herself. "Hey mon, got to go to work!" Her cashier job was the longest and hardest hours she had to work. It was here that she met, Calvin.

Calvin was a student at the University of Richmond, from the lower east side of New York City. He was nerdy and didn't fit in with the other students at all. So, he spent the majority of his spare time either in the library or in the cafeteria talking to Tressa. So, many times, he may have

16

thought he was yapping on and on and Tressa was just being polite listening, but Tressa was soaking in every last word. Calvin spent so much time chatting with Tressa. Calvin thought Tressa favored this beautiful Dominican sister he saw on the subway in NYC. The doors closed behind her and he was too late to stop and ask her for her number.

Tressa and Calvin went out on a couple of dates, but Calvin wasn't really interested in her because his mind was bent on getting money. He was certain that once his bank account was right, it would bring any female he liked. Tressa would never admit it, but minus the nerdy looking glasses and the super shinny penny loafers, the intellectual man that Calvin would grow to be, would be the man she longed to enter her dull life.

Tressa knew that Calvin adored her, but he would never admit it to her or anyone else. Since she couldn't go to her classes, she'd make it her personal goal to absorb five words a day from her conversations with Calvin. Tressa could at least broaden her vocabulary, mannerism and social status outside of work. In addition to spending all of her time looking in Vogue and Elle magazines for the latest fashions and labels, she would read magazines that had interviews with important people over and over again, gradually picking up savvy and intellectual phrases. So overall, she may have been out of college for the time being, but she tried to educate herself.

-3-
Make Your Word Your Bond

While at the city jail, Taj became good friends with a guy named Khalil Foster AKA Lucky Luck. Now, Luck was a live wire, that got his name from being extraordinarily lucky with the dice and never catching any other charges other than misdemeanors. He would always have some kind of beef going on while in jail and on the streets. He wouldn't have any problems doing his time.

Now, although Lucky was a major player in the drug trade, he would always get locked up for petty crimes. Drunk in public, driving with a suspended operator's license, jaywalking, disorderly conduct, urinating in public and simple assault. These were the crimes that were listed on his wrap sheet. Not one of the monstrous, multiple murders or the keys of heroine he conspired to sell on a daily basis, ever surfaced to get him indicted on a murder or a continuing criminal enterprise (CCE) charge. After taking those things into consideration, who would disagree that he owned up to the name Lucky? Khalil hated to be called Lucky because he felt he'd jinx himself, so instead, most people called him Lucky Luck or just plain Luck.

Taj took Lucky Luck under his wing. Luck had heard a lot about the gangsta rep that Taj had acquired over the years. He respected Taj and knew that if Taj's man hadn't snitched on him, he would have never fallen.

Luck was getting money like crazy, it was out of control. But he also knew if he had the right drug

19

connection, his financial status would turn into multi-billionaire in no time.   He had heard rumors of Taj's interactions with foreigners in the underworld. He was also aware of his financial situation and how much he loved his sister. He sympathized with Taj and his plight. Taj wasn't sure, but he knew that Luck had his own ulterior motives for befriending him, but he didn't care.   All he was concerned with was if they coincided with his own agenda. Taj knew that Luck was going home soon and needed a real connect. Taj thought about his faithful sister sacrificing her college dream for him and felt terrible. So, the day before Lucky went home and after a series of loyalty tests during the 60 days locked up, he decided to put Luck on. What did he have to lose?   If Luck didn't play fair, Taj would eventually see him again in the penal system. Luck's life was a revolving door concerning jail. So, Taj would get his revenge one way or the other.

Taj gave him the two vicious plans.   First, Taj needed to get back at his old drug connect, who discontinued all ties with Taj when he got busted and didn't send him one penny, after all the money that he had spent with them, and was caught with their product. Day one, when Luck hit the street, he was suppose to rob the African connect blind and when it was successfully done, then Taj would turn Lucky onto some Dominican guys he knew of and that he was planning to do business with right before he got bagged.

The night before Lucky went home, Taj stayed up all night talking to Lucky. Finally, he told Lucky. "Look man, before we get into this, you gotta give me your word that on your life, you gonna do what we've been talking about over the past few weeks."

After Lucky looked into Taj's eyes, he gave him his word. Taj walked over to his bunk and returned with his photo album. "Look man, this is the dude right here." He pointed to the extremely dark skinned man in the photo and handed him the photo.

"They call him Radda. We took this photo about two years back when we were in Vegas at a fight."

Lucky listened attentively as Taj gave him all the necessary information.   "Look man, dude probably done gained some weight since this flick was taken. I don't know where he lives now, but I do know he likes a lot of young girls, owns a club on Jeff Davis Highway and is real flamboyant. So, when you see him, he'll stand out.

Lucky knew better than to cross Taj. Taj may have not have had any weight on the streets anymore, but he had it in prison. See, it's funny, but the same kind of people that Taj surrounded himself with on the streets, are the same type of people who mostly ended up in the prison system. So, guys in prison knew the power Taj had on the streets, so when he went to jail, he built an empire within the prison system as if he was on the streets. After all, prison is a world within itself. Lifelong relationships are built, friends, enemies and bonds are made behind bars, while principles and rules are applied and broken. Taj was a real gangsta on the streets and only carried it gangsta while in prison. He only dealt with other real guys, he was always put at risk because there was always a sucker or weak dude trying to get "brownie points" by trying Taj. So, there was never a moment that Taj let the least little thing slip when anybody tried him. It was automatic for him to straighten anybody out by any means, with his knuckles or his shank. If it had to be done, it was done.

This gained Taj much respect in the prison system. As far as most were concerned, he was one of the key players in the Richmond team/gang prison system. It was quite peculiar that there were known beefs throughout 233, 644, 321, and 359 neighborhoods across Richmond. However, once the fellas from Richmond were behind the prison walls, many beefs no longer existed. Instead, they all came together and the wars went on from the Richmond dudes with the Tidewater dudes (anybody from the Norfolk, Virginia Beach or Hampton area), or the DC dudes.

Since the relationships built behind bars are taken seriously, it was nothing for Taj to have something done to Lucky if he ever set foot into the penitentiary. It didn't matter what institution Lucky was in, because Taj had family (his prison family) all throughout the system. And if Taj needed to have something done to Lucky, all he had to do was write a letter to one of his boys he knew at the same prison and it was taken care of. This was something that Lucky was well aware of and he wasn't trying to deal with that from Taj. So, the dirty dude that Lucky was, he

21

decided to play fair and map out his master plan to pull the heist off.

Right before Lucky walked out of the door of the Richmond City Jail, Taj gave him a manly hug, and as he did, he whispered one phrase as he pat him on the back. "Make sure your word is your bond."

When Lucky hit the streets, his first priority wasn't sex or shopping for new clothes after being away for 60 days. It wasn't getting at any of his workers or going to see his old supplier. There was no need to, he knew that after he pulled off this move, everything else would come, the women, workers, the shopping, and yes, even his old supplier would become a buyer from him.

Lucky's first order of business was buying a hooptie, a 1978 Caprice classic with a factory radio, no tape deck, CD player, rims or a paint job. Just a good running quiet motor, and the most important feature, was the old round self adhesive .99 cents digital clock that appeared on the dash board of the car. He sat in his hooptie every night outside of the club, with his picture in his hand, studying the actions of Radda and even followed him a few times. Taj was right and didn't exaggerate about it either, Radda was the jackpot with his extremely flamboyant lifestyle, and without a doubt, he loved the young girls. There was only one problem, Radda kept three or four guys with him at all times.

After three weeks of surveillance, and especially after he followed Radda to his house, Lucky felt it was time to pay Taj a visit. When Lucky went to visit Taj at the city jail, Taj was already visiting with Tressa. When Lucky walked up, he spoke to Tressa. Tressa glanced at Lucky who was looking like Wild Man Jack, with a full-untamed beard growing on his face. It was evident that Lucky hadn't had a haircut or shave since he left the jail. It was a pity, he had smooth chocolate skin covered up with hair all across his face. The only thing that was kosher was the snow white on blue Nikes he wore on his feet. Tressa couldn't help but notice the gold teeth in Lucky's mouth when he handed Tressa three hundred dollars so she could walk to the front entrance and put the money on her brother's account. Tressa was happy to do so. This was a big relief, because the $30.00 that she was going to leave her brother, she could now keep for herself. The icing on the cake was that, for the next ten weeks she didn't have to leave her brother any money, because $30.00 was the maximum the jail permitted them to spend at the canteen/commissary every week.

As soon as Tressa was bent around the corner, Lucky skipped the intro of the greetings and small talk, and got straight down to business.

"Look man, let me run this down before lil' sis come back."

"What you waitin' for? Run it."

"Look Shawdy, I seen dude. I have been on this nigga like a pamper on a baby's ass. And like you said, he is getting it."

Taj didn't speak, he just looked at Lucky through the glass and listened attentively as Lucky talked over the two-way phone.

"A few times, I followed him to a mini mansion way out in Bon Air. But he don't dare go every night. But when he did go he stayed in for a day or two straight."

"What kind of cars out there."

"Shiittt nigga, the driveway look like some shit off the lifestyles of the Rich and Famous, a drop top Porsche, a big body Benz, two clover green Rovers."

Taj cut in. "Is the Porsche black?"

"Yup" Lucky said, shaking his head.

"Then that's the house where he lay his head at."

"A'ight, but Shawdy, I ain't going to be able to do this alone, cuz the nigga always have niggas wit him. I'm gonna have to get some other dudes to help me.

"Look, Shawdy do what you gotta do then."

"A'ight."

"Look man, I call my sister just 'bout everyday. So, when you take care of it, let her know that you took care if it. You know she don't know what time it is, so just tell her that you took care of it."

"A'ight man, I got you."

Just then Tressa came back and when she did, Lucky left.

Later that night at the club on the stakeout:

Lucky sat in front of the club with two of his homeboys. They watched a beautiful, young light skinned girl with body for days, waiting in front of the club after using the payphone at the corner two times. Lucky's mind was not really being focused on women since he had been home. He had a few "wham, bam thank you ma'am's". As long as anybody could remember, he had always been weak for a big booty broad and the body attached to this girl, it would be a crime for her to get away from him.

Lucky had put his hand on the door to open it, but just when he was about to get out of the car to make her acquaintance, Radda appeared out of the club, alone and straight into the arms of the girl. Radda was displaying enough jewels that could have amounted to a car around his neck and on his fingers with his gold framed Versace glasses. The multi-colored brown shoes threw off the bright green and gold linen ensemble. The girl didn't seem to notice Radda had on the wrong shoes, for she was looking deep into his eyes while they conversed. Their conversation only lasted a couple of minutes, but the body language told it all, as Radda looked at his watch and uttered a time to the girl after going in his pocket to retrieve some bills to pass onto the girl. As the girl walked away, Radda stood there lusting over the girl, while gripping his penis in his hand. He put up 4 fingers. "I'll be there at 4." He said as he smiled and the girl walked off.

Lucky told the two homeboys in the car. "He's going over Shawdy's house tonight. I know that nigga ain't taking none of his clown bodyguards. This may be easier than I thought."

Low and behold, Lucky was right. At exactly 3:45 am, Radda hopped right into his spanking new big boy Lexus with thirty-day tags on it alone. First, Radda made a turn off the main road, and as soon as he approache the stoplight, Lucky bumped into the back of Radda.

Radda slowly gets out of the car and is clearly pissed off. "What tha fuck?" He says, so mad that he's huffing and puffing, looking at the bumper.

Lucky immediately gets out of his car and is very humbling and apologetic to Radda. The combination of Lucky being clean-shaven, along with his slender build and remorseful attitude, made Lucky appear harmless as he kept apologizing. Radda was not accepting any apologies from anybody, instead, he got very vulgar and started cussing and fussing about his brand new car.

"Man, you hit my shit. I haven't even paid the first fucking payment on it. Then you hit it with that big old ass raggedy car." Radda says, pointing to the Caprice Classic and sucks his teeth.

Radda is too busy looking at the bumper, still being very belligerent and loud mouth, and doesn't even notice Lucky pulling out the gun until it's right to his left temple.

"Nigga get the fuck into the car." Lucky said so serious, and it was a total shock to Radda how Lucky switched from his humble tone to his "this ain't no game" tone.

Once Lucky's homeboys saw the gun, they hopped out the car. Number One automatically helped get Radda into the front seat of the Caprice, while the other sprinted over to Radda's car. Lucky drove straight to Radda's house, while Two followed in Radda's car. Once they arrived at the house, they made Radda use his own keys to open the door. Lucky pushed him face down on the floor with excessive force and asked. "Where da money at?"

Radda didn't respond.

As soon as they were inside the house, Number One moved briskly throughout the house, room by room, to check to make sure no one else was in the house. He went into the bathroom, pulled down the shower curtain. Unfortunately, the very last room he checked, he found a woman sleeping, and right beside the bed was a bassinet with a sleeping baby inside. He quickly pulled the white goosed down comforter off of the woman, only to find she was naked.

"Get da fuck up." He shook her.

As soon as she opens her eyes to the barrel of a black 9mm in her face, she gets hysterical. "Please, please don't kill my baby."

One ignores her and pushes her into the living room buck naked. As soon as Two sees her coming, he takes over and lays her on her stomach beside Radda.

"Where da money at?" Lucky asks, while thinking to himself, how phat the woman's butt is.

Radda didn't say a word, but that's before Lucky saw that Number One was coming back with the baby cradled in his arm.

"Oh, this your baby huh?"

"Pleeaazzz, don't kill my baby!" The woman started screaming and whimpering.

"Shut up!" Number one yelled.

Radda started talking. "Look man, please don't kill my baby. I'll give you the money, just please don't kill my baby! I just had him. He's new. He don't know nothing."

Right away, Lucky and Two got Radda up and Radda took them straight to the room where the money was. The safe was in the wall of one of the closets, and what looked like it could have been a legitimate fuse box, but after Radda jingled the light switch in a certain type of way, there behind the fuse box, sat a nice size safe. Without hesitation, Radda opened the safe.

Two and Radda put the money inside the Louis Vuitton duffle bags. The more money that Lucky saw, the more excited he got. As Radda put the money inside of the bags, he began to cry and his lip was trembling. As he pled and begged. "Please don't kill my baby!"

Lucky stared at Radda whimpering and exclaimed. "Bitch ass nigga!"

"BOOM!! BOOM!! BOOM!! BOOM!!" Three to the dome and one in the heart was what it took to shut Radda up permanently.

When the woman heard the guns shots, she started screaming hysterically. Almost simultaneously. "Boom!"

Number One kills her to shut her up. Lucky runs out of the back bedroom. "Damn, what you kill her for? I was gonna fuck the shit out of her."

Pissed off that Number One shot the lady, Lucky demands him that he goes outside to wipe the Lexus down, because they didn't put on gloves until they got inside the house. Meanwhile, Lucky grabbed the money and instructed Two to grab the baby and the Osh Kosh B'Gosh baby carrier and they rolled out.

Lucky sat in the backseat with the money and the baby. When they were miles away from the house and closer to town, while the sun was rising, they pulled over next to the dumpster of a breakfast restaurant, and dropped the baby off. The whole time in the back seat, Lucky was slyly cuffing the money out of the bag stuffing it into his pants. Not counting the stacks of money that Lucky had stolen while in the back seat, he paid everybody evenly, including Taj.

-4-

On the Road to Riches

Lucky's first priority was letting Taj know that he carried out the heist perfectly. He called Tressa several times, but she was never home. So, he took it upon himself, to take care of some of Taj's business, with Taj's share of the money. He paid Taj's lawyer $17,750.00 that was owed to him, and of course, he got a receipt for it. He put a bankroll on Taj's books to hold him over so he could live comfortably in jail. Not only did he supply Taj with money, he supplied Taj with an ounce of uncut dope (heroine) and paid a deputy to take it into Taj, so Taj could make some money while in jail. Lucky dropped a letter to Taj, and Taj wrote back and told Lucky what time to catch Tressa at home, as well as informed Tressa that Lucky would be calling her. He also gave Tressa Lucky's number and told her to call him ASAP! Tressa wasn't going to call Lucky. She had enough of trying to get money from dudes that owed her brother, and she did not feel like playing the money game. She had been through it time and time again with so many other people who claimed to be cool with her brother. In her eyes, this was no different.

When Lucky was locked up, he had always adored Tressa's mannerisms. Every Sunday night once visitation was over, he would always replay in his mind Tressa's princess wave, the kind of wave that only Miss America would give when riding on the top of a convertible in a parade. Every single Sunday, while Lucky's mother was visiting him, Tressa was visiting Taj. Lucky could not keep his eyes off of Tressa. She was the prettiest thing he'd ever laid eyes on. In addition, when she'd make a few phone calls for him on her three-way, he loved the proper way that she spoke.

Lucky touched base with Tressa a few times, trying to get fit into her busy work schedule. She made it clear she wasn't missing work or being late to work. Especially for something that she knew in her heart wasn't a sure thing, because so many times before, she had been sold dreams and had been given false promises.

When it was time to deliver the money, he called Tressa and got her address. She told him that she didn't get off until 11:00 p.m., so she wouldn't be at home until about 11:30 p.m. He called at 11:30 on the dot. She gave him the address.

Lucky prepared all day for the three minutes he'd get to see Tressa. He got a fresh haircut, even though he had gotten one only two days earlier. He shined up his two gold teeth and he didn't put on clean clothes until 11:00 p.m., when it was almost time to go drop the money off. He made sure his clothes weren't too baggy, although he was skinny as a pole. He wanted to look presentable and make Tressa do a double take when she saw him. He knew when he was dressed and cleaned up, there was no doubt about it, he was a fine dark skinned brother. He popped a Peppermint in his mouth that he had stolen out of the "Jerry's Kids" box at 7-11, and didn't donate one penny to, and rang Tressa's doorbell at exactly 11:47 p.m.

"Ding, Ding, Dong, Ding, Ding, Dong." The doorbell chimes sounded.

Tressa, wore out from work and resting her feet, sat on the couch near the door and was trying to gather some energy to get up. Tressa was so tired and burnt out from working her three jobs, but she would never complain. Before rising from her comfortable position she asked. "Who's there?"

"It's Luck."

Tressa was glad to hear his voice because she knew that he was bringing money, but she did not feel like entertaining any company. She dragged herself up to open the door. "Hi." She said drowsily.

"Hey, what's up?" Lucky said.

Lucky began to look around her apartment, it was not what he had expected at all. He knew she had class. Not only did she talk the talk, but he had no idea that she walked the walk too. He remembered how Taj had talked about her struggles, so the picture he painted of how Tressa lived couldn't have been anymore wrong than he was. Boy, was he impressed. He couldn't keep from looking around, obviously adoring her taste and style. She had mirrors covering every wall, even the cocktail tables and entertainment center were mirrors. The carpet and living room furniture was white with silver flower accented roses on the tables. Even her picture frames on the mirrored octagon stand were silver or mirror. He walked over to look at the pictures on the stand.

"You, ummm, you really got a nice place. This place is beautiful. I know your man must feel comfortable when he comes home from a hard day's work."

"Thanks." She said with a little giggle. "No, there isn't any man shacked up with me. If it was, believe me, you wouldn't be here right now bringing me no money."

He smiled.

"Would you like something to drink?" Tressa offered.

"Yeah."

"What would you like? I have water, OJ, cranberry juice, Pepsi, Mountain Dew, Sprite and Heineken."

"Give me ummm Sprite."

She brought it to him in a Champagne glass. He had already put the $52,000 on the table. He pointed to the money before he took the glass from her.

"When do your classes start back up?"

"They don't begin until next semester, but I have to register and pay for them now."

"That should be enough money to pay for school and quit two of your jobs. I think yo brotha told me your classes cost like 12G's a year. Yo brother's lawyer is paid in full. I got tha receipt in my pocket. Plus, I went down the to jail and looked out for Taj real decent, so he'll be a'ight for a minute on commissary. And when that gets low, I'll stack it up again."

31

"Thank you Luck. I really appreciate it."

"No problem."

He was getting too comfortable when his pager went off and he realized that there was somewhere else he had to be.

He looked at his pager, and stood up. "Duty calls. Thanks for the thirst quencher."

"Anytime."

"Call me anytime if you need anything, day or night."

"Thanks, and be safe OK." She called out to him when he was halfway down the steps.

Luck couldn't figure it out, the way Tressa told him to be safe, really did something to him. None of his other girls or women had even cared about his well being, not even his own mother. All they ever cared about was that his pockets overflowed with cash and how quickly they could spend his money, including his mother. That was the only reason she came to visit him weekly. She wanted control over his cars and money while he was in the slammer. His mother never told him don't hustle, she only held her hand out. But the way Tressa said "be safe", was his conformation that he had to have Tressa. He wanted Tressa bad, real bad.

Sunday could not roll around fast enough. He talked to Taj on the phone, but he knew the only way he'd get to spend some time with Tressa, was to visit Taj. Lucky and Tressa would have to wait at least an hour before they would be able to see Taj. So, he met her down at the jail and sat on the stoop and talked to her. Lucky decided to take what he could get, not his usual style, but she was worth it. Initially, they only made small talk. Suddenly, this guy in a black Cadillac Sedan, with some air shocks to jack it up in the back, and a booming system, rode up and tried to talk to her. She dissed the guy.

Lucky laughed and asked. "Why you giving that dude such a hard time." But secretly, Lucky was glad she rebuffed the fool's advances. He had way more game than that clown.

She casually said. "Because I don't care how many coats of wax are on a brother's car. Can he pay some bills? Can he help me/us elevate to the next level, or is his

32

mentality going to be, how fat my butt in determining what he's gonna do for me? I don't have time for a brotha just trying to make me a notch on his belt. Shoot, I ain't no gold-digger, but if a nigga can't come in and add to my life, I don't need him."

"So, in other words, a brother gotta take care of you better than you can take care yourself?"

Before she could answer, the Correction Officer called. "Visit for Taj Shawsdale." She grabbed her pocketbook and went through the doors marked for visitors and Lucky tagged along right behind her.

The visit with Taj went well. Tressa and Luck were sharing the phone, both listening in at the same time. Taj noticed the way Luck's whole mannerism changed when Tressa was around. He seemed to soften up a little and was less stressed. When Tressa went to the bathroom, Taj bluntly told Luck. "I see you got the hots for my sister man."

Luck hesitated for a minute. "I can't even front man, I'm in love with yo sister."

Taj put down the phone for a minute. He couldn't believe his ears. He was furious. "Look man, you my nigga without a doubt, but I can't give you blessings over my sister. That's my heart. I raised her since she was this high." He said while lowering his hand to just above the floor. "I can't have a slickster like yourself getting her caught up in some bullshit. I just can't have it, and I won't have it."

"Man, I would never hurt her."

"Nope, ain't happening. Plus, you be going back and forth to jail too much and getting in all those stupid ass beefs on the street!"

"Naaahhh man. See, I know if I am with her, she will keep me out of trouble. I know good and well I can't be in that crazy shit, cuz I have to stay on the street with her." Luck pleaded. "Man, I promise, I am going to take care of her." Luck begged Taj, like he was a kid begging his momma to go outside on a hot summer day.

Taj's, temper continued to rise as he could see the determination all over Lucky's face. "Look man, we're partners, you're my brother, she's your sister. How can you love *our* sister in that way?"

"Taj, I'm going to take care of her.   I give you my word man, I got her best interest at heart."

It was clear that Lucky didn't care anything about the incest insinuation, so Taj came at Lucky in a different way.   "Look man, if you cross those lines, our friendship ends."

Lucky's expression showed he was shocked but not surprised that Taj would say that because Taj was so overprotective of Tressa.

"Man, look you are my man. As long as I do right by her, what bearing should that have on our friendship?"

"Look man, I wouldn't even look at you the same and you'd look at me different."   Taj raised his voice as he pointed through the window at Lucky, "SO, if you take it there, everything that we built, consider it gone cause you're tearing it down."

Before Lucky could respond, Tressa walked back up. "What ya'll over here talking about.   It looks mighty intense."

Taj didn't even want to comment. He didn't want to discuss the subject any further, because as far as he was concerned, his sister was off limits to Lucky. Lucky was good for, and could be trusted, to pull off heists for him and to send him drugs while he's in the inside, but over all he was a knucklehead. Lucky was not the pick he had in mind for his priceless sister.

As soon as Taj was ready to give his response, the guard annoyingly interrupted with his loud, deep voice. "Two more minutes." At that point, Taj gave his love to his sister, told them both when he was going to call and before he hung up the phone, he pointed at Luck and said. "Don't make no moves, because this ain't over yet."

As they walked to their respective cars, there was a guy riding by on what looked like a child's bicycle and a book bag on his back. "What up Luck. I got some VCR movies fresh from the movie store."

Lucky smiled and looked in the bag and pulled out the tapes he wanted. He looked at Tressa. "Come and get whatever tapes you want."

She softly said. "I don't have a VCR, its broken."
He looked surprised. "Don't worry, I'll get you one. Just pick the movies you want."

She selected a few tapes that she wanted, but he knew she wanted more. So, Lucky just bought the whole bag from the guy. Lucky paid the dude in cash, but only because Tressa was there. Any other time he would have exchanged some coke or dope for the tapes. He asked Tressa if she was hungry and she said no. He gave her $50.00 to pay for her and a girlfriend to have dinner when she did get hungry.

Later that night, Lucky called and asked if it was OK for him to stop by with the VCR's that he had gotten her. The VCRs were still in the box. He had bought one for her living room and one for her bedroom. He hooked them up and told her to put in a movie. She chose the classic Ghetto Spoof, "*I'm Gonna Git You Sucka*".

As they watched Keenan Ivory Wayans act a fool, they both laughed hysterically and continued to watch more movies. When they finally noticed the time, it was 5:00 a.m. Lucky grudgingly left that morning, but everyday thereafter, he started making all kinds of excuses to visit Tressa, and he always came bearing gifts.

After a few weeks went by, Lucky came over late one night after a long night of gambling. He called when he was in her parking lot and asked for a favor. He needed to come in and get a good night's rest in her other bedroom. *Other bedroom my ass*, she thought. But she agreed and asked if she could use his car. Tressa was pushing a 1985 short body, style Buick a.k.a. "baby 98", that looked like a drug dealers car. It had over 200,000 miles on it and was always giving her one problem or another. Without any hesitation, he handed over the keys and went into his pocket and gave her a crisp $100.00 bill. "Drinks are on me tonight."

Out of all the times she had seen him before, at that moment and for the first time, Tressa really looked at Lucky, this man was fine!! This was the first time that she realized that Lucky was handsome. Lucky had a sensually dark brown complexion with two open-faced crown gold teeth spaced apart. One was on his front tooth and the other was a tooth over. His teeth were gleaming white. He had a fresh haircut, round up and all. His lips were soft and full and he had the longest jet-black eyelashes. He stood at 5'9, weighed about 175 pounds and his very holdable waist was a 34. He wasn't a big dude, but his deep voice and gull carried much weight. He wasn't wearing anything fancy, just some black basketball shorts and a Michael Jordan T-shirt with the new Jordan's that just came out that very day. She glanced below to check out his package, and saw the imprint of his manhood sticking out a little bit and curving a little to the left. *Damn, he's packing,* she thought to herself.

When Tressa completed thoroughly checking out Lucky, she cocked her head to the side, smiled coyly and said. "Peace out." She headed for the door to go and pick up her girlfriend Dutchess. Noticing a small brown paper bag that Luck was carrying, she stopped dead in her tracks and suspiciously asked. "What's in that paper bag? It's not drugs or anything is it?"

Lucky looked at her as if she was asking a foolish question. "Hell no, it ain't no damn drugs! I would never bring drugs to where you lay ya head, its just money."

"Oh, ok." She said relieved. Trying to make it up to Lucky for not trusting him, she sweetly offered. "I cooked some baked chicken. I can fix you a plate if you're hungry. Also, I put a clean towel and wash cloth on the bed in case you want to take a shower."

"Thank you, but I'm gonna warm me something up after I get out the shower. Just go ahead. Have a good time and be safe. I have my cell phone on, if you need me."

When she arrived at Dutchess's house, her friend wasn't surprised to see her driving Luck's car. She had been in Tressa's presence when Lucky was around, and even a blind man could see that Lucky was head over heels for Tressa. "Girl, I see you finally came out of denial, huh?"

"What are you talking about?"

"I see you driving 'Big Money Grip' from the 'Getting Money Strip' car. And you know they say, that nigga don't LET *nobody* drive his car."

"Girl, please it ain't even like that. He's just my brother's friend." Tressa said innocently.

"Tressssaa, you know damn well he's more than Taj's friend. Girl, he ya man!"

Tressa burst into laughter. "Girl please, he ain't even thinking bout me that way. Plus, he got plenty of women I'm sure."

"Chile please, the hell he ain't." Dutchess looked at her and rolled her eyes.

"Where he at now then? Why you got his car out flossing?"

"He's at my house getting some rest."

"Tressa, check this out, a man just ain't gonna give you his car to drive to the club like that. Believe what I am telling you." Dutchess shook her head in disgust. She could not believe how green her friend was.

"Whatever." Tressa responded as if she wasn't taking in everything that Dutchess was saying, but in reality, she was soaking everything in as she continued to listen to the words of Mary J. Blige's song, *Real Love*. How more effective the words sounded coming out of a booming 6x9 kicker box in the trunk of the car, rather than the tiny woofers she had in her Baby 98. *Damnnn, Mary!!!! You make it sound so good. She be hitting home. If I didn't want a real love, shoot, I want one now,* she thought to herself.

Once they arrived at the club, she parked the car and got out. With much swing in their step, they walked toward Ivory's Uptown Lounge. A guy named Motor noticed her walking away from the *only* black on black brand new 1993 Mercedes Benz in town driven straight off the showroom floor, by a young black man a few weeks ago and it was 1992. He spoke first and then asked. "Where Luck at?"

Tressa hesitated for a minute, not sure who this nigga was and if she wanted to respond. "Oh he's at home." She said cautiously.

"Tell him that Motor said what's up and make sho he come round the way tomorrow and give a nigga a chance to win his money back."

"A'ight." Tressa replied nonchalantly.

Tressa and Dutchess approached Ivory's. Tuesdays was College night and there was always a long line. Although it was the designated College night, it was the middle of July and school was not in session. Consequently, the club population may have only been 10% actual college students. The rest were big time, mediocre, nickel and dime or perpetrating, wanna be hustlers of Richmond, VA and surrounding areas. There were UPS workers and the other fellas who worked jobs paying legit money. The majority of the playas in there looked, dressed and wore the jewelry that drug dealers wore. Anybody knows that when there's a club filled with money getting men, money hungry, sack chasing and booty shaking females were sure to follow? The club was filled with all kinds of females, from conservative ones to the freaks.

The temperature outside was a blazing 90 degrees, with the highest humidity level in Richmond, VA. The females' gear made it known that it was definitely summer in the capital city. Barely covering up their titties and asses with the halter shirts and Daisy Duke shorts, the females were clear-cut representing.

Back in the early 90's, the sister's of Richmond, VA, turned Tuesday's College Night at Ivory's into a fashion show. Though there was no cash prize, had there been one, the owner would have to give it to each and every one of them, because every week, the chicks would outdo themselves. Almost all the girls sported the bamboo name earrings that they went to Georgetown to get and the pendants with their names. If they couldn't get to DC to hook up their ensemble for the night, they would go to "Merry Go Round" in Cloverleaf Mall to get an outfit. It was a pity when Ivory's shut down, so did Merry Go Round.

This particular night, Ivory's was off the hook! The party was going on outside too for those who couldn't get in. The dude with the Cherokee jeep illegally parked across the street, opened up his back window and the bass was shaking almost the whole block. It could be heard miles away. People would just stand in Hardee's parking lot and dance and mingle. This didn't concern Tressa and Dutchess, until the club closed, and they too hung out in Hardee's parking lot.

Inside of the club, Tressa and Dutchess had a ball. They hadn't been out in a while, so they were embraced with love from just about everybody. Tressa's new found stardom increased the love she was already being shown. See, Motor was the town's version of Tom Brokaw. As a matter of fact, that's how he got his name Motor, from being a "motor mouth". He was a dude that was cool with everybody, but gossiped like a female. He was always in everybody's business, male or female, he didn't care. He hustled everyday and got much money selling drugs, which was his second priority. Being nosey was his main concern. He kept company with a lot of girls naturally, because he gossiped just like they did. But he also had a lot of homeboys, because he had money and always kept good dope, the dope he got from Luck.

Tressa wasn't in the club fifteen minutes before the news had traveled. Everywhere she went, people were talking about her, "Oh that's Lucky's girl." A dude stepped on her shoe, and another guy told him. "Man you better say excuse me cuz that's that crazy nigga Lucky's girl. Shoot, that nigga might kill you for that shit."

How come people always gotta draw conclusions just because they see somebody driving your car? Shoot, how they don't know I'm not his cousin?

At first, she kept setting everybody straight, because she didn't want the rumor to get out, but soon after, Tressa began to think about the possibility of her being in a relationship with Lucky. She thought about how sweet he was and how giving he was. She sure could use the financial help, and Lord knows his pockets were as long as the New Jersey Turnpike. But would he play fair with her? All kinds of thoughts went in and out of her head. She thought about his bad boy image, and people did say he was a murderer and a psycho.

After the club, Tressa dropped Dutchess off and went home. She kicked her shoes off, and before she was in the door good, Lucky who was sitting on the sofa, looked away from the TV at her and smiled.

"Thought you needed and wanted to get some sleep?" She stepped across his feet and plopped down beside him on the sofa.

"I couldn't sleep because everybody was blowing my cell up wanting to know who the cutie was pushing my whip." He smiled.

"I know they were because they were constantly in my face. Some dude named Motor told me to tell you to come by tomorrow to let him win his money back."

He nodded his head. "I was sleeping good, but every time I dozed back off, somebody else was calling."

"I hope me driving your car didn't get you in no trouble with any of your girls."

"What girls?"

"Please, I seen the looks they were giving me tonight." Tressa looked at him trying, not to let on that she liked the feeling of envy and the thought of being his girl.

He looked her in the eyes and told her with a slight smile on his face. "Oh, they just jealous hoes cuz I already told them you was my girl. So, starting tonight, it's official." He continued to smile as he grabbed her feet and started rubbing them.

He didn't give her any time to respond before he asked her, "Why ya'll females always wear shoes to the club that you know are going to kill your feet?"

"The same reason why ya'll dudes be sticking ya'll dick in some coochie raw dog and you know it may be a chance that it can kill you!"

He laughed. "I don't do that." She giggled. "Yeah, that's what they all say."

"Look, baby I ain't going to do that to you anyway. I am just going to be with you."

"Please, how you going to do that?"

"Because you my girl."

"What makes you think that I even want to be your girl?"

"Look sweetheart, I can and will take care of you better than you can take care of yourself, or any other man can, for that manner."

And Luck meant every word of it too, but before he showed and proved he could, he had to put Tressa through one last test. He went to sleep and left the bag of money in the front room. He folded the brown paper bag that contained over $100,000 in a certain way. He had already counted the money and threw it back in the bag in an unorganized manner. Luck casually mentioned to her that he needed to count the money in the morning. So, if she wanted to hit him up she could have, believing that he would have never missed it. If she didn't take any out, he knew he had a winner.

Lucky had a reputation for sleeping with a bunch of women and now all that was getting boring to him. He really didn't care for any of the chicks, because they all were out for his money. Once he laid eyes on Tressa, a bright idea came across his mind. *Why don't I just get one girl who I can just really get into and she be into me? I can* *just spend on her, instead of giving this one and that one $1,500 here, $200 there, $400 here. I'll invest it all on one female. When functions, shows and plays come to town, I'll know that I got someone worthy to go with me. Instead of having this one and that one on my shoulders, and niggas laughing behind my back because she was just with them the night before. I could do this with Tressa. I'm going to take care of her to the point I am going to make her the envy of the town. If I could get her to just play fair with me, I'm gonna do big things with her. And when I ain't so "Lucky" and the feds come, shit, she won't let the next man get next to her. There won't be any competition.*

When Tressa laid down to sleep, she tossed and turned all night. She couldn't help but think of all the things that Lucky said. But did he mean it? She had been so caught up in her own life, trying to make ends meet, that she hadn't had a man, or any financial help, for that matter. She thought about all the great things they could do together. The Virginia State Fair was coming to Richmond in a couple of months. The State Fair was a big idea to Richmonders. She thought how they could walk through the fair hand, in hand eating cotton candy and he could play the basketball games and win her big stuffed teddy bear. She had always wanted a "real" boyfriend, but due to Taj being so overprotected of her, trying to shield her from the world, a real boyfriend was something she never had. She had sneaked around with boys, but as far as anything real serious, she never had. She hoped with all her heart that everything Lucky said was true and not just talk. She had listened to her brother tell lies to women for no apparent reason, so she was fully aware of the games men played. For the rest of the night, she went back and forth with the pros and cons that came with Lucky. *Well, he's one of Taj's friends so he may be full of it. But Taj wouldn't have introduced us if he would have thought that Lucky could harm me in any way. Overall, Taj plays fair and he mostly surrounds himself with real dudes cause he is a real dude. And birds of a feathers do flock together. And Taj is a real good dude, so there must be some good in Lucky then.* Butterflies just went all through her stomach as she kept trying to fall asleep, but couldn't.

41

The next day, Lucky was up before Tressa. He counted the money, and with no surprise, she had not been in the bag. So, the fairy tale began.

Since the only way he really knew how to show his love was through material possessions, he began to shower her with all kinds of gifts. His first concern was her car. He took her to the car lot and bought her a low mileage, pre-owned, white M30 Infiniti convertible with a black top. He then gave her money to pay the insurance for an entire year, and money to buy new clothes to wear as she rode around in her new whip.

After she got her new car, Tressa went to pick up Dutchess. Dutchess was so happy for Tressa. "Damn girl, who's car?"

"Girl, mine." Tressa happily responded.

"Girl, stop playing. How much ya note?"

"Girl, it's paid for!"

"Dammnnnn, a nigga just didn't put you in a car without a note! You know how some of these dudes come putting down the down payment, talking bout they bought you a car, and all they did was bought the daggone note. Ole boy, Lucky Luck, bought the whole car and paid for it in full! Girl, you got a title out of him already. Just imagine what else he got in store for you. Girl, you know we gotta go strip hopping!" That is, riding around from one drug infested area where drugs, sex and anything else illegal were being sold, to the next one, and on, just to let the hoes know.

With the hot sun beaming down on them, Gucci sunglasses covering their eyes, drop top back and "Summer, Summa, Summertime" by the Fresh Prince, playing with the volume all the way up on the Infiniti factory tape deck, Dutchess and Tressa turned onto Chimbarazo Blvd. where about twenty dudes were congregated at the corner. Tressa saw Motor about to cross the street. "Wooowwww." He screamed. "Oh, SHIT! You got it? That car is pretty as hell! Pull over."

They pulled over to the curb. Motor came over to the car, but called over to the crowd. "Man-Man, come look at this car that Luck bought his girl."

"How you know Lucky paid for this?" Dutchess asked, and of course, motor-mouth Motor gave it up.

"Man, I know he got it for her because that's all he was talking bout when he was beating me out my money at the crap game. How he gonna get his girl a new car. How you going from the bat mobile Buick, to the drop top Infiniti? So yeah, you can thank me. He damn sure took all my money last night."

"Well, thank you!"

Man-Man walked up and set the record straight. "Please, nigga. That lil $35,000 Luck won from you last night wasn't nothing. That ain't going to make or break Lucky man."

"Shoot, that $35,000 was re-up money and now I gotta stand out here and nickel and dime it to get back on." Motor said to Man-Man.

Dutchess heard that and sunk it all in. After they pulled off, she begged Tressa to fix her up with one of Lucky's homeboys. Dutchess wanted a piece of the pie too.

Dutchess and Tressa had been friends for years, since they were in sixth grade. Dutchess was very pretty, but her selfish ways made her ugly. Her sandy red hair went well with her light bright sandy red complexion. She was so pale that she had pink lips and didn't really need to wear any lipstick. She was petite, but was very shapely. She always seemed all right to Tressa, but never played fair concerning the guys in her life. Dutchess's mentality was since she was pretty, there was no need for her to struggle for anything.

Once Dutchess met Lucky, she was immediately drawn to him. She called herself his fake sister.

43

-5-
The Love Games

Over the course of the next fourteen months, Tressa and Lucky became best friends, as well as boyfriend and girlfriend. They communicated so much and sometimes would just sit on the sofa and talk for hours, getting to know the ins and outs of each other's past life and childhood. Lucky shared with Tressa that his government name, Khalil, meant "beautiful and good friend" and he wanted to always be her best friend. He also revealed to her his history with his mother, something he never discusses with anybody. To be truthful, he's glad he shared it with her, because it has had such a great effect on him. He was forced to recall those painful childhood memories when he almost lost Tressa one day, because he snapped and lost his temper.

One night, Tressa got up in the middle of the night and pulled the bedroom door in because a draft was coming in, but still left it slightly ajar. Lucky woke up and felt the door was closed and just about lost his mind. This was the first time Tressa had ever witnessed this type of behavior coming from Lucky. She was scared to death of him and started to cry. After Lucky calmed down, he told her that his mother, Betty, used to make him sleep in the closet when he was a toddler. She would put him in the closet because she only had a one-bedroom apartment at the time. She didn't want her male friends to see Lucky, because then Lucky would "cock block". The more Lucky would cry, the longer she would leave him there, even after her friends were gone. So, he learned to just be quiet and take it, but as an adult, he hates to be in tight, closed-in spaces and behind closed doors. She hugged him and comforted him as tears rolled down his eyes. She also shared with him about the traumatic situation with her mother too. What started out very ugly, ended up being a beautiful moment that pulled Lucky and Tressa closer together. Lucky spoiled Tressa with everything a woman could want. There was nothing she didn't have, and their relationship was the envy and desire of all the chicks in Richmond.

Tressa also spoiled Lucky back. Although her money wasn't as long as his, her love for him was genuine and she showered it upon him. There was no secret about it, she made it known to him that he was her king. One day, as Tressa laid in the bed beside him with her head resting on his chest announced, "Let's play a game."

"You wanna play strip poker?" He asked with a naughty smile, as he put his arm around her.

"No. I want to play the 'I love you more' game."

"What? What's that?" Lucky was intrigued and had never heard of that game. "How you play that, Sweet Cakes?"

"It's real simple, you try to love your partner more than they are loving you. Then the only thing that can go on is a lot of loving!"

"A'ight Sweet Cakes, let the games begin."

And they did.

When Lucky fell off to sleep, she softly kissed all over his face while wearing red lipstick. She wrote him a note, so when he woke up, he could have love waiting on him. If he was sleep at the time, she knew Lucky couldn't out love her this time. So, basically, she'd won the game.

Lucky woke up and smiled as he read the note written in red ink and sealed with her red lipstick prints on the paper. He looked over at her and she looked so beautiful, like a black Sleeping Beauty as she slept. He got up and washed his hands, brushed his teeth, and when he looked in the mirror, he saw the lipstick prints of the soft kisses she placed all over his face. He grinned, as he thought to himself, that he may have bit more off then he can chew with the "love you more game", for Tressa there wasn't any limits. He sat and contemplated on how he could beat her at her own game.

He held her hand while she slept and just stared at her, fascinated that this was "his woman". When she awoke, it really touched her heart that he held her hand while she slept. She got up and used the bathroom, brushed her teeth and washed her face. When she returned, there was a shrimp and fish plate on his night table. *Oh, I know he didn't order some food and not order me something or even ask me if I wanted anything.*

But before she could even utter a word to him, Lucky placed a napkin over her lap.

"I ordered you a snack Sweet Cakes." He said and fed her a shrimp. He cut up her fish while she was chewing on the shrimp and then continued to feed her. As she took the last bite, he looked into her eyes and said. "I love you more." As he kissed her on her forehead."

She laughed, "Oh, this is how you wanna play? All I can say is play, baby!" She said as she smiled.

They both kept playing the "love game" to the T. Tressa went to the mall and picked up a few things she wanted. While in the lingerie store buying some sexy negligees, she thought about Lucky when she saw some paisley print silk men's pajamas that looked so rich that only a king would wear them. Although the pajamas never stayed on long, she had to buy them for her king. She took to this new love game, but either way, she knew she couldn't lose. She had more time on her hands than he did, so when he gave her money, she spent it on both of them, not just herself.

As she opened up the door, she smiled to herself as she thought, *Luck hates to lose and I refuse to be outdone! But he's just going to have to be a better sport. I am about to beat him at his own game.*

Her thoughts were interrupted when she was blinded by a giant stuffed Panda bear on the love seat, with a super fat herringbone laying on his neck, with a side charm that said "Tressa and Khalil", fluttered in diamonds.

A card lay in between the Panda bears legs that said, "I love you more", with a big smiley face drawn beside it.

She called to thank Lucky and put the groceries away. She started preparing dinner, and while it was cooking, she decided to change the sheets on the bed, only to find twelve long stem roses on the bed, with a card also saying, "I love you more".

She just shook her head and said. "Damn it feels good to be loved."

She went into the bathroom to use the toilet, and when she walked in, she almost had a heart attack. There was a giant stuffed arangatan sitting on the toilet with a roll of toilet paper in his hand. She thought. "Real funny Lucky, you almost scared the shit out of me."

She started screaming at the top of her lungs when she saw the three-carat diamond earrings on the arangatan's ears. She had been wanting those earrings for so long. After all the excitement died down, she said out loud, but talking to herself. "Oh, Lucky you got jokes huh?" She took the arangatan downstairs and put the silk pajamas on him that she had brought for Lucky. "He looks just like Lucky too." She joked with herself. Tressa put the negligee on she had brought for herself on the Panda bear. She sat them both on the table.

The phone rang and she looked at the caller ID and saw that it was Lucky. "I love you baby! I think I am starting to like the love war." She said when she picked up the phone.

"Me too. I was at the gas station and went in my pocket to get my money to pay for the gas and I pulled out the little love note you wrote to me and slipped in my pocket. That was a good one."

"Nah, the earrings, now that was a good one. I was getting ready to call you to thank you for the earrings."

"Just thank me by greeting me buck naked when I get there."

She always did. Sex was a routine part of their day. Luck and Tressa would bump and grind two, sometimes three times a day. She hoped on that dick every chance she got. She didn't want to get caught "sleeping". She silently picked this up from Wiggles, Taj's girlfriend. Wiggles always put it on Taj so he wouldn't stray. Tressa was fully aware of the lifestyle that Lucky lived, and knew as soon as he hit the streets, there were all types of women practically throwing their panties at him. Her philosophy was, if there was never a dull moment in their sex life and he was getting plenty at home, he'd be burnt out when the homewreckers and sack chasers came calling.

Tressa will never forget the day Luck took her on a surprise picnic. They sat on one of the huge rocks along the James River, and she admired the beautiful and lavish houses across the street while unpacking the picnic basket. When everything was out, she noticed some keys that appeared to be house keys, in the bottom of the basket. He looked into her eyes, pointed across the street at a white house and said. "That's our new home." She got up and sprinted over to it. She put the key into the door and she couldn't believe what her eyes revealed to her, cathedral ceilings, sunroom, columns in the foyer and living room, fireplaces and spacious rooms. Lucky stood back gloating, pleased at his decision to purchase the house. "I got like 80 G's put up, so you can start decorating. This is our castle, you're the Queen and I am the King."

"Baby, I love it." She said still in shock.

"Can I get some love?" He pulled her close to him and tongued her down.

She hugged him long and hard. "Boo, I know this may sound ungrateful, but when I think about all that stuff at my apartment, I dread packing it."

"No baby, you don't have to pack nothing. All we have to do is move our clothes. I'm going to keep that apartment over there, so when we have out of town guests, they can just stay there instead of here with us or me spending $100 or $200 for a hotel room."

-6-
With Every Good, Comes the Bad

T ressa and Lucky had some very good times, but there was an unbalance in the relationship. Either things were excellent or horrible between them. The thing that Tressa hated the most, but she overlooked, is that fact that Lucky smoked cigarettes. She despised the smell of cigarette smoke because her stepfather smoked. She expressed this to Lucky, but this was a habit he had since he was thirteen years old and he was now twenty-four. As bad as he wanted to, he could never stop. He accommodated her by never smoking around her or in the house, but she still could smell it all over his clothes.

Lucky also owned two rottweiler dogs, Dopeman and Killer. At first, he kept them at Ms. Betty's house when they lived in the apartment, but when they moved into the house, he had special doghouses built for them. He loved those two dogs as if they were his own children. His mother would always say. "Khalil loves dogs more than he loves anybody."

Tressa secretly was against having the dogs in their home. In the beginning, she'd say. "Luck, I was always told that those dogs would turn on you."

Luck always responded. "No, not my dogs." He would have a bit of an attitude, because Tressa would say something negative about his prize possessions.

It wasn't long before Tressa accepted them and started sharing the responsibility of "Lucky's children" with

51

him. They walked the dogs everyday together. Lucky dropped the dogs off to get groomed every week when he was on his way to get his haircut. She'd sometimes pick them up, but most of the time Lucky was responsible for them. Although he said it was charm school that he faithfully took his dogs to twice a week, he tipped the instructor extra cash to teach the dogs attack tactics.

Tressa was surprised when she went for her yearly check up and the doctor told her she was pregnant. She knew that they had sex like rabbits, and never wore any kind of protection. However, after having unprotected sex for over a year, she had dismissed the thought of being able to get pregnant.

At first, she was happy. Once Lucky found out Tressa was pregnant, he made her feel like it was the happiest day of his life. She fixated on the good parts of becoming a parent. She'd be able to dress the baby cute, this would be both Lucky's and her first child, and they'd live happily ever after. Having a child together would complete them as one.

She couldn't wait until visitation day rolled around so she could share the good news with her brother. Taj thought it was the worst news he'd heard since he'd gotten all that jail time.

"What you mean, you having a baby? So, what about school?"

"I am going to finish college after I have the baby."

"So, what you graduated to being barefoot and pregnant now?"

Taj's tone alone sent her into tears. He wasn't screaming at her, but he was firm when he spoke. Once he saw she was in tears, he began to settle down. His sister's tears always made him weak.

"Look, all I am saying is I need you to rethink this. Sugar Gal, I am begging you not to have this baby. I mean you got ten, fifteen more years, at least, that you can have a baby. Get you somebody who is established in life legitimately, not a hustler. Sugar Gal, this dude ain't going to last long in this game. Matter of fact, the drug game ain't set up for no black man. The best thing for a black man, who has no other choice but the drug game, is to get in and get out as fast as he can. And I don't foresee Lucky ever getting out of that game. And what if he goes to jail or gets killed, where does that leave you and the baby?"

"He is going to get out as soon as he makes enough money to get us a business." She said, speaking up in Lucky's defense.

"Sugar listen, when Lucky first got out of jail, I set him up with a job, that if he wanted to go legit, he could have and he didn't. So, Sugar Gal, I am asking you for me to please rethink this." Taj said, practically begging his sister to reconsider.

That day, leaving the prison, became one of Tressa's saddest days. Tressa felt like she owed her brother her life for all of the sacrifices he made for her after their mother was gone. It meant everything to have her brother's blessings, but what about Lucky's blessings. Then she kept trying to tell herself that men will come and go, but this was her brother for life. Tressa wanted to continue to further her education, and Lucky convinced her she could. She was confused and didn't know what to do. With all the pressures from her brother, she decided that the timing was bad and scheduled an abortion.

While at the abortion clinic, Lucky came into the clinic and begged her not to have the abortion "Please Tressa, don't do this. I love you so much and I promise, I will never leave you to raise this baby by yourself. Please, just don't do this to me."

Lucky kept on trying to persuade her everyway he could. "This must be what God wants, because look how much we make love and this is the first time you ever got pregnant." He pulled out every convincing line he could.

"You know I'll take care of this baby, I mean look how I take care of my dogs. I go all out for them, something that I bought. Now, just imagine how I'd go all out for something I made."

She looked into his eyes to try to search for the solution. Her mind was made up, the abortion was the right thing to do, but when she saw the tears rolling down his face, she had to give in.

Throughout the whole pregnancy, Lucky was very supportive of Tressa. They did everything concerning the baby together. He went to every single doctor appointment with her. They went baby shopping together. He did everything in his power to make sure she was as comfortable as she could be. When she was five months pregnant, she found out she was having twins. Lucky considered himself luckier when he found out the twins were boys. Tressa had to admit, he did hold up his end of the bargain. He took care of her to the fullest.

It was after the birth of the twins, when she noticed a drastic change in Lucky. She first became very disappointed when he informed her. "Tressa, nobody's watching my children but their mother. So, until they go to school, you ain't going to school. You'll be at home with them."

This was the first major conflict she had with Lucky. Most women, especially a new mother, would have loved for their man to make this demand. Tressa, without a doubt, loved her children, but she wanted to finish school. There was no win, over this situation, or no other argument. Once Lucky had his mind made up, there was no way he was bending.

Just like a few months before on Thanksgiving Day, the first Thanksgiving in their new quarter of a million dollar house, where his mother brought over a beautifully decorated ham, with pineapples, cherries and maple on top. Well, Lucky didn't eat pork and did not want it in his house. His mother ignored that fact, since Lucky grew up on pork. Just because he didn't eat it now, why should he make decisions for everybody else? Tressa didn't have it on the table, but on the kitchen counter top. Lucky saw it and went ballistic. "Get that damn swine out my fucking house!"

"Your mother brought it to eat. She had to have it." Tressa tried to keep Lucky calm and please his mother at the same time.

Lucky went into the restroom, washed his hands, and when he came back to the kitchen and saw that the ham was still on the countertop, he casually went under his shirt, pulled out his gun and shot the ham. It splattered all across the kitchen, walls, floors, everywhere. Naturally, Lucky's insane outburst ruined their ThanksGiving. This was her first warning to get out, but Tressa was too set in her comfort zone and didn't take heed.

The ominous signs about Lucky's violence were constantly revealed to Tressa, but she never would take a stand against Lucky. She thought the last straw was when she found out who was really residing in her old apartment.

One day, she got a call from the rental office warning her that there are too many complaints coming from other tenants about her apartment. There was always fighting, almost everyday. Tressa was in shock because there shouldn't be anybody in the apartment on a daily basis. Tressa thought the management was lying, until the day she got up early, grabbed the keys to Lucky's rental car, (he had just returned from a "business trip"), left the twins and Lucky sleeping while she went out to pick up a few things from the grocery store.

Tressa ran into one of her old neighbors, a little old nosey lady, who lived in the building next door. She informed Tressa of some shocking information, "I liked you so much better than that other girl that moved into your apartment."

"What girl?" Tressa asked surprisingly. The old lady pointed her finger, moving up and down, as she continued to give the gossip of the hour.

"That other girl is a pure damn winch, wearing those super tight clothes. The heifer don't even speak to me. And, her and that fella that used to come see you in the big fancy car, all they do is fight. I can't stand the little winch."

Tressa could feel the heat come all over her. She literally began to sweat. She thanked the lady and walked away, leaving her basket in the middle of the dairy aisle before the old lady could finish. *No, he didn't move some bitch into my fucking apartment and they over there fucking on my God damn bed. Oh hell no! This nigga really think I am some weak bitch, don't he? That's good, cuz I got something for him and his bitch. Trust me when I tell you.*

In a trance, to this very day, she believed she was having an out of body experience with the episode that was about to play out. Tressa went straight to the apartment, and when she put her key into the lock, it didn't work. She went over to the rental office to get the right key. They never questioned her because the apartment was still leased in her name. The only car in the parking lot was the neighbor who lived in the next building over, whom worked

at night.   Everyone else was at work.   She thought that
maybe the girl was at work too.   Tressa returned to her
apartment, put the key in, but there was a dead bolt lock
on the door stopping her from entering the apartment.   This
only pissed her off more.   So, she knocked on the door.   She
noticed a pair of eyes peak out through the blinds to see
who it was.   Shortly after, she heard a female voice scream,
"Ah, shit!!!"   No one ever came to the door.   Tressa's knocks
just got louder and louder.   Her knocking turned into
banging then she yelled.   "Open up the door, bitch!!!!   Be a
woman!   I know you're in there!   Oh, you bold enough to
live in my apartment, but you ain't woman enough to face
me eye to eye?"

Tressa continued to scream, but the girl on the other
side of the door still didn't respond.   "Oh, that's OK bitch,
cuz I am going to teach ya punk ass a lesson, believe that!"

Tressa went to her car and called "Pop A Lock" to
come out and unlock the bolt lock.   They told her it would
be forty minutes before they could get there.   She sat in
Lucky's rental car with her eyes glued to the window, and
for the next ten minutes, she watched the blinds open up
just enough for the eyes behind them to see she was still
sitting outside.

Forty minutes seemed like it would take forty years.
Anticipating when the locksmith would get there was
driving her crazy.   So, she took matters into her own hands.
She ran up the street to the gas station and returned.

Tressa decided to give the girl one last chance.   She
decided to go at it with a little more calm approach.   Instead
of banging, she knocked on the door.   "Oh, you still in there
playing possum huh?   Lying up in my shit!   I don't think so.
Baby, oh you coming out, one way or another.   Dead or
alive!"   At that moment, Tressa poured gasoline under the
door.

Tressa listened for a minute and counted to thirty
before she lit the match.   She could hear the girl running
around the house.   As she counted and reached twenty, her
cell phone rang.   It was Lucky.   Of course, the girl had
called Lucky in a hysterical panic.   Lucky spoke calmly into
the phone.   "Baby, get out of there because that bitch done
called the police on you.   Get out of there before you end up
in jail."

Tressa hung up the phone because she could care less about what Lucky had to say. He called right back again, Tressa would not respond. "Listen baby, I know you're hurt, but you're not in your right frame of mind. Please snap out of this. I apologize, now please just leave."

Tressa heard him, trying to calm the other girl down who had called him on his cell phone. He told her. "Just calm down, I am talking to her now."

"Tell that bitch to just come to the door, and then I'll leave. You got the nerve to be talking to that BITCH and she done called the police on me?"

"Baby, listen just leave before the police get there." Lucky pleaded with her.

Tressa hung up again, and at that moment, she lit the match and calmly walked down to the steps and then to the window as she sang, "*Burn Baby Burn*". She knew there was no back door, so there was only one way out if she was planning on getting out alive. She could hear the girl screaming, but for some odd reason, Tressa was still in a trance. She couldn't make out any of the words that the girl was saying, it sounded like another language.

Tressa's phone rang again, it was Lucky. She answered and immediately said. "Stop blowing up my damn phone and call your bitch, tell her to just jump out the window, I'll catch her." She said laughing.

"Fuck her. I ain't thinking bout her. The bitch could burn as far as I care. I just need you to get up outta there before you go to jail." At that moment, she heard one of her babies in the background cry and that's when she snapped out of her trance.

She ran to the rental car and pulled off as she heard the sirens getting closer and closer by the second. Once she got to the corner, she looked in her rear view mirror and Tressa saw the girl in the window about to jump. She didn't go back, it wasn't worth it. Lucky or the girl wasn't worth her losing everything, her children, her sanity, her freedom, her self-respect and self-esteem were more important at that moment. Her heart dropped when she passed the speeding police cars, ambulances and roaring fire engines. She could have been caught red handed with the gas can in the car, but she was spared, this time.

As she continued to drive home, her cell phone rang and rang. It was Lucky calling each time, but she never answered. She drove around for a while and when she finally returned home, the twins had the house tore up. Lucky greeted her with an argument, fussing about her not answering the phone, in an attempt to try to side track the argument she had in store for him. "Yo, why didn't you answer the phone? You didn't know if something was wrong with the boys or not?"

"What? Why you didn't find some place other than my apartment for your bitch to live in?"

"Look, now which is more important, your kids or that apartment? Now, why couldn't you answer the damn phone! Were you on the phone with your nigga or something?" Lucky falsely accused her even though he knew better, anything to deflect his cheating ass.

"Don't even come at me like that, with the bull! I am not the one who's unfaithful here. You are!"

"Well, you ain't answer your phone."

"And sometimes you don't answer yours either!" She screamed back at him. "I ain't got to put up with this shit!"

"Oh, yeah?" Lucky asked. "Well, where you going to go with two babies? Who gonna want you? Who is going to treat you like me?" He was enraged. He charged towards her. She thought he was going to hit her for the first time, but he didn't. He just grabbed her cell phone and smashed it into a thousand pieces. She was scared and so were the boys. Her sons just crawled over to their mommy crying. She picked them both up and went into the nursery.

Lucky came to the door. "Tressa, I am sorry all of this turned out this way. That was a girl named Dee that brings work for me from out of town. She liked me, but I promise you, it ain't like that." Tressa didn't respond, she only rocked her twins in the rocking chair back and forth. Before he walked away from the door, he stated in a firm voice. "And Tressa, don't you dare think about taking my children away from this house."

Later she started beating herself up. *What in the hell was I thinking? Am I loosing my mind or what? I just committed arson for this simple ass nigga. I should have set*

*his ass on fire instead of setting her on fire. I really feel bad.
I've got to get out of this relationship and that's for real.*

All of these things were warning signs for Tressa,
but she was suffering from something other than being
addicted to the lavish lifestyle that she had become
accustomed to living. See, Lucky never even raised one
hand to Tressa, but the type of abuse he inflicted upon her
was more detrimental than any bruise, scrape or scar that
could heal. Lucky continuously abused her mentally. He
slowly tore down Tressa's self-esteem, made her lose focus
of her goals, her morals, her capabilities and her strengths.
He controlled her with money, because she went from
struggling and working three jobs, to an extravagant
lifestyle. She had settled so long for Lucky's unacceptable,
controlling and psychotic behavior.

From the ham episode, to cheating with females who
were never the cream of the crop, only the bottom of the
barrel, to the apartment episode. And now this murderous
evening, where two innocent people lost their lives because
of his unjustified jealous rage which could have ultimately
caused her two sons their life.

What kind of father would kill in front of his
children? What kind of father would kill somebody in the
driver's seat, while his kids are in the backseat? Lucky was
just that much of a lunatic that he didn't have enough self-
control over himself. Or maybe, he just didn't care about or
have enough respect for his two sons or Tressa sitting in the
car. He didn't once stop to think that he could have
missed, or the stray bullet could have hit one of the boys.
The thought just never crossed his mind.

Up to this point, Tressa had overlooked a lot of
Lucky's psychotic episodes, but now he had had gone too
far. There was no doubt about it, something had to give!
After this ultimate stunt, it was apparent that Lucky's
performances were only going to get worse. So, Tressa had
to draw the line and this had to be it.

-7-
Hot Sex on a Platter

Meanwhile, **back to Tressa locked in the house...**

She began to ask herself *when I am going to draw the line. Every week it seems like it is something different. When is enough really enough? It's not just about me anymore. I've got two other people I've got to think about. They count on me and I can't let them down. This is it, I've got to go. I don't care where? I don't care if I gotta go live in the projects, but at least I'll have peace of mind. That is worth any amount of money.*

Tressa decided to get into bed and get a good night sleep. But, before she pulled the covers back to get into the bed, she kneeled to say her prayers.

"Lord, in Jesus name. Lord, I know I haven't always been the obedient child that you'd like for me to be, and I would like to ask for forgiveness. God, I ask you for peace of mind. I ask you to look into my heart, and if there, is anything wrong there I beg you to remove it from me. I ask you God, to give me the strength to leave this man. This man doesn't deserve me. I know I have had some shortcomings due to my own selfishness and greed, but God, my children shouldn't have to suffer for my mistakes. God, you said you'd protect fools and babies and my sons are babies and I am a fool. Now, I ask you to replace my spirit of greed with strength, and give me the wisdom to walk away from this

mean, jealous, envious and crazy man.   In Jesus name I pray. Amen."

Tressa stepped onto the stairs to get into the high Victorian style bed, and pulled the satin sheets over her shoulders. Every time she closed her eyes, all she could see was the instant replay of Peako's brains soaring onto the windshield. She rolled over to Khalil's side of the bed and looked inside of his nightstand drawer where she knew he always kept prescription drugs that he bought off the street. She had never taken anything other than a Tylenol, but tonight she needed something strong to put her under. The first thing she came across was Xanax. She took two pills, and before she knew it, she was floating and spaced out and drowsy as hell.

When Khalil returned, feeling guilty as usual, he was horny but he knew Tressa was still upset. Consequently, sex was out of the question. He hopped into the shower and tried to think of ways to make up with Tressa for his foolish impulsive move.

When he came out of the shower, the room was dark. The ambiance couldn't have been any better for lovemaking. He wanted Tressa so bad but he was sure he couldn't get any tonight. He lied in bed and loosely put his arm around her. He could feel her warm, relaxed body in the bed, sleeping like a baby. Her sexy body beside his was making him hot as a hooker on Dollar Day. He pulled her closer and she could feel his pulsing rock hard penis. To his surprise, she moved her butt a little to let him know she was up. He reached around and ran his fingers between her legs, and to his surprise, she was soaking wet and just as horny as he was. He turned her almost lifeless body over on her back as if she weighed 20 pounds. Immediately after, he teased her a little by rubbing his hands over her breast and hardening her nipples. He looked at her in astonishment, as she said in a slurred voice. "Do you see something you want?" But he was so mesmerized, he didn't realize that she was just as high as a kite.

He stuttered when he replied. "Yes, I want you to be my wife." The way he looked into her eyes made her whole body quiver. He started planting little kisses all over her body, moving down her neck, nibbling and sucking. *God*

62

knows his soft lips feel so good, she thought to herself. Tressa wanted him to stop but her body could not resist.

His hands covered every inch of her body making her want more. Grasping for breath, Tressa was moaning and did not want him to stop. Moving his lips to her mouth, he was kissing her so deeply, sticking his tongue into her waiting mouth. She began to quiver under him, needing him to please her.

Tressa could then feel his tongue slowly moving over her ebony thighs, his hands gently, but firmly, opened her legs. She heard him inhale deeply savoring the luscious scent of her pussy. Urging him, she began thrusting her love nest towards his lips, anxiously waiting to feel his mouth on her clit. Oh mercy, she almost lost it when his tongue made contact with her love button. Damn, he had a way of eating coochie. He began directing his tongue in her pussy hole making love to her with his tongue. Eyes rolling in the back of her head, and grinding her twat all up in his face, hands cupping and caressing her breast. At that very moment she began speaking "in tongues". Her body convulsing after waves and waves of orgasms shook her whole body, she gasped for air and sweat dripped from her body. He was still solely concentrating on her pussy even catching some of the juices that squirted onto her thighs.

Lucky was smiling devilishly as he looked up at her. *Oh Lord, no more, oh please, no more,* she thought. He grabbed her legs, placing them over his shoulders and she could see his massive hard penis dangling like a microphone between his legs. He leaned forward, and she felt the penetration of the head of his penis entering into her love tunnel. Thrusting upwards, accepting his deep strokes inside her hot contracting poonannie, moaning and grunting as he was moving his hips as if he was stirring a pot or mixing a cake. He had her simmering and damn it was about to boil over. All she could yell was. "Baby fuck me harder!" Immediately, she thought to herself. "Oh my God!"

She could feel his manhood swell bigger, and an orgasm building again. "Mercyyyyyyy babyyyyyyyyyyyyyy!" She screamed, clawing at his back. "Mmmmmmmmmm." It felt as if his cock was coming up through her throat.

Feeling the head of his penis so deep inside her stomach, she said. "Fuck me baby, yessssssssssssssss."

-8-
Audi 5,000
A.K.A.
Time to Roll Out

The next morning, the phone rang and they were both still in bed. "Yo." Lucky said, when he picked it up. He paused for a minute and then spoke. "I'm in the house, but how much you got? 15? Oh, a'ight, man give me 45 minutes cuz I gotta get dressed and go to the other spot to get it. A'ight, see you then."

He rolled over and looked at Tressa, who was sleeping, and he was disappointed that he had to get up and leave Tressa after their intense lovemaking the night before. But, there was money to be made. He kissed Tressa on the shoulder, who was lying on her side.

"Listen baby, the dude Motor, got 15G's he trying to spend wit me. I'll be back in about an hour and a half, I promise. And today, I'll make everything up to you. You'll forget all about everything that happened yesterday. I promise I'm gonna show you that I'm sho-nuff sorry for all of this."

Normally she would have started an argument, but not this morning. Tressa was making her escape and needed him out of the house. She simply said in a sweet, but groggy voice. "I know you will." She closed her eyes

65

until she heard the door slam and Lucky's 500 Benz speed out of the driveway.

As soon as she couldn't hear the car any longer, she sprinted over to the window pulling back the custom made drapes to confirm that Lucky was truly gone. Tressa ran to the kitchen to grab the whole box of trash bags, and then sprinted back to her children's room as they slept without a care in the world. She went over to their closet and drawers, and in no kind of organization, grabbed everything that she could and proceded to fill the trash bags. She tied the bags, rolled them to the bottom of the steps, and slid them over to the garage door. She then neatly placed them in the car, but most of the space was taken up by the cases of pampers. She grabbed what she could fit into the station wagon of her own clothes. What she wanted to take, but couldn't fit, she just placed in the big, brown City provided trash cans that were out back, and dragged them into her neighbors yard and dragged the next door neighbor's trash can into hers. She would just have to come back for her stuff. As long as she had the majority of her children's clothes that's all that mattered to her.

Tressa looked behind the speakers in the bedroom and gathered the money Lucky kept there. It was about $9,000.00 and some jewelry. She gathered the money, the children, her valuable documents, all of the jewelry, including his 18 carat rose gold diamond Audemars Piguet watch, and one of his clean guns that she knew for sure didn't have any bodies on it. Next, she awoke her kids and hurriedly took them to the car and strapped them into their carseats.

She ran back to the door to get the last bag she had sitting at the door. Before she shut the door, she looked around as the tears filled her eyes. She felt hesitant and questioned herself. *Should I just walk away from all of this, from all the years that I have invested?* Tressa could not believe she doubted her decision.

All it took was one episode to pop into her head that gave her the strength she needed to shut the door on this chapter of her life.

She remembered the day the police took her mother off to jail for killing her abusive stepfather, like it was yesterday. Tressa knew if she stayed, she could and most likely would, suffer the same fate as her mother. Tressa could not let that happen and have someone else raise her boys.

With her heart beating a million miles a minute, she nervously backed out of the garage. She knew time was not on her side. At this point, she knew Lucky would be rolling up at any minute. That was her fear, she definitely did not want to bump into him on her way out.

She drove to a secluded payphone on the other side of the interstate and called Wiggles. She knew that if Wiggles were willing, she'd be the only person Tressa could trust at this moment. Even though Wiggles was a crack head, she was the one person who couldn't be paid off when it came to Tressa and her kids. That she was sure of, but she wasn't sure if Wiggles would embrace her.

Wiggles was the person on every strip whose house all the hustler's hung out in, gambled, tricked in, cut up and bagged up in. Wiggles was a straight junkie, but also a functioning and dependable junkie. She used to be in an intense relationship with Taj years before, but when he took a fall and went to jail four years ago, she got strung out on crack. She has turned so many tricks and degraded herself so much that she's burnt out in the prostitution world. None of the hustlers would dare accept sex from her. They all looked out for her, because over the years, she always kept a house in the hood. The house may have been located on the next street over, or a few blocks up, but always in the same vicinity. When the police would raid one of her houses, she would have to make do on whosever couch she could use. But in a couple days, she'd have another place right around the block. The neighborhood hustlers would keep the water, lights and gas on for her, after all, it was just as much their spot as hers and always more beneficial to them, then it was ever to her.

Wiggles had a dark brown complexion, with bad skin, from picking and scratching at her face when she was high. She had a gold tooth in the front of her mouth and then a space where a tooth once had been. With a shape once to die for, Wiggles curves had withered away. Her once round, fat butt and face were saggy and flat. She was skinny everywhere, except for her pot belly. People who didn't know her always thought she was 6 months pregnant. She wore small cornrows braided to the back, and stood about 5'7". In spite of her being a crack head and a dope fiend, she always kept herself dressed neat, which usually consisted of jeans with a cardboard crease in them and a polo style shirt. Most of the hustlers' girlfriends gave her old clothes and shoes. She'd wash them and iron them to make them look and feel new to her. Although she ravished her body with drugs, deep down, Wiggles took pride in her appearance.

Wiggles' place was nice, considering it was a crack house. The hustlers made it comfortable for them since they spent the majority of their time there. One bought a washing machine and dryer for his girlfriend, but when they broke up before he had a chance to give it to her, it ended up staying right at Wiggles' house and she taxed all the drug boys to wash, dry and fold their laundry. They usually paid her with coke.

She was always cooking and selling dinners. Wiggles might've smoked the pipe all day, everyday, but one thing for sure two things for certain, she could cook her ass off. Wiggles' gourmet cooking skills made it hard on the hustlers' girlfriends. When one of the girlfriends mentioned that they would be cooking, that was never an incentive to make the hustlers run home to their girlfriends. It wasn't anything out of the ordinary for them to get a home cooked meal, because Wiggles cooked a big breakfast and dinner everyday.

Wiggles had very envious and cunning ways. Wiggles use to be the "Prom Queen" back in the day. She was every man's fantasy and now she was every man's sexual nightmare! She was very jealous of any of the hustlers' girlfriends, although she was fully aware she would never be able to have any of the hustlers. She was very protective of them, like a sister would be to a younger brother. In her eyes, she did all the cooking and laundry to spite the girlfriends. She would not make it easy for scandalous little golddiggers to get a come-up. They too would have to work for theirs. Even if the girls ever got out of line, it took nothing but Wiggles to be paid an egg (heroine) or a crack rock for her to go walk the dogs on one of the girls butt.

68

Most of the girlfriends catered to Wiggles because they knew she was an old head. Besides smoking crack, Wiggles had a good head on her shoulders and was sharp on her feet.

Wiggles used to mess with Taj when Tressa was just a little girl. Tressa use to praise Wiggles. Wiggles was her idol. See, Wiggles was eight years older than Tressa, and Tressa adored everything about her. When she grew up, she wanted to be just like Wiggles. She loved to wear her hair like Wiggles, wanted to walk and talk like Wiggles. With Tressa only having a brother, Wiggles was the sister she never had. Wiggles always felt connected to Tressa. She vowed that it would never matter what happened between her and Taj, Tressa would always be her sister.

When Wiggles would come over Tressa's house to see Taj, Tressa would always intrude, straight cock blocking! She'd end up spending all her time with Tressa. Wiggles would do her hair, help her pick out clothes for school, help her with her homework, and just show her how to be a fly girl. Wiggles didn't mind, because she genuinely loved Tressa. Taj always admired Wiggles for the way she treated his sister.

After Taj and Wiggles broke up when he went to jail, Tressa was hurt that Wiggles had left her brother for dead. But as she got older and matured, she realized that Wiggles was only human and had needs too. But at the same time, Taj was her brother and that was were her loyalty was. Tressa rarely got to see Wiggles anymore.

As Tressa grew up, she started meeting people all over Richmond. If they were from anywhere near Sugar Bottom, she'd inquire about her sister, Wiggles. One day, she asked this dude that her friend Dutchess knew about Wiggles, and he made it known that Wiggles was a crack head. Tressa lost her mind and was ready to fight him for saying some whack mess like that. She was pissed! Unfortunately, she later ran into Wiggles and saw with her own eyes.

Tressa was at the 7-11 Convenience Store with Lucky one day playing her lotto numbers when she was pregnant with her sons. Out of nowhere, she heard an excited voice yell. "Treesssaaaa!"

69

Tressa wasn't sure, but she thought she recognized the voice. She turned to look and the person wasn't anybody she knew. Tressa frowned her face because she didn't know who this skeletal looking chick was.

"Tressa, hey baby."

"Who are you, where do I know you from?" Tressa asked, totally confused.

"Tressa, it's me. It's Wiggles." She looked shocked.

Tressa's heart dropped. Speaking before she knew it, she exclaimed. "Oh my God! What happened to you? You look like a shitty mess!"

"I know! Between the dope and the crack, this shit got me gone. I am trying to get it together, but girrrlll, it's hard."

"Wiggles, you gotta get clean. If I can help you in any way, just let me know. You know that if you want to go to rehab, I'll go with you."

"I know you will, but I ain't even gonna front, I'm not ready yet. But I'm gonna let you know when I'm ready."

It broke Tressa's heart to hear the words coming out of Wiggles mouth. Tears began to form in Tressa's eyes when the realness of the words set in that her sister, her icon, her leader, was strung out on the glass dick, the crack pipe. She felt so betrayed that she couldn't even look Wiggles in the face anymore.

"Tressa, don't look at me away from me like that."

"Wiggles, I can't help it." She burst into tears. "You were my sister, and now look at you. I depended on you."

"And believe it, you still can depend on me if you need me. I will come and help you with your baby when you have it."

"You gotta be clean."

Tears started to run down Wiggles' eyes when she seen the hurt written all over Tressa's face. Lucky approached, and Tressa just turned to walk away. "I gotta go."

Wiggles called out. "Tressa, I am still your sister, and no matter what, I am gonna be here for you when you need me. I love you and even at your darkest point, I am going to be here! You know where I live and no matter how much I move from block to block, I'm gonna always have the same number. When you need me, I am gonna be right there for you, no matter how high I'm getting or how clean I am. I promise you that on everything I love, on my life, on the crack pipe, I promise you!"

Tressa never responded. Instead, she just hurried over to the car and broke down crying when she finally got inside. From that moment on, she acted as if Wiggles didn't exist. Wiggles understood, because she knew the hurt Tressa felt. She saw the same hurt on the faces of everyone she loved and disappointed when she became a drug addict.

As Tressa put the two dimes in the pay phone, she wondered if Wiggles really meant what she said. *Wiggles I need you, and you promised me. Promises aren't made to be broken. I hope you meant exactly what you said. There's nobody else I can call. Dutchess's money hungry ass can't be trusted. I know most likely she'll sell me out to Lucky for the right price. Missy is now into church and I don't want to drag her into this mess, but I know she'll be there for me. Please Wiggles, I hope you come through for me. I need you to.*

She listened as the phone rang. "Hello." A guy answered on the third ring.

Tressa was thrown off by a man answering. *Maybe it's the wrong number, maybe she moved or maybe she's locked up.*

"Hello, I am trying to get in touch with Wiggles. Is she available?"

"Who dis?" The guy asked in a hesitating voice.

She was relieved when he asked, but could barely hear, due to the loud noise in the background. "It's Sugar Gal." She said.

"Hole up!" He screamed at the people making noise, with his mouth directly over the mouthpiece of the phone. "Wiggggles, get da phone somebody name Sugar Gal on the phone."

"Damn, is it that serious? I ain't never seen you move that quick." The guy said to Wiggles, as she ran over to grab the phone from him.

Wiggles snatched the phone out of his hand. "Hello." She said in a worried, but happy tone.

"Wiggles, it's me Tressa. I'm in trouble and I need you. You ain't gonna believe."

Wiggles cut her off. "Where are you and where do I need to meet you."

"I am at a pay phone, but I can't stay here long. I don't want to go to your house. Can you catch a cab and meet me. I'll pay for it."

"No, hold on one second. DON'T HANG UP!" Wiggles could hear the hurt, pain and desperation in Tressa's voice. She was talking low to the guy that answered the phone. "Look, I have a family emergency. I need to use the car."

Tressa listened attentively, holding her free ear closed so she could hear better, but keeping a watchful eye on her children sleeping in the car.

"I ain't know you had family." The dude said in a joking way.

"Yeah, crack heads and dope fiends got family too." Wiggles got back on the phone, "I'm on my way out the door, now where do I need to go."

"Ummm, meet me at the service station at Parham and Broad."

"It's gonna take me about twenty minutes to get there, but don't worry I will be there."

"OK, just hurry! Please, Wiggles. Bye." Tressa said.

But before she hung up, Wiggles called out to her to try to catch her from hanging up. "Tressa!!!!" She screamed into the phone.

"Yes." Tressa said, hoping that Wiggles hadn't changed her mind.

"Never say bye, because bye means forever! Simply say see you later!"

"Oh, OK, see you in a few."

"Alright, see you in a few then!"

Tressa looked around suspiciously as she got into the car and began to drive to the meeting place. Tressa arrived right before Wiggles did and she thought about some of the countless times Wiggles had come through for her. There was the time when she got into her first fight, the time when Taj got locked up and Wiggles went down to child protective services posing as her mother to take her home, and the time she got caught stealing fake fingernails out of Peoples Drug Store.

72

Tressa reflected on her very first fist fight and giggled a bit. It was third period at Fairfield Middle School, Tressa's best friend, Dutchess, ran into the classroom with the gossip for the hour. "Tressa girl, I just ran into Michelle Booger, and she said that she gonna punch you in your face because you think you are cute."

"What?" Tressa asked, completely taken aback.

"That's what she said." Dutchess replied.

She had no idea why Michelle wanted to lay a finger on her. She had never done a thing to Michelle Booger, they never even had a conversation before. She did not have the foggiest idea why Michelle wanted to step to her.

Tressa was petrified! The night before, she discreetly told her mother that she might have to call her to pick her up from school because she may be getting into a fight. Cyn asked if she wanted her to call the principal and she said no, because she didn't want to seem like a punk. Amazingly, Cyn just agreed, but if things got to out of hand, for her to just call her. Cyn knew this would be an important life lesson that Tressa had to learn, even though she was just in the third grade.

The next day at school, Tressa raised her hand and asked could she go to the restroom. She went straight to the pay phone. She called Cyn, but Cyn wasn't at her desk. She then tried to call home, but Cyn wasn't there either. Instead, Wiggles answered. Taj was suspended from school and Wiggles had skipped school to be with him.

"Hello." Wiggles answered.

"Hey Wiggles, is my mother there?"

"Nah, she at work."

"I tried calling her at work, but they said she wasn't there. I need her to come and pick me up."

"What's wrong with you, you sick or something?"

"No, I need her to pick me up cuz this girl name Michelle Booger is gonna beat me up!"

"What? You need Cyn to pick you up for what?" Wiggles asked confused.

"Cuz this girl Michelle." Tressa said whimpering.

Wiggles cut her off before she could go any further. "Are you sure she gonna try to fight you?"

"Yes, she skipped class just so she could look for me to fight me, and I know people told her where I was."

Wiggles could not believe her ears. Even though Tressa had never been in a fight before, no sister of hers was going to be pushed around. She knew she couldn't go up to the school and fight for her. She would have to call a cab, and by the time it got there, it would be too late. Besides, Tressa was still in elementary school and Wiggles was too old to mess with those kids. But, she was going to make sure Tressa knew what to do until she could get up to the school and have her back.

The phone was silent for a minute. "Hello." Tressa said, because she thought the call was disconnected. At that very moment, Wiggles put some pitch and authority into her voice. "Look, let me tell you one mafucking thing, you ain't ever gonna run from nobody. You hear me? She ain't no damn body. Now listen to what I'm saying. When she walks up to you, you don't say nothing to her. Don't argue, don't say nothing! Just hit her as hard as you can in the face and just keep hitting her and don't ever stop hitting her. Whatever you do, don't let her hit you first. You hear me?"

"But I don't want to get in trouble." Tressa said in a weak voice.

"Look, if I find out you didn't do what you was told, and you know I know people who got sisters that go to that school, and they will tell me you didn't hit her first, I am gonna whip your ass myself when you get home. Do you understand?"

As she held the phone and listened to Wiggles warning, she wasn't even scared anymore. All she could think of is that she knew she had to do what she had to do. She hung up the phone and headed back to class.

When the bell finally rang, she gathered her things and headed for her next class. As soon as she got onto the main walkway in the campus style school, she saw Michelle Booger coming towards her with what seemed like the whole school following behind her. The butterflies started to flutter in her stomach as Michelle Booger got closer.

Michelle Booger got within an arm's reach of Tressa. She looked Tressa up and down. "Oh, I hearred you said you wasn't scared of me? Did you say that?"

Seeing the silent and hyped look on the crowds face, gave her the push she needed. "Yes, I said it, cuz I don't

74

have a reason to be scared of you or anybody else." Tressa was almost in tears, but didn't let it show. Her heart was beating fast, and although it was a winter day, Tressa could feel the perspiration under her arms.

"What?" Michelle Booger snapped with plenty of attitude, shocked at Tressa's response. Then Michelle Booger started taking off her earrings and fake gold tarnished rings while saying. "Oh, beitch, I'm bout to make you know that you should be afraid of me!"

"Whoooop!" To everybody's shock, Tressa hit her with a right hook that made her stumble, but before she got her balance back, Tressa hit her with another right hook that dropped big, bad, Michelle "Bully" Booger to her knees. Tressa just kept laying Michelle with blow after blow and never letting up. Booger was on her knees, and every lick she was trying to throw was only hitting Tressa's legs, which was doing no damage to Tressa at all. It took the school's teachers, custodians and the assistant principal to try to pull her away and calm her down.

Tressa snapped out of reminiscing when Wiggles rode in a souped up Cadilliac beside her and rolled down the window. Tressa was smiling. "Who Cadi you got?"

"Girl, it's mine. Well, by law it is. It's in my name. The dude Boo-Boo paid me to register it in my name, but really it's his car."

"Oh, Ok. You keep you a damn hustle, girl."

"Girl, they all think I am a stupid dope fiend. But, I ain't a coke smoking or dope sniffing fool all the time. I still got game for days for they asses."

Tressa laughed from the depths of her stomach, although she was ashamed at how she had held such a grudge with Wiggles for so long.

"If you are on the run, I need to get you out of this lighted area." Wiggles seriously stated.

"On my way over here, I ran across this old trick and gave him some head for fifty dollars, but while I was on my knees I stuck him for a $100. So, I got $150 to help get you a room." Wiggles said.

Tressa shook her head at Wiggles bluntness, she always, seemed to amaze her. There was no shame in Wiggles game. It was just like back in the day. Wiggles still had her back and was as gangster as ever.

"Girl, those babies are so cute, I can't believe you had twins."

Tressa parked her car on a side street and got most of her belongings out of the car and put them in Wiggles' car. What she couldn't fit, Wiggles said she would come back later to get. "You need to get settled and put those kids to sleep somewhere comfortable."

Wiggles used her ID to get Tressa checked into a cheap, one story hotel way on the outskirts of town, some place Lucky would never look.

-9-
Money Talks, B/S Walks

The next day, Wiggles came over to the cheap, raunchy hotel room to watch the children while Tressa went to run some errands. Tressa was worried that the twins would drive Wiggles crazy whining because they were so attached to Tressa. Tressa made Wiggles promise that she wouldn't get high around her kids, and she meant it. Wiggles knew this was the last chance for her to make things right between them. One of the reasons Wiggles started getting high, is because she couldn't live with herself after crossing Taj. Taj was a remarkable man. He was her everything and she didn't know how to cope with him being incarcerated and locked away from her. There were so many days she wished she could go back and make it up to him, but she knew after she missed the first month, and had taken his money, that there was no turning back. She knew if Taj was ever released from jail, she would be the first person he'd want to see to seek his revenge on. The wages of double crossing Taj was death and there was no way around it. There was no amount of time that could heal Taj's wounded and broken heart. Wiggles thought that just maybe, if she lived up to all of the expectations that Tressa had of her, coupled with knowing that Tressa was Taj's pride and joy, that just maybe he'd let bygones be bygones and spare her life.

Dressed in blue jeans, a Nike T-shirt and some Air Max sneakers, the first place Tressa went was to the housing authority. They told her that the waiting list was six months. They gave her a list of government subsidized apartment complexes. She studied the list, but she couldn't figure out which was the best place to live. So, she started going to each one, some had three year waiting lists and others were not even accepting applications.

When she called over the phone to get directions to one of the complexes, the woman told her that there was only a three-month waiting list. But when she arrived, the woman took one look at Tressa, and told her they were not accepting applications. When Tressa visited the last complex on the list, she thought, as she parked, *Lord please let this work out.*

While filling out the application, she was told there was a six-month wait. She knew she couldn't live in any hotel for six months and she surely couldn't go back to Lucky. She had to finesse a way to get moved to the top of the waiting list. She looked at the man who worked as an office assistant. He was wearing some balded up shoes that turned up at the toe, with some old Lee jeans with a cardboard crease in it. He saw her looking back at him. She could tell off the back that he was a real buster. He was full of himself, so she made him her mark. She knew all she had to do was stroke his ego a little and maybe, just maybe, he could be of assistance to her.

"Ms. Shawsdale." He called into the waiting room.

Tressa got up and went into the cluttered office. He looked over her application to make sure she had filled it out properly.

With an impressed look on his face, he said. "This is the first application that has been filled out completely and I did not have to ask you to change or fill in missing information."

"Does that mean I get the apartment?" She asked in a humble, soft voice.

He smiled and started to stumble as he began to speak. "Ummm, ummm, ummm, there's a waiting list." The phone rang, he answered it and she could tell by his conversation and uncomfortable tone that it was a bill collector.

Oh, so he needs money. I know good and well he is not going to let this opportunity of free money pass him by. I am gonna try my hand with him and see.

She considered the possibility that if he didn't bite, that she may lose the opportunity for the six-month wait list spot altogether. But what did she have to lose? She and her kids were already living in a raunchy hotel as it was.

"Excuse me, but I had to take that call."

"No problem." She said.

"As I was saying, it's a six-month waiting list and it's important that when you get a letter in the mail advising that you are next to receive a vacant apartment, you must call the rental office ASAP."

"Look, I don't mean to sound forward, but I need a place for me and my two sons to live and I need it before Friday. I'll give you $300 to move me to the top of the list and $300 more the day I get the keys. I noticed when I pulled up that they are working on an apartment. I see you the HNIC, (Head Negro In Charge) and I know if anybody can make it happen, you can. Can you make this my address by Friday?" Tressa said confidently.

His eyes lit up like a big Kool Aid smile. It covered his whole face when he heard the magic words "three hundred dollars" come out of Tressa's mouth.

"If I did make this happen, you have to keep your mouth shut! Take it to your grave, I mean it!"

"Oh, no doubt about that."

"Just come back at 11 Friday morning and we can do your walk through inspection and I'll have your keys for you then."

"Thanks so much! How much will my rent be?"

He looked over the paperwork and declared. "Since you don't have any income coming in, it'll be $25.00 a month. So, you will need your prorated rent of $17.00 and a standard security deposit of $56.00 to move in."

She smiled as he gave her the address to her new place, 3012 Apt J; *J as in thank you Jesus!*

Her next order of business was to get a safe deposit box for her collateral. This should have been the first thing she did because it was very important. This was going to be her assurance that Luck would let them be and not try to get Tressa and the boys to come back home.

She looked at her watch and saw that she still had time. She went to look for a smaller car that she could afford. She called her younger cousin, Gator and asked him to go car shopping with her. Gator agreed to go with her. She remembered that she read somewhere that she couldn't get an expensive car because Social Services wouldn't let her get food stamps if she had a car over $6,000 in her name. Even though the BMW was in both, Lucky and Tressa's name, she got Gator to sign on the dotted line and pose like he was Lucky. She traded in her BMW wagon for a Honda Civic and some cash to make up the difference. The Civic was $4,800, and the blue Kelly book value was $5,800. It wasn't the luxury car that she had become accustomed to, but it was dependable, good on gas, and it was a Honda. Everybody knows Hondas are made to last. She was just happy to have a car that she was able to get for herself.

Next, she went looking for beds for the children's room, and the little necessities she needed to make her apartment a home. She bought towels, dishes and a few other essential things for the apartment. She looked at the clock in the car and realized that she had to get back to the hotel. She dropped Gator back off, picked up some McDonald's for the children and headed back to the hotel.

Before she headed back to the hotel, she stopped to make a phone call to her next-door neighbor, Joan. Though they were never friends, Tressa could tell from the few conversations they shared at the fence, when they were both working in their yards, that Joan was very compassionate and had problems of her own, so she'd definitely understand. Tressa had never confided in her or anyone else about the issues in her relationship, but for some reason, it seemed as if Joan felt so comfortable telling Tressa all her business. Tressa was certain that it wouldn't be a problem to get help from her, after all the times Tressa had allowed Joan's children to come over her house for ten or twenty minutes when their mom was running late.

Joan was a middle-aged, outgoing, white woman, who was fully aware that her husband cheated. She never would have the courage to leave her husband because they both had too much invested. They were loaded and, Joan was a survivor. She put up with all of her husbands bull and rolled with the punches. Joan could see the spunk in Tressa's personality and wished Tressa was Caucasian as well, because they'd surely be closer than what they were.

The phone rang two times and Joan answered. "Hello, the Conner's Residence."

Oh, how corny can she be Tressa thought? "Joan, it's Tressa, from next door." Tressa said.

"Yes, yes, yes. Hold for one minute. I need to get the phone in the study." Joan said in a professional voice, as if it was a business call. Joan picked up the other phone. "Where are you? Are you OK?" Joan said in a frantic voice.

"I have been so worried about you. Your boyfriend came over in a frenzy asking if we had seen you and the babies."

"I kinda of figured that. Well, I left him."

"Oh, really?" Joan wanted to know more, but understood clearly this wasn't the time to pry.

"Yes, I don't have much time to explain. I need you to do me a small favor. If you don't want to get involved, I will understand, but I really need your help."

"What can I do? Do you need money?"

"No, I am okay on the money end." She said but knowing that she wanted to accept the money. She knew the money she had wasn't going to last long.

"I was leaving in such a hurry and couldn't get all my clothes. I put some of my things into the brand new trash cans that the city just gave us a couple of days ago, and I swapped the trash cans so that ours is in your yard and vice versa. I need you to please get the clothes out for me and swap the cans back before he gets suspicious. I will send my sister to get the clothes, but I will have her call you first. Make sure Lucky is not home when she comes, please."

"No problem, I will go do it as soon as my husband leaves. Tomorrow is trash day so I know my husband will be getting the trash together, and this week will be the last week we use the old cans. But what about you and the children? Where will you go?" Joan asked, sounding like a concerned mother.

"We will be fine as long as we are away from him."

81

"Tressa if there's anything, anything at all that I can do, please promise me that you will call."

I will. Oh, and please whatever you do, please don't tell Khalil that I called or made any contact with you at all."

"Oh, I definitely will not."

"If you hear anything about a job, I'd appreciate it if you let me know." Tressa said before she thanked Joan and brought the conversation to a close.

Once she was back at the hotel, she was surprised when she noticed how good Wiggles was with the twins. For some reason they adored her. Wiggles stayed a while to keep the twins occupied while Tressa made the necessary calls to the telephone and cable company. She thought about getting the utilities over at the house cut off, but she didn't. When Wiggles was about to go, Tressa gave Wiggles a big hug and said to her. "You were right."

"Right about what?"

"You'd always be there for me. Thanks Wiggles."

"That's what's family is for."

She informed Wiggles that she needed her to make contact with Joan and Wiggles did. In addition to the clothing, Joan sent $500 for Tressa with Wiggles.

Friday rolled around, and just like the crooked rental agent had promised, he had the apartment ready for her to move right in. She kept her end of the bargain and gave him three new crisp one hundred dollar bills. He presented her with the keys, and after only a week of being away from Lucky, she acquired a "home" for her children. It may have been in the most crack-infested, grimiest, dirtiest government subsidized apartment complexes in Richmond, but at least she was away from crazy deranged Lucky. Guess he wasn't so lucky after all.

The Eastgate Village Apartments were brick with three floors and newly renovated. The city and government kept pouring money into the apartments to try to make them a better place to live. They built new playgrounds and a recreation center. The entrances were all blocked off except one, which made it one way in and one way out. They even went to the extent to install a black iron gate, in an effort to supposedly keep all the rift-raft out, but no matter how much they tried, they were never successful.

They did landscaping on the property to enhance it. They also installed new laundry facilities. The city thought that if they made it a beautiful place to live, the residents would take care of it. But, the fact that it was new, didn't keep certain people from urinating in the laundry room, writing grifiti all over the walls and leaving broken forty ounce beer bottles and trash everywhere.

She drove down to the main street in the complex and as she cruised looking for the apartment address, tears started coming to her eyes. It was 11 a.m. and the hustlers were out slinging their products and the fiends were roaming, looking for their drug of choice, whether it is crack, heroine, liquid syrup or marijuana, or all of the above. They were all at their disposal. Since she was driving so slow, moving at a snails pace down the main street looking around, naturally the dealers thought she was looking for drugs. One dealer ran up to her car.

"Yo, what you want. I got the fattest 20's out here?"

Another came over to the other side of her car knocking on the window. "Look, I got the biggest dope sacks out here and I'm going to look out for you."

She was so upset and offended. She screamed. "I ain't looking for no motherfucking drugs!"

One of the dudes backed up and threw his hands up. "I'm sorry baby."

The other one just screamed at her. "If you ain't looking then get the fuck from round here then!"

The NERVE of him! Now, I see why so many of our brothers get locked up. They running all up to my car, don't know me or my car. Now, what if I was the police? They all would be locked up, begging for somebody to come and get them out on bail. I mean, I don't knock anybody's hustle, but can they not be so aggressive!

Once she approached the building marked 3012, she realized that the apartment was up on the 3rd floor. She parked her car, hopped out and grabbed some of the things that she had bought earlier in the week and had been sitting in her trunk. When she approached the building, there was one guy sitting on the steps replacing the filter out of his Black and Mild cigar/cigarette and about to refill it so he could smoke another one. Another guy sitting beside him, was pulling on a blunt while another

83

guy was just sitting there tying his shoe. There was also a stank looking girl with some old, raggedy braids in her hair that needed to be taken out and redone, examining her, which she would later find out is one of her neighbors, Meechie. All of the guys were in awe of Tressa, but none of them moved out of her way so she could get by without her having to say "excuse me".

She wanted to break down and cry, especially when she got to the top floor and noticed the large crap game that mainly consisted of thirteen or fourteen year old guys, going on right in front her door!

"Excuse me." She said to the fellas, not really wanting to trample over them. None of them budged, and all ignored her. She then took a deep breath, put a little pitch in and raised her voice. "Excuse me, CAN I GET TO MY DOOR PLEASE?"

This still didn't mean anything to them, but one knucklehead said to her. "Wait a minute baby, let him just roll this one." She stood there and waited for this little thug-in-training to roll the dice, about to drop the things she had in her hand. They felt awfully heavy after hauling them up the three flights of steep stairs.

When they finally moved, she put the key in the door to enter her apartment. Once she opened up the door, she couldn't believe her eyes! The apartment building was broke down on the outside, but it was very nice and clean on the inside. It was a three bedroom spacious apartment that consisted of one full bath in the hall and a half bath in the master bedroom. The apartment was even equipped with a dishwasher and garbage disposal. If only the environment was better, she thought to herself, but she decided she was going to make due until she could afford a better place to live.

The apartment itself is nice, but I hate the outside. But at the same time, my children are safer here with me than with that damn nut Lucky. I am just going to use this as a stepping-stone to something better. I just have to keep reminding myself, it ain't where you live, it's how you live. As soon as I can get on my feet, I am outta here. Believe that!

She ran up and down the steps a few more times and unloaded the things she had in her car. She set them up neatly in the apartment, and then waited for the delivery people to arrive with the boys beds. When the beds came, she went to get groceries to stock the refrigerator. When she returned, she struggled with the bags to get up the stairs. A neighborhood drug boy walked up beside her. "What's up Shawdy?"

She kept walking and ignoring him, but he kept talking. "You got a man?" He asked her. Giving him the cold shoulder didn't stop him from trying to pursue her. "Can I take you out?"

She only walked faster as she continued to toil with the bags filled with groceries as she thought to herself, *now here it is I am scrambling to get these bags up three flights of steps, you ain't got a damn thing in your hand, and ain't offered to help me. But you got the nerve to want me to consider going out with you! Picture that? You can't; not even with a Kodak!*

On her way back to the hotel to get the children to take them to their new home, she stopped at a pay phone to make the call that she had been contemplating on all day. Her heart began to race as she looked for a quarter to deposit in the payphone. The "Crime Stoppers" commercial came on the radio as she looked in the console for any kind of change.

"This is Deputy Investigator K. Knowitall and today, Richmond, I need your help with any information on locating the treacherous, perfidious person or people who committed the heinous double homicide this past Monday evening. Jasper Sisco, known by friends and family as Peako, had just driven off the showroom floor with his brand new 4.0 Range Rover that he purchased in expectance of the birth of his first son."

Tressa froze in her tracks and chills began to go up her spine as she started to shake while the man continued with his deep, southern accent.

"Within the next thirty minutes, the perpetrator picked up Dena Dookie, known as Dee-Dee by all her friends, and as they stopped at the intersection of Horsepen Road and Glenside Drive, Peako was shot in the head while still sitting behind the wheel of his Range Rover. Dookie's body was found a few feet away from the vehicle. We are certain that this was done professionally and was drug related. We are working around the clock on this case, but we need your help. We need you to come forth with any information, small or large to bring this investigation to a close. The city has raised $250,000 to be paid to any individual with information leading to the arrest and conviction of the heinous individual responsible for this crime."

Tressa sat in the car as beads of sweat rolled down her face. Her heart pounded as if she had just run a marathon. Her whole train of thought was thrown off. She snapped out of her astonishment, grabbed the quarter she found in the ashtray and continued to carry out her task to make the phone call.

Tressa dropped the quarter in the pay phone slot and the phone rang. "Yeah." The familiar voice answered.

"Hey, it's me," she said in a nonchalant tone.

"Hey baby, where the hell ya'll at so I can come and get you. Me, Killer and Dopeman really miss ya'll. Tressa, we are lonely without ya'll at the house." Although Lucky was heated and had been losing his mind, he played it cool. After all, he had never been happier to hear from Tressa.

"Look, this is the deal, the people around this town want some answers. A snitch is nothing I have ever been, but when it comes to protecting my sons, on everything I love, it ain't no limit to how far I'll go for them. And you know this is right."

"I'm listening." He slowly said, because he knew how deep Tressa's love went for the twins.

"Well, my brother always said an eye for an eye right? Well, let us go about our way and in exchange I'll let you have your life and your freedom. I'll carry what I know to my grave, but should there be any fatal coincidental accidents that come my way, oh trust me, I got it set up so that you will go down like the Walls of Jericho. Do you understand?" She said with every ounce of emotion that she could muster.

"Tressa." He started to speak, but she cut him off.

"So, you better pray brother that no harm comes my way. I better not even break a nail or nothing! If the slightest little thing happens to my kids, it's Independence Day on your sorry ass. So, are we clear?"

He was quiet for a few seconds. Khalil was actually left speechless, but only a few seconds passed before he let his frustration show.

"Oh, you think leaving me and taking my sons is going to be that easy? You think I am going to make your bed that easy to lie in?"

Tressa was quiet as Lucky continued to talk. "Since you want me out of ya'll life, then don't call me and ask me for shit! You play the role of mommy and daddy."

Lucky, I been doing that all along. All this time ya ass been running the streets. It's been me who been holding it together. Not you."

"Well, scrammmm, since you want it like this. I ain't going to help you do shit for the kids.

Tressa wanted to cry when she heard the cold tone of his voice, but she held her own. "You know what? With you out of my life shit can't do nothing else but escalate boo, believe that! You were hindering me."

"A'ight, this is how you want it. I am going to let you go in peace." Lucky calmly stated. "And just so you know, I'll never, I mean never hurt you or my boys believe that, and that's on everything I love." He almost sounded sincere, but Tressa knew differently. Lucky continued. "If I ain't a part of your life, you can't get no type of help from me."

"Oh, OK. This is how you want to carry it? Always remember Tressa gonna get the last laugh. Believe that!"

Tressa started to scream out of her hurt. Although she had known deep down that it was never about her children, it was always about her. This was the first time reality actually sat in. Lucky wasn't going to be a father to Hadji and Ali because he wasn't with her. *What do I have to do with their relationship with their father? I can't understand why he would dare hold it against my babies because I don't want to be with him. I mean, at first I was feeling he doesn't even deserve a relationship with my kids after the fiasco the other night. But in all actuality, every little boy needs his father. I can be the best mother that I can be, but ultimately, there are things that a woman can't teach a little boy. I will never slander Lucky's name to them, I will simply let them draw their own conclusions about their father. I hope that one day Lucky will grow up and get past,*

that it's not about us, but about the boys. It doesn't matter how I feel about him or how he feels about me.
Her thoughts were interrupted when the car behind her blew its horn to signal that the light had turned green. She drove off to the hotel to pack up the rest of their things. She took the twins to their new home in the hood.

THE NEXT DAY AT THE PRISON:

Lucky didn't sleep all night thinking about the powerful words that Tressa told him over the phone. He thought about all the ways he could try to resolve the situation, but there was only one concrete way to keep the situation under control. The one person who had complete mental control over Tressa was her brother Taj. First thing the next morning, he was the first person in the state correctional center's visiting room, ready to seek out Taj's help.
Lucky sat in the dirty plastic chair, hands sweaty and heart racing. Although Lucky was a renowned killer and would try anybody, Taj was the only person to ever put fear in his heart. He replayed the rehearsed speech over and over in his head while he waited. While he was so focused on rehearsing what he'd plan to say, he never noticed Taj walking up on him from behind.
Taj wasn't surprised to see Lucky at all, he knew it would be only a matter of time before he'd show his face. Taj was not too thrilled to see Lucky in spite of all the rumors he'd heard. He didn't know exactly what the final straw was. Tressa always seemed to keep the bad news from her brother. She took into consideration that he was in prison and prison was nowhere for anybody to find out any detrimental news.
When Lucky looked up, Taj gave him a look that could kill. "What's poppin'?" Lucky foolishly asked, trying to break the ice.
"Nigga, I wish I had my glock right now to show you."
"Damn General, you don't want to kill your best soldier. Do you?"

"Man, what the fuck you want. I know you ain't come all the way up here to share no honey buns and chips."

Lucky took a deep breath. "Look Taj, we got a situation."

"I'm listening." Taj responded, unconcerned.

"Look, I fucked up man." Lucky said, as he shook his head. "I really fucked up, I mean big time."

Taj only looked without changing his expression or batting an eye.

"Tressa had me gone. And there was a situation that I jumped the gun on and my actions put me in a place that there is no return."

Tears filled Lucky's eyes as Taj looked at him without any pity or empathy. Lucky continued. "Man, I went into a jealous rage and I lost Tressa and the boys. They ain't never coming back. I never knew how much I loved them until they was gone. I did what I did and now I can't take back what I done."

"So, what you want me to do man?"

"Man, she talking bout turning states evidence on me."

"What you mean?" Taj all of a sudden wanted to hear what Lucky had to say. "Look man, I don't believe that."

"Man, I know I was wrong when I lost my damn cool, but I can't be looking over my shoulder wondering if, when, and how long before Tressa drop a dime on me. Nigga I know you didn't raise no 'snitch chick'. I ain't going to harm her."

Taj shot him a look, and in a firm, soft tone said, "Nigga, I'm going to tell you like this. Don't even think twice about ever putting a hand on Tressa."

Lucky interrupted and started trying to explain with his hands. "Taj, I would never hurt Tressa, I love her more than life itself. She's not just some broad off the street that I could hurt. She is the mother of my kids, the only person beside myself I have ever loved and she is your sister. So, Taj please don't let her turn states evidence on me, I don't deserve that."

"Shawdy." Taj stated as he put his hand up motioning for Lucky to shut-up. "I heard every word you said and no you don't deserve to be here." Taj pointed down making it known he meant prison. "Shawdy, you deserve far worse than this. You'll get yours in due time."

Taj stood up and pointed in Lucky's face. "Nigga, I don't and didn't raise no snitch bitch! So, you are safe from the cops."

"Shawsdale, is everything OK?" The correctional officer asked, noticing Taj was about to make a scene. Taj sat down and looked at Lucky with disgust.

"Taj." Lucky tried to reason with him. "She's holding this over my head like she's my probation officer. That's how she coming out her mouth at me."

"I'll speak to my sister, just make my last payment. When you leave, don't look back. Tressa and I are a closed chapter in your life. Don't worry, you won't be judged by 12. You're more likely to be carried by six. She's not going to the grand jury. Trust me. You're safe. I got her."

On that note, Taj got up to walk away.

"You're a lifesaver, Taj"

Taj stopped in his tracks. "Lucky, I'm not your life saver! That's something only you can do."

"I'll holla back, Shawdy!"

"Kill rocks nigga!"

Taj knew at that moment that Lucky would go all out to rat on him if he ever went under the gun. He shook his head as he walked to exit the visiting room, at how disappointed he was with himself for taking Lucky under his wing. See, he violated his number one rule. "Never confess to anything in this lifetime." He reflected over all the dirt he had done and all the treacherous rumors he confirmed to Lucky in depth. With this info alone, Taj could get life in prison, or worst, the death penalty.

-10-
From Sugar to Shit

Over the course of the next few months, it was a major adjustment, because Tressa basically went from sugar to shit. What seemed at first like a blessing, began to feel like a curse. A combination of empty broken beer bottles, used condoms, crack pipes, trash, dirty stinky diapers, lay all over the ground. For the first two weeks, the strong smell of urine would get into her throat and literally make her vomit. She couldn't help it, although she managed to get over the vomiting, but the pissy smell she could never get used to.

She stocked up on Raid motels and the Raid gel and kept them all over her apartment, due to the apartment being infested with roaches. Although she had bombed the apartment and followed up with all the accessories raid offered, it took about three months for the roach stuff to finally take a toll on the apartment, because it was so roach infested. She was persistant and never gave up on the war against the roaches. She finally got it to the point where she'd only see a roach every now and again. She kept telling herself, look on the bright side. "At least, I don't have any mice or rats."

It seemed like everybody in the complex hated her. The females never spoke to her, they only looked at her up, down and rolled their eyes. At first, she considered entertaining one of the neighborhood guys, so she could have some help to pay her bills. When she thought about the how inconvenient that was, she changed her mind. The guys in the neighborhood began to torment her because she didn't socialize with any of them like the majority of the project chicks did. Naturally, most of the girls who actually resided there would let the guys who lived around there stash drugs, smoke weed, and hang in their house, but not Tressa. She wasn't having any nigga lay up or hang in, after everything she had been through. It wasn't much, but it was hers.

Although she thought the move would have a drastic effect over her boys, but unlike adults, children adapt to change better than adults. The kids were glad to see so many other kids. They were still young, so they didn't know they were living in the hood. Her children did however ask. "Mommy, how come daddy not home?"

She would hug them and tell them. "He's sick, but he loves you both and he'll see you soon."

For the first few months, everyday she waddled in her misery, constantly reminding herself how much she despised the place and encountering situations within the complex that confirmed why she it hated it so much. She decided that until the time was right, she wasn't going anywhere, and nobody was going to run her away. So, she had to stand her ground just to let them know that she wasn't a square, type of country girl, for real.

It was a blazing hot summer July day. Tressa was coming up the stairs looking good with a Church's Chicken box in her hand for her boys. She had on her Guess peach short shorts, displaying her long brown legs with the matching peach and white halter-top that put emphasis on her D cup breast. Her outfit would not have been complete without her fresh, brand spanking new, low top, freestyle, snow white Reebok's on with no socks and a gold ankle bracelet. She was fresh out of the beauty salon. Like all the girls in Richmond, getting her hair done is something she took very seriously.

The fellas in the hood were out with their big, bazooka water guns, and as she pulled up, she saw the damage they had done to the other girls and were doing to any bypassers. When she got out of her car, no victims were in sight. The place was like a ghost town, but with water everywhere. The guys all looked innocently as if they were going to let her pass. When the one named Pondee displayed a slight grin, he let on that they had plans for her too.

She stopped and looked at Pondee eye to eye. "Look DO NOT wet me up. I am not playing in ya'll little reindeer games. So, don't wet me up."

"A'ight." He said shaking his head.

They let her get to the top of the stairs and as soon as she did, it was open field day on her. They all let loose, water was coming from every direction, the front, back and all sides. It all happened so quick, there was nowhere for Tressa to run. She was drenched, her clothes were soaked and sticking to her body. She went ballistic while all the guys laughed hysterically. They were falling down on their knees, crying laughing. "Oh, we got that stuck up bitch good." Because the outfit was so thin, you could see everything! Tressa's large round nipples and the white lace thong she was wearing. The guys started throwing dollar bills, yelling. "Shake what ya mama gave ya!"

"Oh, you muthafuckas think this shit is funny? Oh, okay, ya'll don't know who da fuck ya'll fucking with, cuz I am going to always get the last laugh, baby. Believe that!"

She turned to walk away, tennis shoes squeeching, which only made the scene more hysterical to the dudes. The fellas roared in laughter, holding their stomachs laughing when she screamed out again. "BELIEVE THAT!"

Then to top it off, the Church's Fried Chicken she had in her hand for the twins was ruined! Now, if anybody knows Tressa, they know there are two things that are not to be messed with, Tressa's kids and her hair. When Tressa realized the fact that these scrubs had not only ruined her hair, but her sons chicken, their dinner, all hell was about to break loose!

Wiggles, on a weekend pass from the drug program, was inside of the apartment watching the boys. She came to the door because she heard all of the ruckus going on outside. As soon as she opened the door, Tressa barged through the door.

"What the hell is going on?" Wiggles asked, wanting to know, who was getting as big as a house since she wasn't getting high any more.

Tressa didn't answer. She just walked straight to the kitchen, and screamed to Wiggles. "Put the boys in their room and shut the door, because see these folks don't know who the hell they playing with. See, this shit was uncalled for." She stormed to the bathroom to pull off the wet clothes, leaving wet footprints all over the carpet throughout the house. Coming out of the bathroom with dry clothes on, she was still mouthing off as she went back to the kitchen.

"See, I know for a fact these motherfuckas ain't as crazy as I am. I lived with a psycho, simple ass nigga for few years so they ain't got nothing on me. Believe that. See, I am going to have to show these clowns." She said, as she could hear them at the crap game just right outside of her door, laughing about the expression on her face when the first water jet hit her. Listening to them only made her madder and madder. She walked back and forth pacing the kitchen floor. As she listened, Wiggles could see the smoke coming from out of Tressa's head.

Tressa walked very slowly to the door and she took a deep breath. She opened the door quickly, and before any of the guys at the crap game knew what was going on, the two pans of boiling, scorching, hot water was hitting them and all she could hear was. "Shit!, what the fuck? Goddamn!" And the best one. "That beitch!"

"Didn't I tell you I was going to get the last laugh, you clown muthafuckas?" And she slammed the door.

One Hour Passed:

Tressa and Wiggles sat at the kitchen table waiting for the water for the hotdogs to start boiling, but laughing when the doorbell rang. Now, Tressa was the only person in the whole complex that actually went out and bought a doorbell for her government-subsidized apartment.

"Ding-dong, ding-dong." Somebody laid on the doorbell, then she heard the voice on the other side. "Bitch open up the door, you wanna throw blistering hot water on my man and fuck up his new hundred and something dollar Jordan's. I am about to whip yo ass."

Tressa looked at Wiggles. "Go ask who it is, while I go put some shoes on, cuz see, these people been asking for it since I moved around here."

Wiggles was laughing, getting a kick out of the whole episode, because in all honesty, the people didn't know who they were messing with. Tressa was very meek, humble and the definition of a lady. But don't get it twisted, because her spunk and feistiness would make one think she was a lion.

"Ding-dong, ding-dong, ding-dong." The doorbell sounded, but over top of the doorbell, was the female voice. "You scared bitch, open up the door, cuz I'm bout to whip you like the pigs did Rodney King, since you want to burn my man with some hot water."

At that very instance, that's when the girl, Crumpy, the neighborhood's bad ass, always manipulating and trying to intimidate somebody, was greeted with scorching, sizzling hot water followed by a blow straight in the right eye and another one. Crumpy stumbled and fell backwards. She couldn't really get her balance back or herself together. Tressa had threw the hot dog water on her with the greasy film that comes from cooking the hot dogs. Tressa didn't give Crumpy a chance to pull herself together. Tressa who was wearing her Timberlands, just kept stomping a mud hole in Crumpy.

"Bitch, that ain't fair, you fighting dirty." Said one of the bystanders.

Tressa just went over and punched her in the face catching her off guard. The girl bounced back. She hit Tressa back with what was supposed to be a smack, and tried to take off running down the steps, when her lame plan backfired. Now, everybody knows that when a fight breaks out in the projects, the crowd comes from nowhere and forms a huddle. So, the girl didn't get far when Tressa caught her and started throwing punch after punch and strike after strike, until Pondee, the guy who initially let the first shot of water out, pulled Tressa off the girl. Tressa didn't know what the deal was with Pondee pulling on her, and neither did Wiggles, so Tressa gave Pondee two blows and Wiggles charged him. Together they both was on Pondee, and that's when one of Pondee's boys pulled them

95

off of him when they seen he was not fighting the two girls back, only breaking up the fight.

When the fight was over, the word had spread like wildfire throughout the hood that the girl who lived in 3012 building on the 3rd floor, with the two-lil boys, is not to be fucked with, because she was crazy. So, pretty soon after, just about everybody stopped rolling their eyes at her and gradually began to speak to her. There was still a couple of the girls that tried her anyway, but on the low. And on the low was exactly how she dealt back with them. But those were the ones who were usually the biggest and most deadly snakes.

The only thing Wiggles could say to Tressa was. "Didn't I tell you back when you were in the 7th grade, that if you beat the bully or the one with the most mouth, you don't have to worry about the rest of them. They chuckled together.

Later that night, Pondee knocked on her door. She looked through the peephole. She wasn't going to answer it because she wasn't expecting anybody. When she seen Pondee, she thought he was bringing more drama. *He looks like he's by himself, but maybe he has some other people with him standing to the side of the door.*

"Who's there?" She asked, with her two-shot derringer in her hand.

"It's Slap Jack." He said, knowing that she was probably hesitant about opening the door.

"What do you want?" Tressa said through the door, sure he was up to something devious after all the episodes that had went down earlier.

"Look shawdy, open the door. I just came by to give you the money for your hair, and to tell you that that shit I did today was real fucked up, wettin' you up and shit. But that shit you came back with was on point. I know you think I'm coming back for some mo' drama. Boo, I just want you to know it ain't no beef no mo'. And, I got ya back."

Oh, now you don't want war huh, yeah, yeah, yeah, was what she thought to herself as she continued to talk through the door. She said to him. "Oh, OK, that's nice to know."

"I know you think a nigga blowing smoke up ya ass, but you'll see. I'm going to slide the money up under the door, cause I know you ain't going to open it, but it's cool though."

She looked down and saw the fifty and twenty dollar bills coming through to her side of the door. She looked through the peephole and watched Slap Jack walk away to meet a crack head to exchange some of his product for some bawled up money before he walked down the steps. *Damn, that saying is so damn true, things don't always come when you want them to, but when you need them to. I surely spent my last money to get my hair done and didn't know what I was going to do with my hair.*

Tressa's life had changed tremendously in the past few months since she had left Lucky. A dollar didn't come easy, there was no splurging, impulsive buying, just penny pinching and budgeting. There were so many sacrifices she had to make to be able to make ends meet. However, one of things that she wouldn't give up was getting her hair done. She kept a fresh pair of clean snow white Reeboks and her hair done. Those were the only ways she could reward herself. Most of her clothes were pieces that she had when her and Luck were together. Her other garments were pieces she picked up from the ten dollar store in the white areas. She went through the racks with a fine toothcomb to get the most tasteful things out of there. She could never figure out if she went to the white areas because they truly had better things, or was it because she didn't want to be sited shopping at the ten dollar store in the hood?

Her hair was another story; she spent top dollar on her hair. She believed as long as her hair was right, then everything else would fall in place. A person's hairstyle made a difference with any outfit, was her philosophy. A seven-dollar dress, with the right hairdo and shoes, could get a million dollar effect. With all this in mind her hair was always kept in tip-top condition. Getting her hair ruined during the watergun fight was the major reason she went into a rage. She didn't know when she would get money again to get her hair done.

This weekend was suppose to be a quiet weekend, with Wiggles and the boys. This was Wiggles' first weekend pass since she had finally gone to the drug program after

Tressa had been constantly convincing her to go to for the past few months. With all the commotion and confusion going on, Tressa almost forgot about the cake she had gotten for Wiggles to celebrate her sobority. When she pulled out the cake and went to cut it, a roach ran across the top of the cake.

Tressa was mad and embarrassed. Wiggles just hugged Tressa because she knew she wanted to cry. Instead, Tressa tried to make jokes. "Girl, those roaches be walking around here like they own the place and I am their guest."

-11-
The Art of Hair

Courtesy of Pondee, Tressa was able to get her hair done over again. The next problem she had was getting her stylist to agree to fit her in. So, she called Gypsy, AKA Queen Bitch, AKA scandalous, no good, selfish, self-centered, gossiping, ongoing shit starting, paper-chasing stank hoe, who was also her beautian and could do the best hair in all of Richmond and surrounding counties.

Now Gypsy was no joke when it came to a comb, some curlers, gel and a brush. There wasn't any style Gypsy couldn't do, from ghetto to conservative styles. It didn't matter whether it was long, short, synthetic or horsehair. Gypsy laid it down like tar on a pavement. Unfortunately, Gypsy's was every client's nightmare with her ongoing, forever changing, making up the rules as she go, it made all her clients hate her. But the final, finished result was what made her customers deal with the bull. She came to work when and how late she felt like it. She wouldn't dare dream of letting her customer be over ten minutes late, if they were, she wouldn't do their hair. She never worked on Friday's, Saturdays or any other days if something spur of the moment came up. There were no exceptions for her to inconvenience herself when it came to doing hair, not even for her regular, good-tipping customers. She didn't care what special occasion her clients might have had. If they had a prom or were getting married on Saturday, they either got their hair done on Thursday, were instructed to sleep with a satin bonnet for the next two days, or they could go somewhere else.

Normally, Gypsy worked expeditiously getting her clients in and out. But when she was late for whatever reason, whether she was laid up somewhere screwing, had drama or just simply got caught up, which caused her to be behind and become overbooked, still she took no prisoners. She would bluntly tell her clients, "sit and wait or go somewhere else because there is definitely someone else begging to take your seat".

Not one time did the thought ever cross Gypsy's mind that, without her customers, there would be no her. For she lived by her motto, "Pussy is Power", and as long as she had a well and clean coochie between her legs, there laid the power. There would always be a sucker begging to be with her and to do what she needed to be done. So, gold digging was her first priority over doing hair on any given day. Hair was just a hobby that she used as a back-up plan to get extra money and a ploy to make her victims (men) think she didn't need them because she had a job bringing in plenty of funds. Though she tried to block out the fact that doing hair was a hustle acquired a long time ago while living in the projects, sitting on her momma's porch, charging ten dollars for a hairdo to get the bare necessities that her momma couldn't provide her with because she was too busy hanging out, drinking moon shine.

Gypsy, while growing up, was often teased because of her black, deep, dark complexion. As an adult, her dark skin became her most attractive feature. Her full eyes and lips added to her beauty. Although she was black as midnight, nobody could ever deny she was beautiful. She could have been a model standing 5'9", with a thin curvy build. Her skin was smooth as a baby's behind, no blemishes, moles or acne. Her hair had always been extremely thick, but she learned to tame it when she was introduced to Revlon perms at the early age of eight. After becoming familiar with her newfound straight hair, she maintained her hair in a neat ponytail. She kept her hair up so well, that the other neighborhood girls always asked her to do their hair and she did. Pretty soon people started to come from projects all over, from day in until day out, to get their ten-dollar hairdo. At the age of thirteen, Gypsy was making more money in two days than her mother made in a week. Gypsy was able to buy whatever she wanted and kept up with the latest fashions.

The designer names she wore made her stand out even more, which meant she attracted the boys. Not just any boys, but the older guys that hustled and had money. These guys were interested in her, so she started dating. Juggling her dates and doing hair started to collide. When she had to decline dates because she needed to do hair to keep her money flowing, the guys she dated would pay her double, sometimes triple the money she made, so her hobby, her hustle, to do hair became second to her seeing her male friends. She hated the fact that standing on her feet tired her out. Plus, doing hair was so time consuming and took her away from the easy money, men. It is at this point in her life, she realized that she had the tool right between her legs to get what she wanted.

Girlfriends were never anything dear to her because of the countless times she cut their throats and everyone else's throat to get whatever man she felt she wanted at the time. Then she would have to deal with the jealousy and fighting with her so-called friends.

"If a girl can't control her man, then whose problem is it? Chicks should learn to keep their man on a leash. Then they going to come and tell me, he ain't nothing but a dog. Shit, I am just walking the dog." This would be Gypsy's way of trying to make others see it her way.

Gypsy cared about no one but herself, and the day spa that she just took ownership over. Gypsy, however, ran the spa in a very selfish way. She didn't keep toilet paper in the bathroom. The big screen television that sat in the waiting area had a "Do Not Change Channel" sign. In her mind, the television it was for her, not her customers. However, if they pleased, they could listen and watch the program that she was watching.

Gypsy mothered three children, but motherhood was another one of her schemes. Motherhood was a business investment too. Each one of her children was an insurance policy, assurance that she'd always be able to live the lifestyle she wanted for herself via child support.

101

Her oldest child was by a guy who was older than she, but was a well-respected old head in the town. She slept with him a couple times for money, and seeing the money he had and how he loved his other twelve children, she saw opportunity and purposely got pregnant. It was no big deal to the old head, because he had so many other children, just another one to add to the brood. The old head did everything for the child and was a security blanket for Gypsy. She knew for sure, if all else failed, the old head would look out for her on the strength they shared, a son.

Then there was the middle child that was by a local drug dealer, Pee. She deliberately got pregnant by him because she saw he was a loyal type of guy. He was an only child and hadn't yet fathered any kids. He and his mother, Ethel, were close and Gypsy knew the mother would surely cater to her and her child. The mother, Ms. Ethel, always wanted a daughter and was everything that Gypsy wanted her mother to be. Gypsy was certain that the responsibility for this child would always fall on Ms. Ethel and never on her, she was right. Ms. Ethel took total control over the baby once he was born. Pee was brutally killed while Gypsy was still pregnant, which made it almost natural for Ms. Ethel to keep this baby all the time. Gypsy had Ms. Ethel eating out of the palms of her hands because the baby was the only connection Ms. Ethel had to her dead son. Although the baby spent only 10% of its life with Gypsy, Gypsy maintained legal custody of the baby solely to receive the social security check each month for the baby from Pee's death. The four hundred dollars a month, check was money that she knew was coming in every month regardless of how many heads she did or dicks she sucked. Ms. Ethel didn't care anything about any social security because she too had a healthy insurance policy on Pee. Ms. Ethel vowed to use that money to take care of her grandson. As far as Ms. Ethel was concerned, she was fully aware of Gypsy's kind and her low-life mentality, but if the $400 a month kept Gypsy away, then by all means, she could have it.

Then there was the youngest child, another planned pregnancy, but this was the most lucrative one that she'd cashed in on, as of yet, Lil Merk.

Big Merk was a professional football player that she had met at a celebrity's birthday party. Now, make no mistake about it, at the end of the day, Gypsy is and will always be a no-good guttersnipe. But once she jumps into costume, as she does, no one would ever know. Rolling up in her late model two-year old Mercedes Benz, her "look no further", spunky feisty, "I am the shit attitude", which turns a man on right away. Then to top it off, she has the face and everything else falls right in place. Her well- manicured nails, pedicured feet, picture perfect makeup on her beauty queen face makes any man, white, black, or Chinese feel that it's imperative to know who this woman is. Once they are formally introduced, oh, the show begins. Gypsy keeps the men well entertained from that moment on to the day she gets tired of them or they serve no more purpose in her life.

For some reason, as grimey as she was, the men from coast to coast still lined up to be with Gypsy. This was the same way with Big Merk, but once Big Merk saw through her lies and deceit, he gave her a Navigator truck for the kids and moved her out of her little two-bedroom apartment into a nice one hundred and fifty thousand dollar house, set up healthy child support payments and fled. Gypsy was amicable, but when the word got around that there was a new beauty in Big Merk's life, all hell broke loose.

In the hair salon:

Gypsy agreed to do Tressa's hair Monday, but at 6 a.m. in the morning. The following morning, Tressa was up bright and early off to the salon. Gypsy had a way of making Tressa feel extremely uncomfortable. Tressa couldn't understand why Gypsy was so fickle towards her, for she had never done anything to Gypsy to make her have such a negative disposition towards her. Gypsy most of the time acted as if Tressa and her were cool, but at the same time, she would often have to throw some shade in it. So, Tressa never trusted Gypsy but she played along as if they were super cool.

Today Gypsy's niceness, laughing, joking and trying oh so hard to make conversation out of small talk was so sickening. Gypsy wanted to know, but she didn't want to come straight out and ask, how exactly was Tressa's broke ass able to get her hair done over again, when she was just in yesterday?

Gypsy was thinking to herself, *I know this broke down chick ain't got nobody to replace Lucky's ass that quick. I know she scrambling. Where the hell she get money from? Hum, let me check out her jewelry. She ain't even got all her jewelry no more. She sure ain't have it on yesterday when she was in here, I heard the bitch pawned it all.* Gypsy tried to make heads of the situation.

"Tressa, where all your jewelry at today?" Gypsy casually asked Tressa.

"Girl, it's too early in the morning. Shoot girl, I barely got myself here, talkin' 'bout putting on all that daggone jewelry."

Yeah, yeah, yeah, whatever. All I know is this bitch better have my damn money when I get finished doing her head, Gypsy thought. I don't want no short money and she better not ask me for no credit neither. I don't care if she has been coming to me since back in the day and she referred a bunch of people to me either. I don't owe her nothing. I could give a damn about her doing bad or about her stupid ass leaving her man and now she scrambling. Better believe I don't feel sorry for her. That's what she get, cause I would have never left that paid ass nigga. I don't care what he did, he could've been fucking my damn momma on my bed. I would have just walked in and just asked him for some money. As long as he gave it to me, I wouldn't have cared. She just better have mine when I'm done.

When Tressa's hair was finished drying and she was back in Gypsy's chair to get styled, Gypsy had to continue to pry, but on the down low.

"Girl, I can't remember who it was, but one of my customers was asking about you just yesterday."

"Oh, for real?" Tressa asked, but growing real tired of the small talk.

"Girl, I told her you were just in here."

"Oh, OK."

"Don't you know she had the nerve to ask me, how you going to take care of your kids now since you and your baby father broke up."

Tressa thought to herself, *Naw, baby I know that's really what you want to ask me, but don't have the gall to dare ask me. I am hip to broads like you. But you will never know in your wildest dream how I make it happen for mines and me. Believe that.*

"Oh, what she had some money to contribute or something?" Tressa said sarcastically.

"Yes, girl I had to check her because people always gotta know what the hell is goin' on. Why can't they mind their business?" Gypsy acted like she put the other girl in check, but she know good and well she didn't, because there was no other girl.

Tressa responded with a little giggle. As Gypsy held the hand-held mirror for Tressa so that she could look up close at the finished, beautiful creation.

"That'll be thirty-five dollars." Gypsy informed Tressa.

Tressa, without hesitation, went into her pocketbook, pulled out the fifty-dollar bill and gave it to Gypsy.

"How much change you need?"

"Naw boo, I don't need none."

Although it was only fifteen dollars, she could have definitely put it to use. She knew good and well Gypsy didn't deserve the tip, and she tried to justify and reason with herself. *Sometimes you just gotta pay the cost and take the lost, simply to put a bitch in her place, and to keep their head wondering. See, they think I'm doing bad. They want me to crumble. As long as I got breath in my body, they will never see me sweat. When the dust settles, I'll always be the last chick standing. Mark my words!*

105

-12-
Double Trouble!!!

S tepping out the door of the salon with a fresh do always boosted Tressa's self-esteem. This was the very reason she always wore something cute to the salon. She knew that her hair pinned up in a volcano looking French roll on the top of her head, with not a piece of hair out of place, would only accent her super cute outfit. Today it was some mint green Calvin Klein jean shorts, that stopped at her thighs, and a white and green print Calvin Klein halter-top that matched. What made the simple but cute outfit stand out, were the Calvin Klein white sandals with the same mint green print as the shirt, with the pocketbook to match. Tressa knew she looked good, but now she had nowhere to go. Someone had to see her. Her children were at school, Wiggles had dropped them off on her way back to the program Monday morning. So, she had nowhere to be or obligations until 5 p.m., when she had to pick up the kids. As good as she looked, somebody had to, needed to and was going to see her this day.

Tressa looked at the crushed potato chips the boys had scattered all over the back seat and the floor of the car. It was then that the bright plan popped into her head. She drove to "Big Willie's Car Repair, Custom, Detail Shop", which was a place Lucky always barred her from because this was indeed the place all the hustlers, ballers, pimps and players were known to take their cars, trucks and vans to get washed and hooked up. The fact that Big Willie's had girls dressed in bathing suits washing cars, naturally drew in regular men too. Since this was the designated place where all the "money-getting men" were, that was indeed the place for Tressa to swing by. Although she had no desire for a hustler in her life, after the whole ordeal with Lucky, but she did want companionship, and if he had some money, that would come in handy. She had no intentions of developing a relationship with any guy, not yet anyway, but she wanted to see if she still had *it*. She wanted some male attention like she used to get when she was with Lucky and she was certain Big Willie's was just the place to go and get it. So, it was off to Big Willie's she went.

Tressa was sitting at the stop light when one of her all time favorite songs came on. She turned the volume knob up almost as loud as it could go. The music at the beginning of the song got her excited, then she began to sing word for word. Tressa was "Shaking her thang" just the way Salt-N-Pepa were telling her to!

Word for word, the whole song flowed out of her mouth as if she had wrote the lyrics herself. She had memorized this song and just about every other one of Salt-N-Pepa's songs.

In addition to washing and detailing cars, Big Willie's sold pagers and cell phones, so he had a lot of things going on and a lot of people coming in and out. Although Big Willie's looked like a cheap run down brick building on the outside, inside he only used state of the art equipment. The "décor" consisted of cheap plastic chairs and an old raggedy sofa, with two of the cushions missing, for the customers to sit while waiting. It was rumored that it was definitely a front for the owner, who sold more drugs then a little bit, but so was almost every black owned business that prospered. Tressa decided to go in and pretend she was looking for a new pager while her car was being washed. When she walked in, the men all stared at her because they had never seen her before.

Tressa walked up to the counter and the guy who fronted like he was the owner, but he was just that, a front man. The fake Jake bragged 24-7, around the clock, like all of that was his.   Tressa could see right through it all because he tried too hard.

He tried to hit on her with the weak come on line. "Damn, baby where I know you from?"   Holding his chin, trying to act as if he was figuring it out, while the other guys looked on.

"Boo, that's the oldest line in the book," Tressa said with a slight laugh.

Just then, Boo-Boo walked up and rescued her from whack Jack.

Boo-Boo and Tressa had gone to elementary school together.   Boo-Boo was one of those guys who didn't really have to hustle.   Growing up, he never knew what struggle was, his middle class parents provided him with whatever his little heart desired.   His older sister became a veterinarian, while he went on become a nickel and dime hustler.   He was presented with every opportunity that his sister was, but he wanted to fit in with the street fellas, for it always seemed as if they had the most fun.

"What's up Tressa?" Boo-Boo asked.

"Nothing much." Tressa replied, happy to see Boo-Boo, but at the same time, she wasn't sure if Boo-Boo was really happy to see her since she had gotten Wiggles cleaned up and off the crack pipe.

"You look gooder than a mafucka." He said, shaking his head.

"Thanks."

"You seen Wiggles lately?"

Not knowing what really to say to Boo-Boo under the circumstances, and Boo-Boo could feel the awkwardness, so he spoke up. "I want you to know that I got so much respect for you. The way you had your own issues going on and you took out the time to clean Wiggles up.   I ain't gonna lie, it kinda messed me up at first. But after seeing her progress and her faithfully going to her meetings, I saw how important it was for her and ya kids. She loves them so much, that's all she talks about, are her nephews."

"Thanks Boo-Boo. For a minute there I thought you was a lil' pissed cause I got into it."

"Naw, I am happy for her. But look, let me pull your coat to something."

"What?"

"The old head, Mr. Bill, who owns this place, wanna holler at you.   He the old cat over there in the blue jumpsuit."

She looked over, and all she could see, was a man that was so black he looked dark enough to match the oil wearing a greasy jumpsuit.   Without a doubt, the white around his pupils in his round pop eyes stood out.   He was a slim guy that looked liked he stunk, after seeing the sweat roll down his face, while he gave directions and worked at the same time.

"Who you talking about, the one looking like a grease monkey?"

"Yup, but he caked up.   Dude got money.   Quiet as it's kept, he's the owner, all this is his.   All these dudes acting like they head honchos, are just his peons."

"How though, how he got money?   You know I don't mess with no drug dealers no more."

"He's legit." Boo-Boo assured her.

Just then her pager went off.   She looked down at it and she saw that it was children's daycare center calling.   She raced to the phone to call the school, and learned that her boys had gotten into a fight and needed to be picked up. Before she wrote down her number and gave it to Boo-Boo to give to Mr. Bill, she thought to herself, *you can't judge a book by its cover.   People judge me because I live in the projects, but I may live in the projects, but I'm clearly not project.   So just because he looks like a grease monkey, I'm not going to judge him.*

She wanted so bad to beat their little butts when she walked into the daycare director's office, especially after the director told her that they were suspended for three days from the center.   Tressa was furious, but she held her composure until she got in the car.

Little Ali kept trying to make small talk with his mother, but she ignored him.   Little Hadji, on the other hand knew better.   He figured if he kept quiet, his mother would forget all about it and wouldn't punish them when they got home.

Tressa stopped at the gas station to get some gas. At first she cut the car off, then she thought about how much of a headache it would be to get both of the boys out of their booster seats, and she wasn't in the mood.   So, she

110

started the car back up and hopped out to pump the gas. She glanced at the inside of the service station, decided to pump the gas first before she paid, due to the long line. When she was done, there were only two people ahead of her in line.

Tressa looked at the counter at the Mr. Goodbar, Snickers, M&M's and Starburst candies. It was so automatic for her to buy the boys something when she went into the store, but not this day. Her rule of the thumb was, kids that showed off at school don't get any treats.

"Ten dollars on pump 4." She said and handed the money to the attendant and walked out of the store to receive the scare of her life.

When she looked over at pump four, where her car was, the car was rolling slowly with both of her children in it! She was in such a panic, she instantly froze and all she could do was scream, "Hellllppppp!!!! Please someone help!!! Oh God, HELPPP!!!! My children are in the car!"

Her heart started racing as she saw the bits and pieces of monumental moments in the three years of her boys life replay in her head. At that moment, she started running behind her car, screaming at the top of her lungs, "HELP!" She was running so fast, she forget about her platform boots she had on and she slipped up and fell flat on her face. She continued to scream, all the while trying to get up, and praying at the same time. "God, please don't let any harm come to my sons. God they are all I got."

At that very moment, she saw a young black guy running past her. All she could make out was his gold chain swinging side to side while he sprinted towards the car. Then, a white man appeared with some neon green running shoes, darting over to assist in catching the car. Although both strangers, never laying eyes on each other, worked as if they were indeed a trained team. It didn't matter that one was black and the other was white, or one was old and the other young. What mattered was them coming together saving those two little boys, and that's exactly what they did.

Mr. Gold Chain ran to the driver's side and opened up the door, and neon green jogging shoes somehow caught up with the car and open up the passenger side of the car. Gold chain hopped in, while neon green jogging shoes failed

111

the first time he attempted to jump in, but succeeded the next time and got in. They were both surprised to see that there were two little mischievous boys in the car. Lil Hadji was at the wheel, but it was Little Ali that was in the floor trying to figure out how to make the pedals go faster. Gold Chain reached over and put the car in gear, while neon green running shoes grabbed Little Ali off the pedals.

Tressa, now on her feet, ran over to the car, although it felt like the pounding of her heart weighed her down. She had broke put in a cold sweat, although it was close to 90 degrees outside.

Even though the car was stopped, and her boys were safe, Tressa's heart continued to beat fast. Was it the fact that she had made the mistake of leaving the car on? Was it the fact that she was so angry, she wanted to whip her sons' butts from the gas station all the way home? She ran over to the car and demanded that both boys get back in their car seats.

"I don't know what's wrong with ya'll? I promise you, you are going to get it when you get home." Tressa said.

Hadji looked at Gold Chain with his big convincing eyes. "Please tell my momma don't beat us. Please." He begged and tried to con Gold Chain.

No words could ever express how truly grateful she was as she walked over to thank both guys. Neon green jogging suit simply said. "Glad I could help. Next time, don't leave the car on." He simply walked off, happy that he had been a good Samaritan.

On the other hand, Gold Chain just kind of hung around. This was the first time she had got a really good look at him and he was FINE!!! She looked him over and realized that he was the suave and debonair type, and she would really have to stoke his ego. She could tell that he wasn't the Superman type of guy to rescue anyone. For he was too much of the pretty boy, fly type of guy. Gold chain was the kind that would get a haircut twice a week and surely threw a tantrum if his Timberland boots got one scratch or scuff on them. Gold chain's Versace sweatpants were fresh out of the cleaners, with no creases down the middle, but an inch away from the side stitching on the Versace sweatpants. The collar of the zip up sweat suit jacket rested flat, indicating that it too was fresh out of the cleaners. He was a deep dark chocolate complexion, with a mouth full of gold teeth.

Ullll, she thought to herself. *I hope his breath don't stink.* Damn, I wish he wouldn't have even opened up his mouth! But since he did, let me see what he has to say.

With what sounded like a fake whine to Gold Chain, Tressa said to Gold Chain. "Thank you so much. Thank you, thank you and thank you. I can't thank you enough."

He shook his head. "No problem, I'm always happy to help a sister out. Those lil' dudes you got is off the chain."

"Yeah, I know."

"What's your name honey?"

"Tressa, and yours?"

"Jacko"

"No, sweetie your government name. I know good and well your mother didn't name you Jacko."

"No, it's Jack, but they call me Jacko."

They talked the small talk a couple more minutes and then he popped the question. "Look, you look like you are having a pretty fucked up day. I'd like to take you out for a drink or something."

Tressa was a bit flattered that a male was finally asking her out. She hadn't been with a man since she left Lucky. Just the hustle and bustle of being mother and father, trying to make ends meet, which seemed like such an easy task only eight months earlier, was keeping her so busy that she had kind of lost sight of finding companionship for herself. Then not to mention, she had to keep up her guard up. She was fully aware that Lucky was not going to let them live in peace, not over his dead body anyway. Lastly, could he be trusted? He seemed nice, but he could be just another Lucky in disguise?

-13-
Meal Tickets

Rinnnng, Rinnnnng, Rinnnnng. *I wish this heifer would answer the damn phone.*

"Hello, you have reached the voice mailbox of Linda Blue, social worker with the Richmond City Department of Social Services." *"Now ain't this some shit."* Tressa said, shaking her head while continuing to listen to the recording. *Is this chick ever at her desk? What are they paying her for, to retrieve messages?*

"I am away from desk or interviewing another client. Please leave your name, number and a brief message and I will return your call at my earliest convenience. Please remember to report all changes in your household." Beep.

"Yes, this is Tressa Shawsdale. Ms. Blue, this doesn't make any sense. I have been leaving you messages for days, and now it's been a week, and you have still have not returned my calls. I have turned all my paperwork in and I still haven't received my food stamps yet. I have two young boys who do not understand why there is no food in my house. I hate to have to call your supervisor to report your lack of attention to my predicament, but I will." Tressa slammed the phone down.

These people make me sick. This is so humiliating. I hate having to depend on the government, especially to eat. It used to be cute not having to pay for food and being able to apply that money to something else, but at the same time, I

115

hate feeling like I am begging them to give me a handout. Shoot, I remember when Lucky used to come home and hand over six or seven hundred dollars worth of food stamps. I had no problem using them then, and our refrigerator stayed stocked with the best meats, poultry, seafood and snacks for the kids. Now, I just gotta go make it happen for us.

Tressa continued to think how screwed up the system was. She had never had any dealings with the welfare system until now. She needed food stamps to eat, Medicaid for her children so they could go to the doctor, and state funded daycare to watch the children while she worked. She knew now she had to work. But, she realized that the system was put in place for those having hard times and needed a break to get ahead. But how so? She could never understand. The welfare system, in her eyes, seemed to be set up and only works for those who sit on their asses and collect a check. Not for the working individuals that are really trying.

I wonder why, as soon as I got my little seven dollars and fifty cents an hour job, it seemed like I was doing worse than when I didn't have a job. At first, my rent was only $25.00, now it's gone up to $303.00. My daycare was free when I was laying around not working anywhere, only pretending to look for work, now they have raised it to $130.00 a month. I know $130.00 is good for two children, because before I was paying $130.00 a week per child, which is still crazy. Some women are better off just staying at home raising their own children. Shoot, I used to get over four hundred dollars a month in food stamps, and now all I can get is $127.00 to feed all three of us. Then to top it off, this worker takes all day to process my damn food stamps. She got the nerve to tell me to be sure to report all the changes in the household. Shoot, for what? For them to continue to cut my benefits all the way off, I don't think so. If I make four, five or six hundred extra dollars, you think I am going to tell them? I used to laugh and look down on people who get locked up for welfare fraud, but I can't much blame them. Seems like you have to commit some fraud just to stay afloat.

Tressa's old neighbor, Joan's sister, Shelly, owned an interior decorating firm. Now, Shelly was so much different from Joan. Shelly was in her late fifties, had been

116

divorced three times, and all her ex's were very wealthy men. Each husband paid off like Big Game lottery tickets, which left her bank account as big as Texas. She possessed much attitude and spunk. She weighed a hundred and twenty-five pounds, had dyed dirty blond hair, and a beautiful flawless red tan, that made her complexion resemble that of a light brown black woman. Shelly stood 5'4", and had tried every kind of plastic surgery to enhance her physical appearance, from liposuction, tummy tuck, breast implants, face lifts to hormone shots to enlarge her behind. The physical enhancements, combined with her money, made her hell on wheels. Shelly loved to brag about and spend her money. She may have looked like a bimbo or a kept woman, but she was a hell of a businesswoman.

With Shelly's cold, bitter attitude, there would always be someone fed up with Shelly and eventually they would quit her. So, Joan managed to convince Shelly that Tressa would be the perfect candidate for the receptionist position, which later, the responsibility of buyer was eased into her lap, though there was no wage increase.

Although Tressa had no prior experience in interior design, Joan always admired the eye she had for decorating the house that she used to reside in with Lucky. Shelly was certain that Tressa would just mess up, but as a favor to her sister, she gave her a shot. And to her surprise, Tressa, the lowest paid employee, worked harder than any other staff member Shelly employed.

It took everything in Tressa to give her social services income verification forms to Shelly to fill out. She was so embarrassed that the cat was out of the bag that she received welfare benefits. Shelly would surely let Joan know exactly how hard life was without Lucky. She didn't want anybody feeling sorry for her or looking down on her. The humiliation really sat in, when she thought about how Shelly would look at her as a charity case, and maybe dog her out concerning her job responsibilities. She thought Shelly would try to talk down to her, and lose all respect for her because she knew Tressa needed the job.

Frustration filled Tressa's body after examining the whole scenario. Her pride was fighting her to not give the forms to Shelly, and just doing without the benefits. Then next, she thought about how there was nobody else to help her provide for her children, and her low paying job was barely enough to make the basic bills. Taking those things into consideration, she swallowed her pride and handed the forms to Shelly to fill out.

After facing the humiliation, mortification and embarrassment of her bourgeoisie boss having to find out she was a welfare recipient, the social worker still had not completely processed her food stamps application. Tressa still was forced to execute her street survival skills and take matters into her own hands. On that note, Tressa slipped on her 9 West slides, grabbed her cordless phone and ran down the steps of her third floor based brick style, government subsidized apartment. She stood in front of the building, scooping out the area, looking to see whom she saw.

"Rosey!" She yelled. "Girl, who out here got some food stamps they trying to sell?"

Nosey Rosey, a.k.a. Mouth All Mighty, a.k.a. Mouth of the South, was a short, stubby bright skinned girl, with fat cheeks who walked around the projects all day, every day with the same print scarf wrapped around her head.

You would think she would get another damn scarf, being that it's a permanent part of her everyday attire. If she wears it every single day, when does she ever wash it? I know it has got to stink!

Rosey sat on the bench in the front of apartments, and positioned herself so she could be in view of who came in and out of the main entrances, and basically every building of the apartments. Nosey Rosey looked around the neighborhood, took a deep breath, and smacked her lips as she began to talk.

"Girrrrll, you know food stamps came out like seven, eight days ago, so it's pretty dry round here. The only person I know who haven't got theirs yet is Meechie. Hers should be coming today, I'll let her know you're looking for some. "

"Thanks, girl."

Meechie was really somebody that Tressa did not want to deal with, she was larceny-hearted. She lived right under Tressa and could not be trusted. Meechie was a dirty girl, who had six kids, but only two of them lived with her. Her whole existence was getting high all night and

118

scamming people all day. The two kids that lived with
Meechie, never even had the bare necessities. They were
ashy and dirty kids. The only clothes they ever had was
hand-me-downs. At first, Tressa used to try to look out for
them since she felt so sorry for them. Their constant
begging got to be too much for her to handle.

As Tressa was about to walk up the steps, Meechie
walked up and asked Rosey. "Do you know anybody who
wanna buy some food stamps?"

She turned to look at Tressa. "Or Tressa if you
know somebody, let me know."

"How much you trying to sell?" Tressa asked.

"Well, I wanna sell 'bout $200.00 for $100.00."

When people sell food stamps, it is usually double
the amount of food stamps for the cash money.

"No problem, I'll get them. Are you trying to do that
now?" A relieved Tressa was happy to catch the break even
if it was from Larceny Meechie.

"Well, in the next hour when the mailman comes, I'll
be ready."

"Well, I'll be in the house, just come upstairs when
you get them."

"You sure you going to get them?"

"Yeah, I am sure." Tressa assured her that she
wanted them. She knew she had to really act pressed,
because if she didn't, Meechie would sell them to someone
else.

Lord, thank you! She said, to herself.

Tressa went back into her ghetto, but plush
apartment that was like a home featured in Better Homes
and Gardens magazine. Although Tressa lived in the
ghetto, she didn't live like she was ghetto. When people
visited her place, they would have never known they were in
one of Richmond's most cracked-infested projects. Even the
landlord could not believe what she had done with the
place, and often used it as a model to the top officials.
Tressa may have had twin boys, but that wasn't a valid
reason why one wouldn't be able to eat off the apartment's
floor. She had upscale brown expensive leather furniture,
with leopard print pillows and curtains. On the opposite
wall, she had two mini brown leather recliners made for her
twins. She had removed the dingy shades the complex

supplied in the windows and replaced them with matching vertical blinds in her living room and kitchen. The brown and black marble lacquer dinette set, with the hutch to match, had leopard placemats on the table. She had even went as far as getting a mini kiddie lacquer table to match her sons.

When people asked how she could afford the expensive furniture, she wanted so bad to say, because she lived in the projects that how. Her rent was cheap, that was why. But she mostly shopped at scratch and dent departments, that way, she could afford what things she wanted. Then to add to it, when she first moved, she wanted new furniture so bad that she combined the boys and her social security numbers together to make up a fresh social security number so she could get the furniture she really wanted.

The original kitchen floor had wax build up. So she stripped it, re-stained it and finished it with a high gloss.

Tressa had worked wonders with that apartment. She had done every stitch of the work herself. She had three bedrooms and two walk in closets. One of the closets was in her room and the other was in the hall. The hall closet was turned into a sewing room. She sewed as a hobby, which was a skill she picked up from her grandmother. The other closet in her bedroom was filled from top to bottom. As much as she tried, it never stayed organized. Her bedroom furniture was filled with French dovetailing, and an impeccable quality wood bedroom set that took up practically all the space in the room. Her curtains, comforter and Persian rug matched. The twins shared a room with two blue Little Tikes car beds, dressers and desks. The décor was race cars. The border, carpet, bedspreads, curtains, lamps, light switch cover and pictures on the wall had race cars.

The third bedroom, she transformed into the boys playroom. There was two of everything so the boys wouldn't fight, and there was a television. The room was painted blue, and in the middle of the floor was a plastic Little Tikes playground. The playroom was a privilege for the boys. They had to earn the right to go into the playroom. She never allowed her children to play outside on the playground, because at any given time, there would be roaring gunshots, or just drama at the playground. The type of drama that would tempt her to have to beat one of the ghetto chicks down and violate her probation. The only time her boys got to play outside was if she took them to a playground elsewhere, or if they were over Wiggles' house.

Tressa was a good mother to her children, in spite of her circumstances. She just didn't spoil the boys materially, she spoiled them with knowledge, books and learning toys. As any devoted mother would, she spent time with them reading and showering them with love. Her boys were now three years old and were developing nicely.

Tressa was in the house sitting on her leather sofa, when the doorbell rang. *That must be Meechie.*

"Who is it?" She stood beside the door. There was no need for her to look out of the peephole, because she had a wreath on the door blocking it.

In a rough women's voice. "It's Meechie."

Tressa opened the door partially. "Oh, you got dat?"

Meechie, with a pitiful look responded. "Girl, I don't know what I am gonna do. The mailman came and didn't have my food stamps, and I ain't got no food in my cabinets or refrigerator. I called my caseworker and she said they should be here tomorrow."

"Well, I can wait until tomorrow." Tressa said briskly.

"But, could you go loan me like $30.00, and I would take it off the money for the food stamps tomorrow when I get them. I really need to go buy my kids something to eat, plus I wanna get me a beer and some cigarettes."

Tressa hesitated for a minute *I really don't trust this bitch! I don't think she'll really burn this bridge because I live right over her. Plus, I don't wanna say no cuz if I do, then she won't sell me the food stamps tomorrow.*

"Look, I was going to have to run to the bank and get the money anyway, but I do have like $15.00 that I can give you. Hold on."

Tressa shut the door and went to get the fifteen dollars. She came back to the door and handed her the money. Attentively looking Meechie in the eyes, she said in a subtle tone. "See you tomorrow, right?"

"Yes, Tressa thanks." Meechie replied as she turned to walk away with a big Kool-Aid smile on her face.

As Tressa put the dead bolt, bottom and top locks on her door, her phone rang. Rinnnng...Rinnnng...Rinnnng. *I hope this is the damn worker calling me so I won't have to be dealing with that larceny ass bitch Meechie.*

"Hello."

"What's the deal baby?" She had heard this greeting so many times from this familiar voice. She paused for a minute, surprised that he had acquired her number after so many months had passed.

"How you manage to fall off the dead beat dad wagon to make this call?" She said in an abrupt tone as she caught an instant attitude.

"Oh, you got jokes, huh. But I'm going to let that one slide cause I know I've been carrying it real fucked up concerning the boys."

She listened because she didn't know what to expect next. Lucky was so unpredictable and was capable of anything at this point. She wondered just what it was that he wanted.

"Look, I got some stuff for the boys. I am downstairs in front of your building. I know I am not welcome in ya house. Oops, I meant ya project!"

That low blow really packed a mean punch! She'll never let him know that he hurt her feelings. Plus, she just fantasized about the things Mr. Big Spender had for her sons as she listened to him continue.

"So, just please come downstairs to get the stuff. I'll pay one of these nickel and dime niggas to help you carry all the stuff back up stairs."

So, she slipped on her 9 West slides, glanced in the mirror to make sure her hair was in place, and exited the apartment.

As soon as Lucky caught sight of her, *Damn my baby still look good, still fat to damn death. Shit, it don't look like she starving. I guess she probably got one of these lil' neighborhood busters looking out for her.*

"Hurry up cuz my car getting hot sitting out here in this war zone." He said to her as she walked over to his big body style LS 400 white Lexus on eighteen-inch chrome rims that the fellas around Richmond hadn't even been introduced to yet.

She didn't comment, she only grabbed the huge shopping bags from Hecht's, the Gap, Nordstrom's, Macy's and Foot Locker. He motioned to one of Pondee's workers. "Shawdy, come help her carry this stuff up the steps. I'm a look out for ya."

The worker grabbed the bags, as Lucky told her. "This is some boxes of fish sticks, chicken tenders, some steaks and some other things. I figured the boys would probably want some of their favorite foods to eat. Oh yeah, I almost forgot to mention, it's about $200 worth of roach motels and raid so those roaches can check in, but won't be able to check out!" Khalil snickered.

She walked away not showing one ounce of emotion towards him. That in and of itself pissed Lucky off, because he wanted to see a reaction from Tressa. At least some small talk to open up the doors of communication between the two of them. She didn't show the slightest bit of appreciation after he'd gone out of his way and spent his $3,500.00.

"Damn, you mean to tell me a nigga can't even get a thank you?"

Tressa stopped in her tracks, gave a slight giggle, made direct eye contact with Lucky. "A thanks shouldn't be required because these are the type of things you're suppose to do for your kids. I don't get a thank you when I feed and clothe your children every day, now do I?"

By the expression on his face, she could see she had him where she wanted him, now she went in for the kill. "Oh, and by the way, we may be in the projects, but guess what boo? This is our safe haven away from Alcatrez, the prison we used to call home, just minus the bars. I know your Don Coleon, shoot' em up, bang-bang ass not afraid to sit out here in this hood. Let me find out I got more heart than you."

Tressa turned to prance back up the steps, never looking back at Lucky. She knew she had gotten up under his skin and knew all the right buttons to push when it came to him. Once back in her apartment, she realized at that moment, that all the items that boys brought over were not because he wanted to do right by his boys, it was simply his way of letting her know that she couldn't hide from him, and he knew exactly where she lived. She was certain that Lucky was about to set it off. She was still unsure what he had up his sleeve, but whatever it was, she wasn't taking it lying down. Her guards were up and her game face was on.

-14-
Lucky's Lucky Day

Tressa ran into "Bills Bar-B-Que" to pick up some food, leaving Wiggles in the car with the children. As Tressa gave her order, she overheard some screaming that sounded like Wiggles. She looked out the window and saw a flatbed tow truck. She observed through Wiggles body language that she was having an intense dispute with the tow truck driver. She gave the cashier her money and ran outside to see what all the chaos and commotion was all about. By the time she reached the door, the tow truck driver was attaching what looked like a chain to her car. It was then she realized the man was towing her car!

"What the hell you are doing with my car?" She screamed at the fat white man with a big belly that was hanging over his belt.

"What does it look like?" He screamed back at her.

"Why?"

"I don't owe you no explanation. I'm just doing what I was hired to do, get the car. Remove your personal possessions." He said to her in a nasty tone with a giggle and continued to hook her car up.

"Get this fucking car down, so I can get my kids out." She screamed at the top of her lungs, wanting to punch him so badly.

She ignored the police siren as a police car rolled up behind her. She didn't care about any police car. There wasn't a police officer in the world that could stop her from getting to her children.

As the tow truck driver went back into the truck, he started pushing buttons to lower the car. The children were in the car screaming, but not because they were scared, they actually enjoyed the lights and movements on the tow truck. Then all of sudden the screams of excitement turned into screams of being afraid, because they could see their mother's frustration and they could tell something was wrong with her and their aunt Wiggles.

One of the police officers approached Wiggles first, trying to make heads of the matter. They next went to talk to the crowd of folks that had come out of Bill's Bar B-Que to be nosey. The other police officer approached Tressa and the tow truck driver.

"Sir, what seems to be the problem?" He asked the driver, but Tressa spoke before the driver could.

Screaming at the top of her lungs, Tressa excitedly replied. "The problem is I wasn't parked illegal, over the lines or anything. And this man is towing my car with my children and belongings in it, and won't give me an explanation!"

The officer looked at the car and saw Lil Hadji in the window screaming, and Lil Ali trying to escape through the passenger side window. Wiggles was running trying to rescue him. When they realized he was on his way out of the window, everyone, except the tow truck driver, ran over to the window as the other police officer told the driver to shut the truck off.

Once the children were out of the car, the police officers were too frustrated with the tow truck driver. It took everything in Tressa not hit the tow truck driver with a right hook. The driver handed some papers to the police. The officer looked over the papers thoroughly.

"Both of you wait here." He instructed the tow truck driver and Tressa, while the officer proceeded to his police cruiser to dissect the writing on the papers. He used his cell phone, as well as called over the cb radio, to try to gather the necessary information.

126

The officer returned after fifteen minutes with a disappointed looked on his face.

"Ms. Shawsdale, I regret that I have to tell you that this bill of sale for the vehicle, in exchange for *dog food,* is very legal." He said, as he held out the bill of sale to her. "I will let you gather your valuables out of the car."

"But I don't understand. It has got to be a mistake." She said to the police officer, totally upset, but still trying to stop the tears from rolling down her face.

She looked at the bill of sale in depth, and at that very moment, abhorrence, disgust, revulsion, hostility and hatred for Lucky filled every bone in Tressa's body. Tressa couldn't believe how desperate and determined Lucky was to make her life without him a living hell. Wasn't it enough that she had to fend for herself? Wasn't it enough that she had to be on welfare to make ends meet? Wasn't it enough that she had to explain to her kids where daddy was and why he wasn't there with them? Wasn't it enough that she lived in a roach infested housing project, taking a risk everyday, not knowing at any given moment, if her or her sons were going to get hit with a stray bullet? Wasn't all this humiliation and agony enough?

While he's rolling around in his array of cars; Lexus', B'mer's, trucks all suited up, living the life of luxury, we're over here with the bare necessities struggling, scrambling, scuffling and barely making it. All he can do is to continue to find ways to try to bring me down. I can't believe this dude hates me, the woman who bared his two sons, the woman who rubbed Preparation H on his ass when he had hemorrhoids, the woman who was his best friend, who listened and consoled him through the good and bad, happy and sad. He hates me so much that he's going to sell my damn car for a car that he wouldn't dare drive around the block in or be caught dead in. A car that his children gets from point A to Point B in, for a bag of fucking Purina Dog food and two cans of Alpo! I can't believe he did this! Why? So what the car was in both of our names, and so what I got Gator to sign his name. What difference does it make, shit, that B'mer was my car. I don't mess with him, I stay out of his way and I don't contact anybody he knows. And yet, still he won't let me be. This clown had the nerve to sell my four thousand dollar car for a bag of dog food. I can not believe it, a bag of dog food! It's all good, though. Since he wants to have jokes, and wanna play games, he better step up to the major leagues because believe me when I tell you, it's on!

Tressa, Wiggles and the two boys waited while Tressa called Jacko for a ride.

"Yo." Jacko answered the phone.

"Hey Jacko, what are you doing?"

"I'm about to go get me some'in to eat, why, what's up?"

"My babies father just had my car towed, and me and the kids need a ride."

"He had your car towed? Damn, what type of time is that dude on? He had the car towed that you drive his kids around in?"

"Yup." She said. "Oh, I forgot to mention and sold it for a bag of damn dog food."

"What?" He smacked his lips. "This guy is bananas! Where you at?"

"We at Bill's Bar-B-Que on the Boulevard." She answered him.

"I'll be there in fifteen minutes, and don't let that get you all upset. I'll make sure you get back and forth to work and the kids get to school."

Tressa and Jacko had been conversing over the phone for the past few weeks. Always reluctant, and especially not ready to deal with Jacko in an actual relationship, due to the drama that went on with her and Lucky. She never explained in depth just how far Lucky would go, but she made it clear that he was deranged. Her inner self also restricted her from even developing a relationship with Jacko, because if Lucky found out about Jacko and their relationship, she was sure it may cost Jacko his life. Jacko wasn't afraid of Lucky, although he had heard stories, but he never pressured her at all. He knew if he played the background, and was the understanding, consoling friend, what was due to him would surely come.

For the next two weeks, Jacko came to take Tressa back and forth to work faithfully every day. She was grateful for that. Shelly observed that Tressa didn't have a car, and Tressa never confirmed the details of what happened to her car, but Shelly automatically thought the

128

car was repossessed. Unbelievably, Shelly sympathized with Tressa, having two children, needing to get back and forth to work. By, no means, did she want Tressa to lose focus by getting frustrated with having to depend on someone else to give her a ride to work every day. Shelly took into consideration the money that Tressa was making for the company with her impeccable taste. Tressa had made the company six times the amount the other buyers had made in a year, in such a short time. Tressa never received a pay increase. Shelly, at any point, easily could have bought Tressa a little used car as a gift and wrote it off on her taxes at the end of the year. The reality of the matter was, no matter how big the dividends were that Tressa's expertise brought in to the conglomerate, Shelly wasn't buying any black girl a car. Why would she? For her to think she was almighty and leave her. Shelly did ask around the office, and found out that one of the other employees, Wanda, had a car for sale.

Wanda boldly approached Tressa. "I heard you don't have a car and needed one. Well, my husband has a car that used to be my son's. Now, I am warning you, the car is not beautiful, but the motor runs like clockwork. Nothing else is wrong with it, but it needs some bodywork. I can talk to him, but I am sure he'll sell it to you for about $350.00. I mean, it's nothing fancy, but I am sure it will get you to and from work and ride your children around safely until you can do better."

She wanted to hug Wanda. Wanda's news was like music to her ears. Although it was a real hoopty, it beat thumbing it, busing it or begging for a ride any day. Where was she going to get $350.00? She didn't get paid until Friday and it was only Tuesday. Even after taxes, her check would only be about $240.00. She didn't care if she had to spend her whole paycheck on the bucket (usually an ugly small car), but where would she get the rest? Plus, she will have to get insurance and tags from DMV, since the tow truck driver took her car with the tags on it. Then, not to mention, she would still need gas to get her back and forth to work.

For the rest of the day, she began to brainstorm where she could get the money. She called her cousin, Gator. He said he couldn't give it to her because he had just purchased a barbershop with all his money and did not have one dime to spare. She fully understood, due to the fact that Gator had always assisted her in other matters where Lucky fell short. Like for instance, he took the boys to get a haircut every week, and afterwards, would take them to dinner somewhere. This was the closest thing to any male bonding her boys had, her thugged-out, younger cousin Gator.

Gator was a few years younger than Tressa. He dressed like a thug, complete with cornrows braided to the back, barely weighing in at 150 pounds, baggy pants sagging down, which gave him an extra fifteen pounds. Gator was a brown skinned handsome guy with fat, chubby cheeks, and wore gold Versace glasses. He was one book that couldn't be judged by its cover. He was raised up by the same principles and rules that Taj had instilled in Tressa, but a gangster he wasn't. He was fully educated by and was affiliated with, many people who lived the life, but Gator's number one goal was to get rich legitimately. He read all kinds of management and business books. He'd just put a major accomplishment under his belt at only twenty-one years, owning a barbershop. This was just one of his many goals he had set for himself. He loved Tressa as if she was his sister. There wasn't anything he wouldn't do for her, and if there was some way, somehow he could give her the money, the money would be hers without a doubt.

She called Wiggles, who also now worked a 9 to 5. Wiggles agreed to give her $75.00, and offered to help pay back whoever Tressa would borrow the rest of the money from. Wiggles also said she would ask Boo-Boo for fifty dollars too. Within a matter of forty minutes, Wiggles had $125.00 for Tressa towards the car. Now, all she had to do was work on getting the DMV tags and title fees, which was about $240.00. As far as the insurance, she would transfer it over from the Honda and would still have to pay them a down payment to add it. That wasn't a major worry for her, she'll get that in a week or so when she could.

Then she called her faithful girlfriend, Missy. If Missy had it, she could get it. Missy was her devoted friend, although it seemed as if Tressa spent more time with

Dutchess. Missy was one of the most positive people she knew. Though they didn't talk everyday, she knew Missy was someone she could count on regardless of the storm. A lot of times she wouldn't stress Missy out with the everyday, day-to-day drama she experienced. She only called Missy when she needed words of wisdom, a positive input. Missy was heavily into church, so sometimes, Missy's religious take on things wasn't what she needed. Missy informed Tressa that she had just paid a slue of bills, so she wasn't able to assist Tressa either.

Tressa wasn't going to call and ask Dutchess for the money. Dutchess was cool with her, but at times, Dutchess got on her nerves. Tressa would never admit it to Dutchess, but she was very ashamed to go out to a restaurant with Dutchess because she always embarrassed Tressa. They could never go to a restaurant without Dutchess bringing the drama. Dutchess would order the most expensive thing on the menu, and eat more than half of it, and then have the nerve to say when she's just about done with it, "ullll, there's a piece of hair in my food! And they must be crazy if they think I am going to pay for this."

And Dutchess would make a big scene at the end of meal, and guess what? She wouldn't pay for it either. As broke as Tressa was, by all means she wanted a discount if she could get one, but at the same time, she had no problem paying for her meal. This was one of the things that Tressa overlooked when it came to Dutchess, for Dutchess and Tressa shared so many laughs and they talked faithfully everyday for hours. Tressa loved hanging out with Dutchess, but to save herself the embarrassment, she just never went to dine with Dutchess.

But when it came to matters of the heart and her innermost feelings, she kept them away from Dutchess. She believed with all her soul that secretly, Dutchess was happy that Tressa was going through such hard times. Not to mention that Dutchess was friends, well a fake sister, to Lucky. Although she said, and swore to God, "crossed her heart, hoped to die, stick a needle in her eye," that after Tressa caught the girl in her old apartment, that she wasn't dealing with Lucky anymore.

As convincing as Dutchess sounded when she promised Tressa, it was a promise that Tressa didn't ask for, because she knew that Dutchess and Lucky called each other brother and sister. In Tressa's heart, she never fully believed it. So, as bad as Tressa wanted to call Dutchess, she didn't. She knew the routine, Dutchess would probably ask her all these questions and then say she didn't have the money. She wasn't giving Dutchess the satisfaction of knowing that she needed her, and she wouldn't come through.

Hoping nobody spotted her going into the pawnshop on her lunch break, she tried to pawn her rings to try to get the money. To her surprise, the two rings she thought was worth over $2,500.00 a piece, the pawn shop owner was only trying to give her $50.00 for each one and wanted her to sell them outright, due to the fact they already had so many other cluster rings. She was deflated. As desperate and disappointed as she was, she told them. "Before I give you my rings, I'll sell them on the streets and get way more than that."

Is this what all single mothers go through when the father refuses to give them child support?

For one second, she thought about asking Jacko, but she couldn't bring herself to ask him. See, asking any man to do anything for her was such a hard thing. Prior to meeting Lucky, she was very independent. She never had to actually ask Lucky for anything material because he always made sure it was there. She never felt dependent on him.

Her mother, Cyn, couldn't escape her abusive husband because she was dependent on her stepfather. Her mother wanted the better life for her children, so, instead of leaving, she put up with the abuse.

Tressa reflected that she didn't want to put herself in the situation of making Jacko think, for one minute, that she needed him. She was already grateful to him for transporting her and her kids to and from work and school. Him inconveniencing himself was already enough for him to do. Plus, she didn't want to feel "needy". So, she destroyed the thought of approaching Jacko for the money that she was positive he would give to her.

Tressa took a deep breath, swallowed her pride and picked up the phone to make her final call, the one phone call she dreaded to make. Before the phone could ring, she hung it up. She took two more deep breaths, picked the phone up and dialed the number. As soon as the voice answered. "Yo." She got an instant attitude. Lucky's voice made her sick.

"Lucky, this is Tressa."

"Hey baby." He said in a sweet tone. This was one call he was glad to receive. "Do you think I could ever forget your voice?"

She ignored the question and took a deep breath while she got her lie together in her head. She knew she couldn't be honest with him. He wasn't going to contribute to the "Tressa's car fund". After all, he was the reason she had to scrape up money for a hoopty.

"Look Lucky, I'm in a bind. I received a cut off notice for the lights. I don't get paid until next week. I have half of the money. Do you think you could give me the other half?"

"Baby, look you know that's no problem, no matter how much it is. Why don't you and the boys just come and stay with me a couple days. I'll give you a bankroll. I miss you so much. I hate that you live over there in that hole and I want you to just give me one more chance. I love you so much. I'll make it up to you. All I am asking is for one more night, and if you don't want me after that, then I'll give you a few g's and let you be."

She paused for a minute and thought about the lifestyle that Lucky could provide for her and the boys. Then reality set in when she reflected on how Lucky's jealous rage almost landed her sons dead, as well as herself, not to mention as an accessory to a double homicide. Then not to mention, how he'd gone to such extreme measures to make her life a living hell. After all the scrambling she had done, the prior nine months would be in vain, if she went back to him. So, her even entertaining the thought, would not be an option. She didn't want to go off and tell him exactly how much she hated him because she needed his help.

"Lucky, I don't want to lead you on, it's over between us. All I need is for you to help me with the light bill."

Lucky cut her off and screamed through the phone. "Use the half of the money you got and buy some candles, because you gonna be in the dark if it's left up to me." He slammed the phone down.

Before she knew it, Tressa had tears in her eyes. She picked up the phone and called Lucky back. As soon as he answered, Tressa let him have it. "Look motherfucka, the whole nine months I've been gone, I ain't never asked your ass for shit. I could have, so many times, ran downtown to the white man and took you up for child support, but I didn't. I just did what I had to do for my babies. You showed up one time with a few outfits for your sons, and got mad because I didn't fall to your feet thanking you. Other than that, I held it down. All you did was try to strip me of my self-esteem, constantly trying to do everything to make me crumble. But baby, you can't make me disintegrate. You'll be the one who's going to wither like grass. You'll be the one who's going to need me." And with every once of emotion, she put emphasis on. "Because when the dust settles, I'll be the last one standing. Mark my words."

"I ain't going to need you." He started, but she slammed the phone down in his ear before he could get a word in.

That night when she got home, emotionally whipped, the phone rung.

"Hello." Tressa said, somewhat nonchantly.

"Uh, hello, can I speak to Tressa?" Mr. Bill said with caution.

"Speaking." She said with slight attitude, not really feeling like talking to anyone after the day she had.

"Tressa, it's me, Mr Bill, I was calling to see if you wanted to go out for dinner and a drink?"

Mr. Bill had been calling Tressa, wanting to take her out on a date since he had seen her at his shop. She had been declining, but today was different. His call was truly perfect timing. After Shelly had worked the shit out of her (Wiggles had taken the boys for the night), she needed a drink. The people downstairs had been fighting and the ruckus was driving her crazy. Without any hesitation, she agreed to have dinner with Mr. Bill. Mr. Bill hadn't seen her since they met, and she hadn't been out since God only knows when.

It was March, but it felt like June outside. Having been bundled up the whole winter, she was no different from all the rest of the girls when an "Indian Summer" day came along. Tressa, by no means, was attracted to the old grease monkey, and none whatsoever did she want to turn Mr. Bill on. All she wanted was a drink and a free meal. She put on a cute little short sleeve Ralph Lauren Polo T-shirt dress that she had the summer before. Along with the dress, she dug out her Polo ankle socks and Polo deck, bo-bo tennis shoes. The ensemble was nothing too revealing, but it was working for her. The dress wasn't tight and it didn't show any cleavage, but it hugged her and breast in a way that made Mr. Bill, and every other man, eight to eighty, blind, cripple or crazy, want her.

Mr. Bill picked her up in front of her building in his gray Mercedes Benz. She couldn't believe how good the old grease monkey cleaned up. Mr. Bill could have made millions if he'd done one of those "before and after" motor oil removal soap commercials. The only thing that she still remembered from their first meeting was Mr. Bill's deep southern accent and dialect. If it wasn't for that, she may have never known who Mr. Bill was. She didn't realize until that moment, that Mr. Bill was a fine old man. She looked him over in his Armani silk pants suit and his gator looking dress shoes, his glistening diamond jewels only complemented his blue/black complexion and was kind of sexy to Tressa. However, Tressa was a little turned off by his yellow teeth that were obviously stained from smoking.

Tressa was usually ashamed at the thought of anyone visiting her. That's the very reason that, besides Wiggles, nobody came to visit her. From the guys hustling and hanging out in front of the building, handing drugs to the crack heads, the dope fiends begging, the winos drinking their Wild Irish Rose bottles, to the babies walking around with pissy pampers, and not to mention the individuals whose whole existence was to just sit on the bench and loiter in the parking lot ignoring the "No Loitering" signs, were a great embarrassment to her. Mr. Bill didn't care anything about it, he saw potential in Tressa. He had seen her plight so many times and knew that this would only be a short stay for her. She would be different from the other females who had roots and generations that lived in the projects.

Mr. Bill and Tressa ended up going to the Olive Garden Restaurant, and though not surprised at all, he was quite impressed with Tressa's class, in spite her present residence being Eastgate Village. Mr. Bill wanted Tressa, but knew because of the age difference, they could never be. He'd settled for being whatever she needed him to be. He was certain there was only two ways he could lock her in and become an official player in her life. The plan was one that he knew well, but was sure the younger "whipper-snapper" that Tressa had dealt with in the past wasn't hip to yet.

The dinner went well. Mr. Bill was a perfect gentleman, until he needed to stop by his house to get some movies he wanted to drop off at Video World. She timidly stood by the door while he went to get the movies. He came into the foyer and put the movies onto the bottom of the steps and then told her he wanted to give her the grand tour of the house. Once he got to the master suite, it was then he asked her. "Look baby, let me lick that sweet clit. That's all I want, to taste you I'm going to look out for you real big."

After the long day she had, she wasn't turning down Mr. Bill. Although this was there first date, right at that moment, it wasn't any shame in her game. Getting some release from all the built up stress that she'd been dealing with for months, and the day she had at work was just the tip of the iceberg. So, the song Mr. Bill was singing was something she needed and wanted. So, why the hell not let him show her what he was working with? She stood by the door as he walked around her licking his lips taking in her gorgeous body. The countless hours of working out during her lunch break at the YMCA wasn't for nothing. He moved behind her and then carefully leaned forward so that she could feel his breath on her neck. She tensed up for a second, but he whispered into her ear, "relax baby," as he undressed her and laid her diagonally cross the big California king size bed.

Tressa's nipples tightened as he began kissing along her neck and ear. She didn't speak when he whispered into her ear how hot she looked, instead groans escaped her lips. Slowly he moved forward, she could feel his breath on her nipple before he enclosed his mouth around her nipple sucking tenderly at first, then releasing it. Her mind was racing, keeping pace with her heart. Tressa arched her body, wanted to tell him to cut the chase and explore more of her. Instead, he began giving her other nipple the same attention, bringing loud moans from her. By this time, she was gasping for air, and he could tell just how hot and ready she was.

She could smell his cigarette breath on her lips as they shared a hot kiss. When he was trying to kiss her, she kept trying not to. She didn't want to mess up the mood, so she held her breath and tasted the nicotine. As his tongue flicked in and out of her mouth, the taste of the nicotine was making her feel like she was about to vomit, but she kept her compulsure. He whispered in her mouth, "not yet baby" and moved away.

"Oh my god." Her mind is screaming. "Mr. Bill, Mr. Bill, I am ready to cum. I don't have the time for these damn foreplay games, just handle your damn business."

All of a sudden, he moves behind her taking her breasts in his hands squeezing them, her nipples didn't need any help getting harder. Squeezing and releasing, "mmmmmmm" he says, as he moves closer she can feel his rock hard penis pressing up against her butt. She could feel his hips swaying against her butt. She was thinking to herself, *he better know I don't take it in the butt, but on the real, this damn ole man knows how to work his stuff.* He began rolling my nipples with his finger, and by this time, she was begging, whimpering and squeezing her legs together. She felt him pulling her back towards the bed. There she was, laying smack dead in the middle of the bed, body glistening, squirming legs spread, Mr Bill began running his hands slowly down her stomach, watching as she drew in deep breaths as her chest heaved up and down, his hand slipped underneath her to remove her soaking wet thong, revealing how wet her pussy already was. Moaning as his fingers moved up to run lightly over her sensative clit, nearly brought Tressa off the bed. He leaned in between her legs, and anticipation was killing her as she felt his hot breath blowing on her pussy lips. Her hips slowly rose to greet him. Mr Bill's tongue slipped up and down Tressa's clit, slowly and tenderly drawing it from its hiding place. Her legs were shaking like jelly. Now, make no mistake about it, Tressa has experienced oral sex before, but dammmmm, not like this, not with such expertise. She felt him slowly and carefully run his tongue from her clit down through her wet lips. He felt her hips bucking as he moved back up and slides his tongue deeper into her hot pussy. Tasting her excitement as she tried to grind back on his tongue, Tressa begans begging for release as he brought his tongue up through her lips to run the flat of his tongue along her clit. Then slowly but firmly stroking it.

"O shit, got dam, what da!" Tressa screamed. That was all it took, it was a done deal! She arched her back telling him suck harder, begging him. "Please don't stop." Tressa began hitting one orgasm after the other, grinding her pussy on his tongue, bucking wildly. Mr Bill placed his hands behind Tressa knees allowing him to take her even further. Once Mr. Bill was done working his magic, Tressa lay on the bed for a minute wondering why Mr. Bill wasn't hugging her. She snapped out of her trance, opened her eyes only to see Mr Bill walking to the bathroom to wash the cum off of his face.

The orgasm sure fitted the bill. Boy, did Mr. Bill have her climbing the walls for the next two hours. When it was all over, Mr. Bill gave her a bubble bath and a long message. Once he was in front of Tressa's building, he handed her a wad of cash, and said. "Told you I was gonna look out for you real good, here's a little something to help you out." She happily took the money and went up to her apartment.

Once she was upstairs in her apartment, Tressa thought, *damn I can't believe this man gave me five hundred dollars just to lick the clit. Shoot, where has he been all my life? And he did it just like it was his profession! Life is good! Tressa didn't feel like a prostitute at all, she was getting paid for her services and doing what she had to do.*

The next day at work, she gave the money to Wanda for the car, and on their lunch break, Wanda took her to the DMV to get the tags and title transferred over. She knew Wanda told her that the car needed *some* bodywork, but she had no idea that literally, the only thing on the car in great condition was the motor, which ran great.

The car was every aspect of a bucket. The liner in the roof of the car was hanging down. The outside paint job was shot to hell. The original paint job was black, however, there were rust spots all over the car, and to top it off, one of the fenders was red. None of the remaining three hubcaps on the tires matched. The trunk didn't even open, it was tied down with a piece of rope. Only one windshield wiper worked. The driver's door handle was broke, which meant she had to roll down the window and open the door from the outside. She had scrambled, begged and went through the agony of giving Lucky the satisfaction of asking him for the money, to buy a 19 year old 1978 Z-28 Camaro that was all banged up.

After a few days of driving the car, she actually came across some other things that were not working on the car. She found out that the gas hand never moved, it always stayed at a full tank, weather it was gas in it or not. There was a hole in the bottom of the car under the floor mat on the driver's car. Without the mat, she could see down to the ground of the car. The driver's seat could not be adjusted at all, it was stuck in the last notch all the way to the back. So, when she went to sit in the car, she had to put a pillow behind her back to bring her closer to the steering wheel. See, that was the an issue that she had to accept with having a bucket, everyday something else surprising would pop up that was wrong with the car. Tressa was sort of embarrassed at the appearance, but she thanked God for her transportation to whatever her destination would be.

When she'd go places, she always parked two blocks away because she didn't want anybody to see her get out of the car. Two weeks after she got the car, she went to the beauty shop to get her hair done and, of course, Gypsy had some dirt to throw. Although she tried to keep the Z-28 a secret, Gypsy saw her getting out of the car two blocks up the street from the salon and, of course, Gypsy decided to throw some mud and rub it all in Tressa's face.

"Girl, ooohhh, I love your Coach bag." Gypsy complimented Tressa.

"Thanks."

"Where you get it from?" Gypsy could tell that it wasn't a bag that the bootleggers had been coming into the shop selling.

"Oh, I got it from Hechts."

"Girl, how much was it?"

"It was like one something."

"Congrats on your new car, girl!"

"I don't have a new car." Tressa tried to play it off.

"One of my customers, who work at the DMV, was telling us about your car. And how your Coach bag is worth more than the car you drive."

Ouch, that hurt! I really can't wait until I get in a better position where I can just floss on these hoes. As a matter of fact, I am not even giving that hoe Gypsy one more penny of my damn money. She always talking down on me, but she going to get hers too. That bitch!

That was a low blow. That one statement is what sent Tressa off the deep end. Although she wanted to punch Gypsy in the face, her frustration and rage turned towards Lucky. She vowed to herself that this would be one day that Lucky would feel a portion of her pain and frustration.

Tressa stormed out of the salon and held her tears in until she got into her car. She cried hysterically, not even able to catch her breathe. The more the tears rolled down her cheeks, the more determined she felt to do something to Luck.

Once she started the engine on the car, the radio was playing. She was thankful that if nothing else worked, the tape deck did. She pushed the cassette tape in and her theme song came on. She listened to the first verse, but the chorus is what dried the tears from her eyes, *she wasn't gonna let nobody hold her down*. The last verse of the song is what gave her the will to pull deep within herself and clear her mind to think straight.

The song "Juicy", by Biggie Smalls, a.k.a. the Notorious B-I-G, was her instant gratification. This song reminded her that there was hope, the world was not over and her situation was only temporary. It was through this song that she was reminded there were brighter days ahead and that no storm lasts forever. Not only did this song give her inspiration but it pulled her out of her pity party

140

mindset and gave her a clear mind. With a clear mind, she was able to come up with a plan to make her feel better for the moment.

Tressa stopped at a pay phone and called Wiggles to tell her she needed her to come over later to watch the boys. Without hesitation, Wiggles agreed.

When Wiggles arrived, to her surprise, Tressa was dressed like a Ninja, wearing all black. She wore a tight fitting spandex jumpsuit, some black Reebok classics, and carried a small black leather backpack.

"Where are you going?" Wiggles asked.

"To combat."

"Well, you need to call somebody else to watch the boys because I need to be with you then."

"Nah, Wiggles, I've got this under control and I need you to be here with the boys. You know they're not going to stay with anybody else anyway."

"If anybody calls, tell them that I am sleep, but whatever you say, don't say that I'm not here."

"Got it."

"I will call you if I need you."

"OK." Wiggles said, but unsure and scared of what Tressa was up to. "Please promise me you'll be safe."

"I will," Tressa said with a devilish grin on her face.

Tressa took a drive to the West end part of town, a route she hadn't taken in close to a year. She reflected on how the neighborhood, she once loved so much, hadn't changed one bit since she'd left Lucky. She drove two streets over from her old place of residence, but still Lucky's dwelling.

She checked to make sure she had a spare set of keys to the Z28. She pulled them out of her backpack, took her black leather jacket off, placed it in the car and locked the main set of keys in the running car under a big weeping willow tree. With her backpack placed securely on her back, she raced across the street and hopped over one of the houses fences. One more fence would put her in Lucky's backyard. She crept slow and cautiously like a thief in the night as she approached the fence that separated Joan and Lucky's property. She took her backpack off, got her bait out and placed her backpack on. With one hand, she threw herself over the fence, while clutching onto her bait. When she landed on her feet, she saw the two rottweiler dogs headed her way. Once they approached her, although it had been close to a year, they recognized her scent and began to lick her. After all, she was the person who had taken care of them for over two years. She fed them 75% of the time and faithfully took them to all of their veterinarian and grooming visits. When they approached, she threw them a peace of turkey rolled up with two Tylenol PM tablets in it while she continued to pet them.

I hope these daggone Tylenol PM's make them sluggish and go to sleep. Shoot, they put humans to sleep at the drop of a dime. I wish I had had a Valium. The other day Jacko took me to see that new movie called "Congo". I remember they gave the gorilla a valium to put him to sleep. I should have bought some from somebody around my way. That's OK, I am here now. It ain't no turning back.

Before she knew it, within five minutes, the wild hyper attack dogs were getting sluggish. When the first one, Dopeman, dropped down, Tressa's heart started to beat fast.

Dag, I hope I didn't kill him. I am not here to kill the damn dogs.

Tressa quietly crept over to Dopeman, then she looked over at the other dog, Killer. Killer was staggering in slow motion, eyes watery, tongue hanging like he may have been taking his last breathe. She got close to Dopeman, relieved that he was still breathing. When she glanced back over at Killer, she watched as he collapsed. Then Tressa went straight to work. She pulled her barber clippers out of her backpack and began to shave the dogs fur. When the fur got just low enough, Tressa used the clippers to write. "MY OWNER IS A FAGGOT."

Once she was done, she hurried and fled the scene. She didn't want to take any chances on her car not starting up when she got done, that is why she left it running. The whole way home she laughed hysterically, wishing she could be there to see the expression on Lucky's face. She knew Lucky would be furious because he was as homophobic as they come. Plus, rottweilers have a quality, thick coat of fur and the season was still winter outside.

142

This was enough to set any person off, and it was a known fact that it didn't take half as much to piss Lucky off.

This was the first night she slept well in a while knowing she had made Lucky just a little upset. The next morning, she was awakened to the doorbell and banging on her door. She hopped up as she heard Wiggles say. "Who is it?"

Tressa got her small 380 gun out of the shoebox on the top shelf of the closet, and ran to the front room as she asked Wiggles silently, using only body language, who was at the door.

"Meechie." Wiggles responded.

Both were puzzled, trying to figure out what she wanted this early in the morning.

This begging ass chick better not be knocking on my door like she the damn police begging for a daggone thing.

"Oh, my God. Wiggles, I need you to get Tressa quick. It's important!" Meechie screamed from the other side of the door. "She gotta come quick."

"Hold on!" Wiggles screamed back through the door.

Tressa and Wiggles both slipped some sweatpants and shoes on and opened up the door. Meechie was looking like she had just seen a ghost.

"It's horrible and it don't make no sense. I am sorry for waking you up so early, but I had to. I just got up to walk around back to get me a hit, and I, oh my God."

They only walked faster down the steps, and Tressa could not believe her eyes!

Dopeman and Killer were laying on the hood of her car slaughtered. Blood covered the windshield and the side windows of the Z-28. One dude walking by came over to be curious, and he vomited everywhere. Tressa just shook her head in disbelief and Wiggles couldn't understand why someone would put two dead dogs on Tressa's car.

"Don't worry baby." Wiggles said, as she hugged Tressa.

Just then a crack head walked up. "Look, I'll clean all this up for $40.00 and have your car looking like new."

It doesn't make any sense, a crack head will do anything for a dollar to get a hit.

Tressa didn't dare say what she thought out loud, she would never want to hurt Wiggles' feelings. After all, she was a recovering drug addict.

"Nah, I am going to take some pictures first, but I am going to need you to clean it up, but probably not until later tonight. OK?" Tressa told the crack head.

Tressa went back into her apartment to get the camera and cordless phone. She checked on the boys, and couldn't believe, but was relieved, they were still sleeping through all the drama.

As she walked back outside, the phone rang, *who is this calling at 6:26 am?*

She answered, before looking at the caller ID. "Hello."

"Bow-wow, yippee yo, yippee yea. Guess whose dogs ain't in the house?" Lucky jokingly sang to the melody of Snoop Dogg's song.

Tressa knew exactly who it was, but she pretended that she didn't because she was totally caught off of guard. So, again she said. "Hello."

"See how you make me kill?" Lucky asked in a cold, heartless tone.

"What?"

"You really don't understand do you? See, it's nothing for me to kill something that I love so dear."

Tressa was so stunned that Lucky was on the other end of the phone, she could not reply. His words sent chills up her spine. Lucky only continued to torture her through his words.

"As much as I loved the dogs, they were my fucking world, but in a New York minute, those dogs don't mean shit to me! I don't want nothing that you can get next to, because you'll never get next to me again. As a matter of fact, anything that you can get next to don't mean me any good, it's better off dead. Everyday you ride around in that raggedy ass car of yours, always remember, the second best thing to me is laid dead on your windshield."

Before she could respond, Lucky hung up the phone. Wiggles could see the expression on her face as she held the phone.

"Who was that?" As soon as Wiggles asked, Lucky's Lexus slowly drove pass with the passenger window down as he made eye contact with Tressa, a satisfying smile on his face.

After all the excitement calmed down, and Tressa got her head together, she really felt bad that the prank was taken this far. After all, she cared about those dogs, she had lived with and taken care of them for over four years. She felt that it was her fault that the dogs were dead. She wanted to have a funeral for the dogs, but she couldn't afford to, so she paid the crack head to dig a hole in the open field behind the projects and bought two storage totes to put them in.

-15-
Can't Knock The Hustle

Tressa called the insurance company to file a claim. She was thankful that she had just gotten insurance a week before. They agreed to give her a check for $538.00 to get the car cleaned and detailed. Mr. Bill gave her another car to drive until her car was taken care of. He told her it'll take about two weeks for her car to be ready.

After making that phone call, she asked Shelly for a raise. Shelly said. "No." Tressa loved her job, but Tressa decided that she'd play hard ball with the Shelly. *See, this broad don't know who she dealing with. I practically run this place and she can't give me no raise. I got something for her.*

The next day, Tressa called into work sick and she stayed out of work for the rest of the week. Monday afternoon, just as Tressa predicted, Shelly called Tressa at home.

"Tressa, how are you feeling?"

"I am coming along." Tressa said with no emotion at all.

"Well, we have had a crazy week around here, with you being out."

"Yes, I am sure you have."

"So, after our last conversation, and after looking at the big picture, I need you here and decided to give you a $2.00 raise, and I also will be giving you a bonus every

147

quarter." Shelly said in a jolly voice. "We love you over here and value you as a part of our team."

"Oh, OK." Tressa said, still not showing one once of emotion. Shelly was expecting Tressa to be doing cartwheels, but she didn't.

Tressa really liked Mr. Bill. Mr. Bill always came to her rescue. She was able to reach Mr. Bill by phone anytime day or night. He started giving her a minimum $250.00 a week, although he only spent a few hours with her on Thursday nights and every other night they talked on the phone until the wee hours of the morning. Tressa was definitely grateful because that money came in handy and she was able to gather much of Mr. Bill's wisdom.

Whenever Mr. Bill would give a present, money or any thing, whenever she'd tell him thank you, "she'd say thank you." He'd always say didn't I tell you I was going to take care of you?

Tressa listened to Mr. Bill and took in everything he said. So, seeing Mr. Bill on Thursdays, was always beneficial for her. She'd get treated like a queen, top of the line of everything. Mr. Bill always took her to a nice dinner, and afterwards, a romantic evening at his beautiful house. He gave her an expensive present and always licked her clit, which always gave her multiple orgasms, but she never understood why there was never any penetration. She didn't care that Mr. Bill's penis was the size of a pencil. So many times after he had pleased her, she wanted penetration, but he never gave it to her.

Along with no penetration, there was one more thing that Tressa didn't not like about Mr. Bill, he too was a smoker, and it drove her crazy. All the men in her life that had ever hurt her, smoked. Her stepfather smoked Salem's and he hurt her by taking her mother from her. Lucky, he smoked Newport's, and he broke her heart and tried to tear her down in any way he could think of. Now, what kind of pain did Mr. Bill have in store for Tressa? He smoked Marlboro Lights 100's, and oh, did they stink. She stressed to him that she hated them. He tried not to smoke around her, but it was very hard. Like most smokers, after he finished a meal, he had to have a cigarette. She resented the fact that his house smelled like smoke. She tried not to nag him about it after voicing her opinion once. So, she simply overlooked it, because he was so good to her. When she'd arrive home after spending the evening with him, she'd jump straight into the shower to get that cigarette smoke smell off of her, and spray Finisheen on her hair to get the smell out of her do.

Mr. Bill had also fixed the Z-28 up to look like a new car, fresh paint job, new tires and all the quirks were fixed. He found a buyer for the car and sold it for $1,500.00 After all, the car was equipped with a good motor. Mr. Bill gave her the money so she could get a new car.

Her credit by now was a little shaky since she paid most of her bills late. Before Mr. Bill came along and starting helping her out on the financial tip, her bills, two boys, and household necessities, always exceeded the amount of her income. There was no need for a budget, because she had to always rob Peter to pay Paul. She went to a "Buy Here, Pay Here" car lot. They agreed to finance her a Mazda 626. Since she had blemished credit, they enrolled her in a special program, "The On-Time Program". The On-Time Program resembled that of a prepay cell phone, instead it was pretty much a prepaid car.

They installed a programmed device under the steering wheel of the car that looked like a phone jack that had a light on it. Sometimes the light was green, and sometimes it was red. They gave her another device, on one end, there was a numeric keypad, and the other end, a phone cord to hook into the jack under the steering wheel. Every other week, when the payment was due, the red light would come on to remind her that the payment was owed. If she wasn't in by noon that day, the device would start beeping. Once the payment was finally made, the dealer would give her a 4-digit code to punch into the device and the red light would turn to green, until another two weeks, when the payment was due again. If she didn't or couldn't make the payment by close of business that night, then the engine would not start up the next day. She agreed to these terms because she knew she was certain that she'd be making the payments in a timely manner.

Even though Tressa had a rocky start with the neighborhood girls, the girls and Tressa eventually gave each other a mutual respect. Although they never hung out together, if one needed something, Tressa pretty much loaned them whatever they needed. In return, they paid her back and watched her back.

Tressa was no fool when it came to loaning money. She never loaned more than one hundred dollars, and for every dollar, she charged an interest rate of 30%. So, this became her hustle, everybody's got one. She knew she could have done like her brother did in prison. Anything he loans out he gets double back of what was borrowed.

There was this one girl, Britta, from the projects Tressa would see from time to time. Britta was beautiful. She had light skin, long hair and a body to die for! Britta was only eighteen and already mothered two young children. Both of her children stayed with her eighty year-old grandmother most of the time. Britta was a girl that Tressa felt sorry for and she tried to get her on the right track. Britta was young, dumb and full of cum. Britta had all kinds of rudy-poot dudes running in her house and was always broke, begging to borrow money from Tressa.

One day, Britta explained to Tressa that she was about to get evicted because she hadn't paid her $46.00 rent in three months.

"Tressa, I know you don't loan more than $100, but I can't get put out. I'm not going to have no where to go."

Tressa had to ask. "Why do you have all those niggas running up in your house, and it never seems like it's never beneficial to you?"

"They promise me they're going to look out, but they never do. I wish I had a way to get some money other than my $291.00 welfare check, I need a hustle. Do you know of one for me?" She asked Tressa sarcastically.

"Well, I might. Let me think about it. But in the meantime, don't let them niggas run up in your house. Especially if they're leaving you to borrow money for your $46.00 rent!"

"The truth of it is, I like the attention." Britta said.

Tressa never commented on Britta's stupid and naïve statement, but a bright idea popped in her head. "Let me check on something and I'll get back at ya."

Tressa met back up with Britta and loaned her the money. When they met, Pondee saw them talking. Pondee immediately called Tressa over. "What's up with your girlfriend?"

"What you mean?" Tressa asked.

"I'm trying to hit that." Pondee said.

"Well, go over there and talk to her then.   I'll introduce you." Tressa said.

"Look, I ain't got no whole bunch of time to be lollygagging, taking a chick out to dinner and playing the dating game. Straight up, a nigga trying to fuck." He went in his pocket and pulled out $150.00 and handed it to her. "Give this to her, and if she bites, I got you. Since you my peeps, I'm going to give you some money for the hook up." Pondee said.

"Shoot, you better give that girl more than some damn $150.00 then." Tressa said.

"Look, by the time I take her to the movies, dinner a couple of times, and give her money to get her hair done, that's what it would have took to get her to give me some. So, I am just trying to cut through the chase. Now make that happen."

"I'll see" Tressa said smiling.

Tressa set it up for Pondee to screw Britta, and he gladly accepted her fee. A few days later, Pondee approached Tressa asking her to also set up strip parties for him and his homeboys. She would never have to come off of anything, except make the arrangements to get the girls together. He expressed to her that she could make good money, and Lord knows, she needed all the extra income she could get. But after thinking everything over, she decided she wouldn't pimp any more females, instead she'd just keep on loan sharking.

The lone sharking alone, combined with Mr. Bill's money and her legit job salary, enabled her to get ahead a little. She was able to bank some money, but still not enough to move herself out of the projects.

-16-
M.M. Ordeal

Everything was going fine between Mr. Bill and Tressa. Tressa wasn't in love with Mr. Bill, but very content with their friendship, until one day when he was dropping her off. Mr. Bill had just taken Tressa to the mall to buy the boy's Easter outfits, and "Nosey Rosey" was sitting on the bench as she watched, with green-eyed envy, while Tressa got out of Mr. Bill's car struggling with all the shopping bags.

How in the hell this girl get this old man to peel off paper like that for her? Shoot, she makes me sick. She think she better than everybody else cuz she got a job, and now, she got that old man looking out for her. I can't stand her! I remember I used to go up to that man's shop, trying to get him to notice me, but he never would. Now, tell me what she got that I don't have? It's all good, cause I'm about to burst this bitch's bubble, while she thinking she all that, Rosey thought to herself.

Tressa made eye contact with Rosey, who was plastered in her usual spot, on the bench. "Hey Rosey."

"Hey Tressa."

Tressa walked past Rosey, tussling with all her bags, when Rosey called out to her. "Tressa."

Tressa stopped, but turned to make eye contact with Rosey.

"Look, Tressa, I can't believe you been dealing with that married man as long as you have."

"What?"

"Yes, Bill is married to a girl name Angel. She's young and they have been together for a while now, since she was about sixteen years old."

"Oh, for real. Thank you girl for putting me down with that info, I really appreciate it."

"Yup, I am only telling you for your own good." Rosey was attempting to seem concerned, but she knew she was only telling Tressa to steal her joy. Rosey hoped that Tressa would stop messing with Bill, because married or not, Bill took care of Tressa and her boys, and that was something Rosey didn't have.

Tressa started feeling sick and dizzy. She felt a cold sweat come over her body. However, she managed to hold herself together while she was there in front of Rosey. The walk up the three flights of stairs was the longest walk up those stairs in a while.

All kinds of things started running through Tressa's mind. *If this were TRUE, where was his wife? When did he possibly spend time with her? What does she have to say about him not coming home on a regular basis? Maybe she worked at night. Maybe they are separated. Maybe she lived in another city. Maybe she was away at college or tending to a sick family member. Where was his wedding band? There wasn't even a tan line on his left ring finger to indicate that he'd ever worn a wedding band.* All these were possibilities, but she had could not understand how he could be married. There were not any signs. *Maybe Rosey was lying or exaggerating,* she thought. No, Rosey never gets the negative reports wrong.

Tressa had expressed to Mr. Bill, how Lucky had hurt her feelings with the all the lying and cheating, and now him too. She held her composure until she got into her apartment.

This situation needed her immediate attention. She called him. Tressa informed him that she needed to speak to him. He could sense in her voice that something was definitely wrong. *Had she found out what he had concealed from her?* He insisted that she tell him what was wrong, because he'd surely fix it. Whichever secret she knew about, he'd have to come clean and explain. How would she ever accept his betrayal?

Tressa wanted to ask him face to face. She always felt that it was indeed better to approach a person who she was unsure about face to face. Their body language would usually speak for itself, and she couldn't read body language over the telephone. Tressa drew the conclusion, a while ago, if there was chin stroking, lip pressing, earlobe pulling, nose touching or rubbing slowly, covering the mouth while talking, the person is lying. She was certain when there is an increase in hand to face motions, that was a sure sign of deceit or trickery of some kind. Other parts of their bodies project the truth as well, their legs and feet. As bad as Tressa was trying to hold it in and wait to ask him face to face, she couldn't, she had to know.

Tressa bluntly asked him. "Are you married?"

"Where you get that from?" He asked. Because he didn't deny it right away, at that instance, Tressa was convinced it was true.

He began to ask Tressa. "Does it seem as though I'm married? How could I be married, if I'm either working or on the phone with you day in and day out?" Everything was starting to look like a blur. Tressa never responded to him, she simply hung up the phone.

The rest of the day, Tressa did not accept any calls from Bill. It wasn't the fact that she was heart broken or anything of that matter, it was just the principal that he put her in a very dangerous situation. He called her repeatedly. He left her all kinds of messages about how he needed to talk to her on her answering machine. He expressed how important it was for her to call him back. After two days of totally ignoring him, he showed up unannounced on her doorstep. She didn't answer the door. She was so hurt and confused. She was disgusted with him, simply because they had put so much emphasis on honesty in their friendship, and he was the one living a lie.

Tressa was leaving out for work, Bill was staked outside of her apartment in the parking lot. He approached Tressa. He expressed that he desperately needed to talk to her. She listened to him, hoping just maybe, this was all a big misunderstanding. He denied being married. His body language declared his guilt. She could tell he was lying.

155

Lucky had played Tressa time and time again, but make no mistake about it, Tressa was very clever. She told Bill that they were never going to get anywhere with him lying to her. She told him she knew for a fact he was married, because she had seen his wedding pictures. His mouth dropped to the floor. Of course, she hadn't seen anything. She also told him that he should've been totally up front and honest with her from the beginning. She should've had the prerogative to decide if she wanted to be involved in a triangle or not.

Bill used the same excuses that EVERY single married man who cheats uses. How he's not happy at home, how his wife doesn't cook or clean anymore. He proceeded to give her this lame story about how not a day went by that he wanted to tell her, but he knew the type of woman she was. He knew that she wasn't going to accept the situation. He didn't want to risk losing her, so he kept his secret from her.

All kinds of things started running through Tressa's head. The biggest issue was, he was somebody's HUSBAND! REGARDLESS OF WHAT HE'S SAYING, HE'S STILL SOMEBODY'S HUSBAND!!!!! That was kind of a hard pill for Tressa to swallow. The next fact was, this man had been parading her around town, not only hugged up, but she was driving one of his cars for a few months when the dogs were slaughtered. He was not concerned as to who may have seen them. His wife's cousin, sister, girlfriend or the wife herself could've seen them! What if the wife would've seen them together, and Lord forbid, killed Tressa for being with her husband. Tressa would be dead and her family wouldn't have a clue as to why.

Tressa discovered that it was many issues that came along with the M.M. (married man) ordeal. At that point, as much as she wanted to continue the relationship, she knew she couldn't. She felt they'd developed such a connection, that she considered being undercover with him. Maybe just a little more discreet. She knew she deserved more than a being a down-low lover. She owed it to herself. Although, she was fully aware of the fact that there was a black male shortage of good men in Richmond.

Tressa contemplated, *what kind of future could I possibly have with this man? In the long run, I'd only be left with a broken heart. How would I ever be able to trust this double-crossing, two-timing man anyway? If he double-crossed the one he said, "I DO" to, just imagine what he'd do to me.*

She remembered he said that he didn't love his wife. She may have believed him, if she was his girlfriend, but she was his wife!! That was a fact. Tressa continued her thoughts, and reflected on something that Foxy Brown once said, something to the effect of:

Anybody can be in a relationship for eight or nine years. Anybody can go through struggles with you, anybody can have sex with you. It doesn't take a lot to luck up and have a baby or two with you, BUT a man's GOT to love you if he makes you his wife!!!!!!!!!!

After taking all these things into consideration, she simply said to herself. "Tressa, A GIRL'S GOTTA DO WHAT A GIRL'S GOTTA DO!!!" And she ended the relationship with Bill just like that.

Bill continued to pursue Tressa. Tressa made it clear that it was over between them. Tressa discontinued any contact with him.

-17-
Everything that Glitters Ain't Gold

She wanted to get the film developed quickly from the boys birthday party, because she was anxious to see the pictures. When she approached the one-hour photo stand, there was no one there. She went to the very front of the long line, and nicely asked the cashier. "Excuse me miss, is there anyone working the one-hour photo booth?"

People looked very agitated, because there was only one cashier working. The fact that Tressa had walked to the front of the line, practically jumping in front of everybody else, pissed the people off. She overheard the gestures people made, but Tressa blocked them out. She simply said to herself, *shoot, I need help in one-hour photo, and I'm not going to stand in this line just to get to the front, and ask for help in one-hour photo. That's crazy!*

The frustrated cashier said. "I'll call someone." And she did. Two girls wearing CVS vests walked up at the same time. One was very petite and timid looking. The other was obese and very sloppy. The petite lady gathered Tressa's film, and asked for her last name. Tressa told her. "Shawsdale."

"Ms. Shawsdale, your photos will be ready in one hour, would you fill out an envelope for each roll of film, please?"

"Sure." Tressa answered, and started filling out the envelopes.

The obese girl walked up to Tressa, and said. "Ain't your name Tressa?" Tressa said. "Yeah," And never looked up.

The girl stood there looking at Tressa from head to toe, with her nose turned up, rolling her eyes with a negative emotion written all over her face. Tressa continued to fill out her photo envelopes, never acknowledging the girl at all.

"Don't you want to know who I am or where exactly you know me from?" The girl said to Tressa in a stank tone.

Tressa could sense the tension in the air, although she'd never seen this girl before. Tressa responded. "Yeah, since you insist.   I'm sure you were going to tell me anyway."

"YOU ARE FUCKING MY HUSBAND!!!!" The girl screamed and turned and walked off down the aisle.

The statement shocked Tressa, as well as every one else, in the long line, waiting to be checked out.   They all turned and looked at Tressa in shame.   There were two little elderly ladies, both wearing wigs and hats that women usually wear to church, standing behind Tressa waiting to be served at the one-hour photo booth.   Tressa shouted to the stout girl. "Excuse Me?"

One of the two old ladies said. "You home wrecker!" And the other added. "Acting all stuck-up!"

The plump girl said.   "Did I stutter?   I said you fucking MY husband!" As she rolled her neck around, she said. "Don't try to deny it, because I know all about you."

Tressa was embarrassed, to say the least.   She took a deep breath and proceeded down the aisle after the obese girl.

The girl was in the shampoo aisle straightening and pulling forward the hair products. "What are you coming down here for?   Cause I damn sure don't have nothing to say to you." The girl said, rolling her eyes while continuing to work.

"Look, I really don't have the foggiest idea what you are talking about?"

"Yeah, right." The girl said.

Tressa thought to herself, *what is she talking about, whose wife is this? I know for a fact we couldn't have a man in common. She's got to have me confused with someone else.* Tressa spoke in a sure tone, while shaking her head. "Look ma'am, I apologize that your man is a cheating bastard. I truly sympathize with you, because I had one of those myself that I was glad I got rid of. Face it, he's a loser and what do you do with losers?   YOU LOSE THEM!!" Tressa said, trying to comfort her. The girl only looked at her. Tressa said. "There's been a big misunderstanding, because I don't know your husband."

"Yes you do." Responded the girl in a frustrated tone.

"Ma'am what is your husband's name?" Just out of curiosity, Tressa wanted to know, so she could straighten this out.

She screamed at the top of her lungs to Tressa. "Bill, as if you don't know!"

You could've bought Tressa for a penny at that very moment.   She stood there in astonishment.   She was shocked that this was indeed Bill's wife. *How could this be?* The way she looked! She was out of shape and had truly let herself go.   She was not well groomed at all.   Tressa took into consideration that she was at work.   She wasn't expecting her to be Versace down while working in a drug store, but there were certain things that a person maintained anyway.   Especially with a man as neat and clean cut as Bill was.   Tressa expected that his wife would be model material, very pretty, slim, with a flat stomach and a figure to die for.   Even if Bill's wife would've been overweight, Tressa guessed she'd be very pretty and neat as a pin.   Tressa was fully aware that it's not the flesh of a person that matters, but what's inside.   Maybe she did have a wonderful personality, but it was certain things that made Tressa say, hum.

Wifey was really tacky!   Her cornrows looked as though they should've been removed two months ago.   She wore glasses that were broken.   And taped together with masking tape.   She had a Gap T-shirt on that was two sizes too small.   Not only could she see the mustard stain on it, her belly was hanging out, because the shirt didn't cover her stomach completely.   Her teeth needed dental work extremely bad, she spoke with a lisp, and her breath reeked.

Tressa felt sorry for her. She developed a little compassion for Bill's wife. She explained to wifey, in a very subtle tone. "You know from day one, I never knew Bill was married. There were no indications that he was married. The very instant that I found out, I approached him with the information that I'd received. He denied it. After playing a psychological game with him, he finally admitted it and still wanted to pursue the relationship. At that very moment, *I* broke off the relationship. I haven't had any contact with Bill since. That was over a year ago!"

The wifey felt stupid. She was upset at the fact that Tressa was pretty, that she held her head up when she walked. Tressa was everything she wasn't. The whole idea of the way Tressa actually pretended she felt empathy for her, pissed her off even more.

Wifey never looked Tressa directly in her face. She was speechless for a minute. Her voice was very abrupt. "Well, it don't matter, because Bill gives me everything. The only thing he could offer you is a wet ass!"

Tressa said to herself, *look you broke down winch, I was trying to be respectful, because after all, you are his wife and I know you must be hurt, but at the same time, don't try to hit me with the low blow!!*

"What makes you come to that conclusion?" Tressa asked while laughing as if it was a joke.

Wifey responded. "Oh, I get it all, he pays me off like a slot machine."

Tressa looked at the wife up and down while saying. "Oh really? I can't tell!"

"Well, you wasn't nothing but his little project chick anyway!"

Oh, those were fighting words. Tressa was about to kick off her shoes and punch those old braids out of wifey's head.

"Well, honestly speaking, you should have been his project. And Lord knows he had his work cut out for him. He should have had the mission to fix your broke down ass up. Boo, it looks like to me that you are the project chick aiming to be somebody's project. You know when you get

162

ready for your makeover, the girls over at the Professional Hair Studio does wonders."

"Well, you know what, since you feel you are the better woman, you can have him." Said the wife.

"No thanks." Said Tressa. "I'll leave him to you."

Tressa was about to turn to walk away, when the wife said. "You can have him because he's a dog anyway."

"Nah, sweetie. I don't have any room in my life for K-9's." Tressa said.

"Well, just so you know, I don't want Bill!" The wife said in a hostile voice.

Tressa laughed right in her face as she asked. "Then why did you cause a scene in front of all these people? I know love hurts and you're in denial. I can only pray that you get the strength from your inner self to move on past this whole ordeal."

The wife said in a harsh tone. "Whatever bitch."

Tressa simply looked in wifey's face and took in a mouthful of air. The wife was sure Tressa was about to smack her.

"Maybe you should consider watching Lifetime, I am sure one of those movies may be therapy." She turned and sashayed away. She thought to herself, *I handled that so well.*

Tressa thought about all the times she secretly envied Bill's wife and it was one thought that came to her head. "Everything that glitters ain't gold."

-18-
The Head Banger

Taking in all the drama that Tressa had gone through with Lucky and Mr. Bill, Jacko decided to step up to the plate. He started wining and dining Tressa whenever she had free time, and Wiggles or Betty had the boys. They went on friendly outings, but Tressa knew Jacko really liked her.

He called Tressa and said. "Look, I know your baby father been giving you a whole bunch of drama, and I know you are under a lot of unnecessary stress. So, look, I want to take you away this weekend to Atlantic City."

Tressa agreed. She needed a break. Lucky's estranged mother, Betty started coming around to spend time with the boys. At first, Tressa was unsure if she should let the children go with Betty, because she knew the games Lucky played. Also, she had second thoughts about Betty being able to keep her children, because she was fully aware of the way Betty locked Lucky in the closet when he was little. Betty understood and assured her that the children were safe with her. She expressed to Tressa that she had made big mistakes when it came to Lucky and she wanted to make up for them through her grandsons. Tressa felt her boys were old enough to tell her if anybody did anything to them. God forbid if they ever came back and told Tressa that Betty did something to them, she'd beat the brakes off Betty. After the boys spent, an hour here and a day there, gradually Tressa started letting Betty get the boys on every other weekend. After all, they were her grandchildren and the boys deserved to have a relationship with their grandmother. Betty mentioned to Tressa that Lucky had fathered other children too, but she didn't acknowledge any of the children but the twins. *Isn't that something, how a guy's mother is always trying to say whose child is their sons. Like they were actually there when the humping, bumping and grinding was going on,* Tressa thought to herself, while Ms. Betty went on and on. Finally, she reminded Tressa that this was the weekend that she got the boys. So, Tressa was clear to go to Atlantic City.

Tressa was actually looking forward to going to Atlantic City for the weekend with Jacko. She hadn't had any sex, penetration anyway, in almost a year, so she couldn't wait. She thought about how much of a good friend Jacko had been to her and how fine he was!

Jacko surprised her and purchased a nice Coach duffle bag to put her clothes in, and tried his very best to accommodate her in every way on the ride up to Atlantic City. When Lucky and Tressa had gone on road trips, as soon as Tressa seen they were on the highway, she was out like a light. However this road trip was different, she stayed up and kept Jacko company while he drove. When they stopped at the Maryland House to get gas, she ran in to use the restroom. When she returned, he gave her a Mountain Dew soda, and pulled off from the gas pump to near where the air pumps were located.

He got out the car and stood near the back of the car. After two minutes, she was curious, hoping that it wasn't any car trouble. As she was about to get out to check on him, he opened the door and got back in.

"Everything OK?" She asked.

"Yes, it is."

"Oh, what was wrong?"

"I had to smoke. I know how much you hate the smell of Black and Milds and any other smoke so, I just smoked outside."

How sweet and considerate. Most dudes would be like, it's my car and I'll do whatever I want to do, she's just got to accept it. Jacko had been my friend throughout everything and never ran away from me because of the drama in my life. He has his own legit business, although sometimes, I wonder if he did a little hustling. He drives a nice car, spends a lot of money, and flosses like a hustler. But, all in all, he's a perfect gentleman.

Once they arrived to Atlantic City, they checked into Caesar's Palace where Jacko had reservations. Tressa took a shower and changed clothes. They had dinner at a classy five star restaurant located in the hotel.

Their first stop was the casino. Jacko gave Tressa five hundred dollars to gamble with. She wasn't really a gambler, but she played the games for fun. A waitress walked up and asked her what was she drinking?

"Strawberry daiquiri." She responded.

Jacko jumped in. "Look, we came to have fun, so loosen up a bit." Jacko said to the waitress. "Give us a Grey Goose and cranberry juice."

Tressa didn't realize Grey Goose was vodka, but she tried it anyway. The drink wasn't strong. It wasn't until later, she realized that the cranberry juice is what camouflages the Vodka. After two and a half of those, intoxication snuck up on her. Jacko could see Tressa was getting very tipsy, and being the gentleman he was, he knew the night had to be cut short. He had to get her back to the hotel room, she was in no shape to be out.

On the way back to the hotel, as the man pushed them in the cart with wheels on the boardwalk, Jacko asked him to pull over. He ran over to a flower stand and bought Tressa a bouquet of white lily's. The gesture was nice, but Tressa was so tipsy, she couldn't give Jacko the reaction that she wanted to. All Tressa remembered, was getting on the elevator to go to the room, and when she awoke the next morning, she was comfortably nestled and tucked in under the covers, wearing her bra, panties and Jacko's T-shirt.

She slowly sat up in the bed, and to her surprise, she didn't have a massive headache that drinking any liquor usually would give her. But she did have the smell of liquor all over her body, and that had to come off. Once Jacko felt the bed moving, he asked. "How did you sleep?"

"Good. Thanks for tucking me in."

"No problem." Jacko planted a kiss on her cheek.

"Give me twenty minutes, I'm going to take a shower." She hopped out of the bed, headed over to the bathroom as she pulled a wedgie out of her big voluminous butt.

Once she hit the bathroom, she saw the oversized sunken tub, and decided to take a bath instead. She poured bubbles in the tub, lit votive candles that the hotel provided, and climbed in. Jacko came in to join her. He started fondling her breast and round, juicy butt, and boy was it feeling good! Between the jets, the water and the bubbles, they all combined to make sexing in the Jacuzzi very awkward. So, she told him that she was going to stand up and wash all the soap and bubbles off of her. He grabbed an oversized towel, left the bathroom and laid on the bed to get his manhood right and erect to give her the treat she had been waiting for. He did this by repeatedly stroking himself and thinking of Tressa bent over with her ass in the air.

Once she was done thoroughly washing her body, she wrapped herself in an oversized towel and headed to the bedroom. Slowly and seductively, she walked over to the bed. She reached to grab the Victoria Secret Pear lotion, and the towel dropped to her feet. Jacko's tongue fell out of his mouth, lusting and wanting all of her. His heart was racing, mouth watering, and body yearning for her, and his penis stood up rock hard. All he could say was. "Come here let me put that lotion on you."

She handed him the lotion, but she had plans to give Jacko a sexually pleasing treat that she had mastered with the lotion. She knew for a fact it would have Jacko climbing the walls, begging her to stop!

Jacko squirted the lotion in his hand and began to rub it all over her. First he started at her beautiful smooth feet. As he raised her feet to get in between her toes, he placed his tongue in between each of her toes. He continued to methodically massage the rest of her body until he got to her inner thighs, which was about to boil over anyway.

The air conditioner in the room was on full blast, but the temperature in the atmosphere was as hot as a desert day. He rubbed her clitoris for a while. He began to wonder why it was taking her so long to climax. As soon as his fingers started getting tired, she started trembling, moaning and groaning for the next sixty seconds and all of a sudden it was over. Although she would never turn down oral sex, this orgasm wasn't any different from ones Mr. Bill gave her. She still desired, longed and craved to feel a rock hard dick inside of her.

She bit the bullet and rolled over, poured some lotion in her hand and grabbed Jacko's erect big, hard cock. She moved her hand up and down over the whole shaft the first couple of strokes. Boy, did Tressa know how to give a hand job. Shoot, she beat his penis better than he could do it himself. Then she focused more on the tip of the head, moving back and forth, around and around. She gripped it, but still managed to be as gentle as a summer breeze. His eyes rolled in the back of his head as he drooled out of his mouth. It was something she did with her hands, that made him feel unlike any woman had ever made him feel. He wanted to look down to see if it was a toy or some type of device she had that was driving him crazy, but he couldn't get the strength to sit up and see. It didn't take long for him to get his climax, and when he did, he squirted all over the place. Although he had just been in ecstasy, he needed more.

Damn, if she can work her hands like that, I wonder how she works the middle? Was all he could wonder after that breathtaking, have a brother weak in the knees, show stopping performance with her hands.

He looked down at his soft cock and tried to stroke it to get it hard again so he can finish off what he brought her to Atlantic City to do. His fondling was clearly not working quick enough, so he abruptly blurted out in a rough tone, "Suck my damn dick to get that shit hard."

"What?"

"You heard me. Suck my dick to get it up."

"What, nigga?" The whole atmosphere got as cold as the 63 degree room. So much for the desert.

Wait, first off, this is the first time this dude has ever touched me, and off the bat, he's going to ask me to give him some head. How he even know I do that? Maybe I never have. Thirdly, he isn't any man of mine, so what makes him think that he can show up and get some head? That's royal treatment that is reserved for a special man. If he was my

169

man he could demand head all day long and I wouldn't have no problem giving it to him, because that is my obligation to satisfy "my" man. How he know I'm even comfortable enough with him? He must be out of his mind. He didn't even try to go down on me and please me so I would feel compelled to give him the same pleasure.

He definitely caught her off guard, not necessarily by what he said, but how he said it. In an attempt to compromise, Tressa was about to suggest to him that they 69, he does her and she does him. But, before she could, Jacko hoped up off the bed and told her. "Get dressed. Pack ya shit because I am ready to go."

"What?"

"I said, get yourself together. I am ready to go!"

All this simply because I am not going to give him any head? Damn is it that serious? I guess he's used to any and everybody putting their mouth on him. But I am not the one. He's in the wrong place, maybe he should have stepped it up a notch and went to Vegas instead of Atlantic City, where he could have paid a prostitute to give him some head. It would be perfectly legal. Shit, I would have paid one if I knew he was going to carry on like that about a daggone blowjob. The hell with this dude.

The whole way back to Richmond, Jacko didn't say anything to Tressa and Tressa didn't say a word to him. With no conversation going on between the two, Tressa had a lot of time to try to analyze the whole concept of the "head banger".

Funny how when it comes to oral sex, everybody wants to be on the receiving end and never on the giving end. Very rarely will you ever come across people who genuinely want to give head in general. Not just the head banger episode, but in life in general. Nobody wants to drive, but everybody wants to ride. Everybody wants to receive a present, but nobody wants to give a gift. Even me Mr. Bill ate me out on a regular basis and did it well. Not one time did I ever take the initiative to go down on him. It was always kosher for me to receive, but now I am put in a position to give, I throw a fit. But shoot this dude, Jacko, wasn't even worth a drop to my knees having a brotha eyes rolling in the back of his head.

She laughed a little to herself, but her thoughts continued, *stupid ass nigga, shoot, he ain't no real playa, cuz all he had to do was play on me.* *He should have just gave me some head, and put his head game down so well and have me feeling so good, that I would have no choice but to reciprocate the feeling back and wanted to suck the skin off it.* *But no, he gonna get an attitude with me.* *But do I give a damn, shit I got a free trip, and won me some damn money and got a nice Coach duffle bag.* *Shoot, I am coming back with more than I had.*

After crossing the Delaware Memorial Bridge, Jacko pulled over to the side of the median strip and said one word to her. "Drive."

Jacko then got into the passenger seat, put the seat back and tried to act as if he was going to sleep. Trust and believe, Tressa had another plan in store for him, he wasn't going to sleep on this ride if she could help it. She knew he only made her drive out of spite because he knew Tressa hated to drive long distances. She knew he wanted her to argue, but she didn't. Instead, she just listened to the music, hit every pothole and bend she could and tried to drive the wheels off his car

171

-19-
Smiling all up in the face...waiting to slip in the place

AKA
The Backstabbers

Tressa exited the car, walked to the back of the car and reached into the trunk of Jacko's 300 ZX to grab her duffle bag. She slammed the trunk down so hard, hoping it would break a window. As soon as the trunk closed, Jacko sped off not even making sure Tressa had made it into the house. Rosey looked on as she noticed two things, the tension between the two of them and the soft leather Coach duffle bag set that Tressa was carrying. It was clear that Tressa possessed the real Coach and not the bootlegged stuff that flooded so many shoulders and hands of women. Rosey looked at Tressa from head to toe, and the sight of Tressa just made her sick to her stomach. Tressa may have lived in the ghetto, but it was obvious that Tressa wasn't ghetto. Tressa scrambled and struggled to pay her bills just like everyone else. The only difference between Tressa and the hood-rats was, Tressa never shared her business regarding when, what or how she paid her bills. So, for someone in the "p.j.'s" on the outside looking in, it may have appeared Tressa had it going on. Especially when she looked at Tressa's flat stomach in the tight fitting dress that hugged every curve.

This broad had two babies, twins at that, and her stomach is flat as a damn pancake. BITCH!

Tressa was wearing a super cute, red sundress that stopped a little above her knees. The dress crisscrossed in the back with two splits on the side. The python print red and black strap sandals dressed the ensemble up. She had some fresh micro mini-braids in her hair, and had it pinned up in a sophisticated style, with a couple of braids hanging down on the side coming over her left eye. She wore some medium-sized gold hoop earrings.

That bitch thinks she's all that, with her little outfit, Rosey thought to herself.

Rosey examined Tressa's outfit to try to find a flaw, but there wasn't one.

Rosey never would have imagined that the dress was purchased in the white area of town at the seven-dollar store and the dress was on clearance for five dollars! The shoes were on sale for thirty dollars. How pathetic that Rosey was jealous over a $37.00 outfit!

Rosey's envy continued. *Then she got the nerve to have some name brand luggage. Why she toting that four hundred dollar bag? Why don't she move up out of here then, if she's so damn big time! I'm so mad she got that bag, I wish I had it. I ain't worried about her because she didn't buy it. That nigga bought it for her, I am sure. I betcha she probably sucked his dick to get that. Or maybe she did him and his friend. Damn, I wish I knew something about him, because I daggone sure would throw it right up in her face. That's all right, because I got some dirt for her that would make her bite the damn dust. She might have had a good little time on her so-called vacation or whatever she wanna call it, but guess what? The bitch is going to feel like the only getaway she wanna go on, is one to the mental institution.*

"Hey Tressa." Rosey's jealous hearted self said.

"Hey Rosey, how are you?"

"Girl, I came up to your house last night looking for you, because I had something to share with you."

"Oh, is that right." Tressa hesitantly said to Rosey.

"Gurl, Gurl, Gurl, I hate to seem like I'm always gossiping and shit, but gurrrrllll, I had to know how you felt about your baby daddy fucking your best friend!"

"What are you talking about?" A stunned Tressa asked.

"That girl you be with Dutchess, and Lucky, that's right, they been messing with each other for a minute. You didn't know that?"

"Nope, I didn't know." Tressa barely said, after the wind was knocked out of her, by the news of this latest betrayal.

"I figured you didn't. Well, now you do."

Tressa walked away stunned, astonished, surprised, dumbfounded, and most of all, hurt. At this point, she would expect something so low and grimy from Lucky. Now, Dutchess was a different story, her and Dutchess went way back. Dutchess was her road dog, her comrade, her friend, and partner in crime. Dutchess called and talked to Tressa everyday, and constantly reminded Tressa how she loved her as a sister, and truly wanted the best for her. For one second, she thought that Rosey was lying, but then she thought again. She knew in her heart that Rosey was telling the truth. Dutchess had never given Tressa any type of indication that there was something going on between the two of them, so she had no reason to suspect them. She realized that this type of accusation was something heavy to place on somebody, and especially a so-called best friend. But there are some things in your heart that you just know, and for Tressa this was a hard pill to swallow.

Tressa never called either of them to discuss the matter. As far as Lucky was concerned, she could give a damn. But Dutchess on the other hand, oh, that was a different story.

The first person she called to try to express her crushed feelings to was Wiggles. Wiggles had truly lived up to her promise to Tressa to be there for her. Wiggles was Tressa's backbone now, at times, Tressa wondered what she'd do without Wiggles. Wiggles' first reaction was. "Boo-Boo told me something like that too, but I didn't pay him any mind."

"Well, it's true." She started talking fast, pouring out her heart and pent up tears.

"I never liked that hoe anyway. I told you she wasn't shit when she didn't help you fight back in the 7th grade when that girl Michelle Booger was looking for you."

"Yeah, you did."

"I'm going to smack the cowboy shit out of that broad when I see her. Just for the principle of the matter."

Tressa changed the subject, because she knew how Wiggles could get carried away when it came to somebody trying to bring harm to her and her kids.

"So you picked up the boys, huh?" Tressa asked, redirecting the conversation to something she knew would calm Wiggles down.

"I picked up the boys this evening from Ms. Betty's house. She called and needed them to be picked up early because she said she had to go to Bingo."

"See, she said she didn't need me to pick them up until Monday afternoon. She'd drop them off at daycare and I could just pick them up. She makes me sick, always reneging." Tressa said, getting a little frustrated.

"It's no big deal. You know I love those babies as if they were my own. I picked them up and took them to the mall to get some ice cream. Gurl, I had to have a long talk with them, especially that Hadji."

"What? Hadji? You mean Ali?" Tressa asked, trying to correct Wiggles because she knew Ali was usually the bad one.

"No, I mean Hadji." Wiggles assured her.

"What did he do?"

"Girl, he showed out for Lucky, both of them really, but Hadji more. After I handled it, I brought them home, gave them a bath and now they are fast to sleep."

"Thanks Wiggles. It's always nice to have a big sister."

"But while we were at the mall, we ran into Lucky. Girl, I swear I felt like just killing that nigga!"

"Gurl, don't I know it." Tressa said.

"If I thought I could get away with it, I will kill him. Not because he's so damn disrespectful to me, but because he lives to make your life a living hell."

"Gurl, later for Lucky. Don't worry he'll get his."

"I know, but if I ever catch him slipping, he's a done deal. Believe that."

"Gurl, what did he say at the mall." Tressa said, growing inpatient.

"Well, first off, he has this thing that he has established with the boys. When they first see each other, they put their fingers up like guns, aim them and act like they are shooting each other. Then whoever shoots first, the other one falls on the floor like he is dead."

"What? Oh, HELL NO!"

"Then when I corrected the boys, he had the nerve to say to me. 'What the fuck you doing with my damn kids, you junkie bitch. How about I give you fifteen dollars to suck my dick? Or, what about a rock?'"

"Gurl, stop playing?"

"Nope, I am not. I didn't even respond to him because the boys were with me. But girl, he was dead serious."

Tressa couldn't stand to hear anymore. Her blood was boiling, she had heard just about enough about Lucky for one day.

"Wiggles, I gotta go. I'll call you back."

Tressa couldn't even think of Lucky's number, she was so mad that she dialed the wrong number while pacing the floor back in forth. When she finally reached him, she let him have it.

"Yo." Lucky said as he answered the phone.

"Why in the hell you got my sons playing Shoot'em up Cowboy and the Lone fucking Ranger?"

"Because when they grow up, they're going to be gangsters, they need to practice." He said arrogantly.

"You know what Lucky? I asked you to leave us alone and you can't. Why? Tell me why? You keep trying to attack me every way you know how. Why?"

"Cuz, I hate your dumb ass and I plan to hurt you in every way I can."

"You know what Lucky, one day you're going to get yourself boxed in and you're going to need me."

"Need you? Need ya ass for what? You a broke ass bitch! What can you possibly do for me? Please tell me?"

"You are going to crumble, watch what I tell you. You are going to wither like dry grass. You think you up

177

now, but watch, you are going to come tumbling down like the walls of Jericho. And when you lying on your back, you're going to need me. Mark my words!" She screamed into the Uniden brand cordless phone. "And, I won't need your ass, that's for sure. Believe me, I got enough people in my corner who'll die to be there to watch you fall."

"The only way I am going to crumble is if you go to the police about that double murder you made me do."

"What, nigga? Oh, the one thing you don't have to worry about is me going to the police. I don't have to. I'll let you do that, you'll bring them to you. And when they come for you, I hope you don't think Dutchess' going to be there for you either." She slid the fact she knew about Dutchess in there, just to get his reaction.

"So, what you know 'bout Dutchess? I don't give a damn! She has been around just as long as you have. How you think I knew where you lived? How you think I've always been one step ahead of ya dumb, stupid ass? Because of ya girl Dutchess. It was a close call when you set the apartment on fire." He laughed. "Now, that was some funny shit. You were so close and still didn't catch on. I've fucked all your friends and it ain't going to be, but a matter of minutes, before I get to Missy and Wiggles, one way or another. Believe that."

Tressa was left speechless by the words that came out of Lucky's mouth. She couldn't believe what he said about Dutchess being the girl that was in the apartment when she set fire to it years ago!

At that, Tressa slammed the phone down.

Tressa cried for a minute, out of hurt and pain that her friend would do something like this to her.

Now it's all coming together. When it first went down years ago, Lucky said the girl's name was Dee. He threw me off when he said she was from out of town. But I didn't even think nothing of it when I saw Dutchess and she had a bandage over a burn. I would have never thought, in my wildest dreams, that she would dare do something like this to me. It's one thing for a female to mess with my man behind my back, but to act as my friend. To have the gall, the audacity, the fucking nerve to call me everyday and portray herself as my friend, and the whole time, she's laughing behind my back. Oh, hell no! I might seem like a fool, because so many times I have turned the other cheek and never went off on nobody. But a pipe can't take but so much steam before it bursts.

Tressa grabbed her car keys and went over to Dutchess house. She began banging on the door like she was the police coming to raid the house.

"Open up the damn door! You made your bed now lie in it!" Tressa continued to bang on the door and screamed at the top of her lungs. "I know ya punk ass ain't going to answer the door, same as you'd rather jump out the window and get burnt up than face me."

It never dawned on Tressa that Lucky had already called Dutchess to warn her that the cat was out of the bag. Tressa kicked the door and the door didn't budge. Dutchess still never answered. For some reason, the neighbors never came outside to look. Maybe it was because Dutchess always has something going on at her house, so they were used to these types of behavior.

Tressa was still in a fury. On her way home, she passed a paint shop and a bright idea popped into her head. She purchased some cans of spray paint and went back over to Dutchess' house with a stepladder. Tressa waited until every light on the block was off and spray painted in black paint, "Bitch, Whore, Slut, Backstabber", all over the freshly painted white aluminum siding on Dutchess' house.

After doing this, she felt better. Payback is a bitch!

-20-
The Breaking Point

Two weeks later, she began to look through the mail and there was a letter from the rental office and one from her brother.   She knew her brother would have something positive and motivating to say, so she thought about saving that for last.   She changed her mind and decided to read her brother's letter first.

Peace Sugar Gal,

First off, let me say I love you more than life itself. Can you try calling MCI to get the block off your phone? I know they probably placed it there because you haven't paid the bill, but see what you can do. I need to talk to you. I know things are tight for you. I really wish I wasn't on this racist-ass plantation, because I would damn sure send you some money to help you out. But don't worry, I have only a couple more years and I will be home shortly. All your worries will be washed away. I promise.

I got a letter from that hoe Dutchess. I told you a long time ago that hoe was not your friend and you never listen when I tell you about people. Don't you know that hoe had the nerve to write me and tell me that she wants me to talk to you about her fucking that no good snake Lucky! She tried to act like she

181

was so concerned about you getting into trouble because you fucked up her house. But I know she scared as hell. She is shaking in her boots, and rightfully so! I laughed so hard when I read the part of the letter that you spray-painted her house. You are gangster!

I ripped that letter up and sent it right back to her. I am not speaking on her behalf. Sugar, all I'm saying is, don't get into no trouble behind those two cruddy suckers. They're not worth it, the boys need you out there, not behind bars. Don't worry, they'll get theirs in the end. I promise!

Write me back ASAP! I love you and give my love to the boys!

Love, Taj

Tressa was furious, but all she could do was shake her head. This winch Dutchess is crazy! *Now, why would she tell my brother? Like he can control me. I'm a grown ass woman and that only makes me want to whip her ass even more. I had made up my mind that I was going to leave it alone. But some people won't let sleeping dogs lie. I can't wait until I see her.*

She was certain the rental office was simply writing to address something negative. She was right. The lady who had just moved in under her, told the rental office that the twins are making too much noise over her.

Whatever! I have more important things to worry about! They always writing about B/S, they never ever address the real issues. People are getting murdered right on our playgrounds where our children play, and not to mention, the selling of the narcotics right at our doorsteps. All these things clearly go on everyday, and they got the nerve to send me a letter about this crap!

Come to think of it, this broad downstairs looks in my face everyday, and still decides to go to the rental office and complain. Instead, she could have simply came upstairs and asked me to keep it down. She don't have a problem sending one of her begging ass kids to my house to borrow some eggs, sugar or Kool Aid. I mean, what do she expect? She lives in apartment, not a house and I have kids. But then again, she doesn't even have any furniture in her apartment, so I'm sure it's really hollow in there and she can hear everything. Shoot, it's not my fault she can't afford furniture! Taking all these things into consideration, she felt conquered, and overturned like everything in her life was going down hill. Every single person in her life that she even cared about had deceived her or let her down. Her mother and brother both went to jail, and left her out here to fend for herself. Her mother later committed suicide. The men she chose, Lucky, Jacko and Mr. Bill, and allowed in her life, were all poor choices. At first, all kinds of things ran through her head, like maybe somebody put a curse or a root on her. Then she thought about, maybe, she was being punished for going against her brother's wishes and dating Lucky. The final thought was, maybe God was punishing her for having her children out of wedlock and for all the other sins she'd committed. Tressa was about to crack the fuck up!

The girlfriends that she selected, whom she played fair with, crossed her every chance they could and she did not know why. Her only thoughts were when was Lucky going to take Missy and Wiggles away from her too?

(One Year Passed) Now 1996:

After the three past experiences with the men she choose, Tressa became bitter towards men. She withdrew from dealing with any man, and she didn't allow any new people into her life. She was also certain she'd never be in a close relationship with a woman again, that was not even an option.

Although there was nothing that could replace a warm body in her bed at night, Tressa learned to improvise when it came to her sexual needs. Like numerous women, even those afraid to admit it, she settled for vibrators. The "Rabbit", the "Butterfly", the "Penguin", and she couldn't forget about old faithful, the "Penis Pleaser!" filled her lonely nights. She reasoned with herself that self-pleasure was the way to go, to try and ease the pain of being alone. Tressa accepted the fact that she was going to be alone, just she and the boys.

I'll be A-OK. Well, at least I don't have to worry about a man not doing his job properly, and not being able to make me cum or to the dick going down. I control the size, width and shape, and how many times a night I want to cum. Furthermore, I don't have to worry about any man cheating on me or another girl sitting on my man's dick when I leave to go to work, cause see, I own that. It'll still be sitting in the closet waiting on me to return and give it some action. So, whether I work it everyday or once a month, as long as I have some fresh batteries, I'll be A-OK!

Tressa's new focus became to rise above the poverty stricken life that she had accepted for the past two years. She knew things happened for a reason. She just had a feeling she had put in her dues, and now it was her season to come up. Her pity party was over. She decided that she'd have to accept a few things. One, that it was not meant for her to have companionship! Two, that Lucky would never step up to the plate and be the father that she so yearned for him to be for her children. Although there were some things that she couldn't teach her boys, she'd do the best she could. Her whole life revolved around her boys. She participated in every activity she could with them.

She worked on building a better life for her boys and threw herself into their lives. She put them in karate lessons, and all her spare time revolved around her boys. She picked up a second job and didn't report it to the rental office. With the monies she made from the second job, she sacrificed and put it in a savings account that she didn't touch. This was going to be her way up out of Eastgate Village. Whenever her children were gone for the weekend, she didn't hang out, instead she worked. Wiggles pretended she had a part time job, but really she was selling weed. She only sold fifty-dollar bags or better to help Tressa move out of the hood. Wiggles rolled the money in. Everybody knows that there is no better hustler than an ex-crack head or drug addict. Even after they no longer have their addiction, the hustle is still instilled in them, since their habit depended on it when they were using. So, as sober as Wiggles had been for the past three years, she still had the hustle in her that once satisfied her addiction.

Tressa on the other hand, wasn't any drug hustler, but she too came across a hustle that she liked too, the "Bootlegg" hustle. She begin catching the Greyhound bus up to New York. Carrying only a small bag with her toothbrush, toothpaste, cash, her ID, and a pillow, she'd hop on the bus that left Richmond late at night, so she'd arrive in New York City at 8 a.m. Her routine was the same, she'd leave her pillow on the Greyhound, to her it was worth it to leave the $5.00 pillow. She'd stop by the bathroom in Port Authority to freshen up. Then go to have a small bagel and a cup of coffee. By this time, China Town and the garment district would be open and she'd make deals all day for the Coach bags and other knock off items. This was back in 1996 when Versace, Gucci, Coogi and Fendi was hitting Richmond's fashion scene hard, so these things were in big demand. At this time the closest place the divas and dons could go to get these items were Northern Virginia/DC areas, which were about two hours away. A few people did take that two hour drive, but most didn't. So, Tressa brought these things to Richmond and a real bankroll it brought to her.

Tressa, unlike other bootleg artists, she told the people that her things were imitation. A few other people did it in the town, but they lied and told people that their products were the "real deal". She could have easily gotten over on the same people, but bridges were not what she was trying to burn. She wasn't trying to beat anybody over the head with her prices. She was just trying to make her money back and get a profit out of the deal. For instance, she'd buy Gucci shades and would pay $5-7.00 per pair, and come back and sell them for $30-40.00 a piece, or Coach watches for $7-10.00, and come back and sell them for $30.00. Tressa was making more money in a week then she made on both her jobs combined in a month. The part time job she dropped almost instantly, but the first job she kept because she knew if she wanted to get a house it would be so much better with legitimate employment.

Tressa ran into Calvin from back at the University and he now owned a lot of property. Sometimes it isn't what you know, it's who you know. He introduced her to some government programs, and before too long, Tressa was able to move into a three-bedroom house, nothing too fancy, but it was hers. She was uncertain when this time would come, but her freedom was finally here. The day Tressa moved out of the projects, a lot of thoughts were going through her mind. She was grateful for two things, that she didn't have to live in such a degrading environment, and that the experience made her a much stronger person than she was when she went in.

-21-
The Clown

Tressa had been around the house all day cleaning, until Missy called and asked Tressa to give her a ride because her car was in the shop. Tressa didn't hesitate to say yes.

Tressa was wearing her black Calvin Klein faded jeans that she would never, under normal circumstances, do anything else in, but clean her house or wash her car. On top, she had on a gray, black and red Calvin Klein T-shirt that she had tied in a knot in the back exposing her flat stomach. She pulled her long ponytail through the buckle on the back of her baseball cap. She couldn't dare leave the house without her lip-gloss neatly painted onto her lips. She threw on some black Reeboks and grabbed her bag to play taxi to her dear friend.

While out, she swung by the barbershop to pick up the boys, they had been hanging out with Gator getting a haircut. He told Tressa to come by later to get them. She was hoping they were ready when she pulled up in front of the shop and blew the horn, but Gator signaled for her to come in. Gator's barbershop was a nice, modern looking barbershop. Just about everything in the spacious barbershop was black. The chairs and counters were black, and the mirror frames were outlined with black and gold. The back of the shop looked like a bachelor's pad equipped with a small refrigerator, a black leather sofa and a big screen television.

Tressa always felt so uncomfortable sitting in the barbershop, and especially in her "scrub the floor and toilet" clothes. There was always a bunch of men and she didn't fit in. Most of the guys there she knew, but there was a few she didn't know. There was one particular dude that was sitting over in the corner. He was quiet and the average person would not have noticed but being as attentive as Tressa always had to be, she noticed everything. He especially caught her attention when her son, Ali walked over there to talk to the man, and to her surprise, hyper, energetic with ants in his pants Ali, was listening to him! Being the overprotective mother she was, she called over to Ali. "Ali come here."

When Ali dropped his head and walked slowly over to her, she scolded him. "Baby, you know you don't talk to strangers."

"Mommy, he's my friend. He's funny and he helped me draw this picture for you." It was a picture of some flowers. "Hadji was crying when Uncle Gator threw away the flowers we got for you."

She smiled as she looked at the picture. "Ohhh, isn't this beautiful!"

"Yeah, mommy we made it just for you." Ali excitedly said. He was obviously happy that his mother loved the picture they both drew for her.

Gator spoke up while holding the clippers in his hand. "Before you jump to any conclusions, I let them go outside since you keep them exiled from the world." Gator continued as he talked with his hands. "When they were outside, they picked you some flowers. Hadji knocked them on the floor, and the flowers fell apart and I threw them away by mistake. It started raining and I couldn't let him go outside to pick anymore. Hadji threw a tantrum since he wouldn't have the flowers for you when you came. My man Indie calmed him down and helped them draw flowers for you instead."

Tressa gazed at Indie, there was no doubt that he was fine. He had an exotic looking, reddish bronze complexion with high cheekbones. He had a razor sharp chin and a beautiful perfectly shaped nose with a protrusion in the middle. Although he was sitting down, she could tell that he stood well over six feet. He was slim but with a nice build. His coal black hair was cut close, but the curls were still present. He wore blue jeans, a gray T-shirt and moccasin style shoes. The moccasin shoes he had on threw her off. She didn't care if they were by Polo, they were still moccasins!

He was so handsome and sexy to her that she could have ran over and tongue kissed him. The strangest thing was, as good as he looked to her, he managed to turn her off at the same time. She was certain that he'd be more of a headache than he was worth. Shoot, as fine as he was, she was convinced he had women lined up as long as the free cheese line.

She put on the boys' little windbreaker Nautica jackets and left the shop. Once she was outside, Indie ran out behind her. "Excuse me, miss, you forgot your flowers." He extended his hand to her holding the two pictures with a big Joker smile covering his face, as she walked to meet him halfway to get the pictures.

"Thank you for helping out with my sons. I know they can be a handful at times."

"No problem at all. I like those little dudes." He looked her up and down, and spoke bluntly in his soft voice. "I'd like to take you out." The last part of the comment caught her off guard.

This dagonne moccasin wearing clown think I am going to go out with him. That's a joke, she thought, as she looked him up and down. *And he's so sure of himself!*

Before she could say no, he cut in. "Look, I see you are a little uncomfortable going out with a stranger and that's OK. Well, at least let me call you then."

He looked into her eyes in an aggressive, take control way. When their eyes met, she couldn't refuse his sexy, deep, dark brown eyes. If she didn't know any better, she would have sworn his eyes were black. In the past year, it had never been hard at all for her to reject any man. She had determined in her mind that they were all full of it. She wanted to cut Indie down, but somehow she couldn't be as bitter as she had been over the past twelve months.

"OK. I'm ready for your number." Indie aggressively said in his soft, sexy voice.

"I don't have a pen to write it down."

"Baby, I don't need you to write it down. I can put it up here." Indie responded, by pointing to his forehead but referring to his mind.

She was caught off guard, so she had no choice but to ramble off her number to him.

A week later, Missy and Tressa were up late in Tressa's kitchen eating some Alaskan king crab legs when Tressa's pager went off. She didn't recognize the code 101 behind the number. She called it back.

A man's voice answered. "Peace."

"Hi, did someone call Tressa from this number?"

"Yes, Ms. Tressa, it's Indie.

"Oh, how you doing?"

"I am blessed."

"Likewise." Tressa said.

Missy asked Tressa with a look. "Who is that?"

Tressa covered up the phone. "The clown from the barbershop."

Tressa heard a loud noise and could tell something was going on in the background. So, she asked. "What's that loud noise?"

"The game is on."

"What game?"

"The Wildcats verses the Sooners."

Just then Tressa remembered that the game had been on earlier that day, but she didn't mention it. Instead she only made small talk. "Who's winning?"

"The Sooners are up 15 points."

"OK, who you going for?"

"The Sooners, they are my team."

"I'm telling you the Wildcats are going to win." Tressa said. He took it as a general accusation, but he knew the Sooners were going to win.

"No, they are not. Too bad you don't bet." Indie said.

"No, too bad you're going to lose the bet, baby.

"I wouldn't bet you anyway."

"Why?" Tressa wanted to know. Still not really feeling him, but since she was only killing time, she figured she would just play along with him.

"Because I could never take anything from you. You're a lady and I don't take away from women's lives, I only add to them." Indie said cockily.

Just then he got another call on his other line. "Hold on baby." He said, as he clicked over to answer the other call.

Tressa covered the phone and spoke to Missy. "Girl, don't you know this clown got the nerve to try to bet me on a game that I already know the outcome of."

"Really?" Missy said. "All I say is go ahead and make the sucker into what he is, a clown!"

They both burst into laughter as Indie came back to the phone. Tressa had the perfect trick for this clown.

"Sugar, I'm back."

"Wait a minute, where did you get the name Sugar from?" She wondered how exactly did he know about her childhood nickname that her brother had called her since she was born, "Sugar Gal".

"Sugar? Because Sugar is the sweetest thing I know, and it seems like under all that hardness and bitterness, you may be the sweetest thing that I have met in a long time."

"Oh, that is very 'sweet' of you to say. The reason I asked is, because that's my childhood nickname that my brother gave me and still calls me by to this day."

"Swoosh." Indie said in excitement. "Damn, that nigga just dunked, no, he slam dunked the ball." Speaking back into the phone. "Sugar, you still up for the bet? I know you don't want to bet.

"Look, I have always believed in the underdog." Tressa assured Indie.

"Me too, but I am betting on my team."

"So, I am rolling with the Wildcats, we are down two touchdowns right?" Tressa asked playing dumb.

"No, Sugar. This is basketball, not football. Ya'll down about 7 baskets."

"Oh, OK. I got it now. So, yes we can bet."

"OK, what do you want to bet? You are clear, that the Sooners are up 15 points, and the second half is about to start now, right?"

"Yes, now it's on you, what do you want to bet." Tressa put the pressure on him.

"Umm, let me think. I don't want it to be any money. So, if I win, then you go out on a date with me."

"And if I win?" Tressa asked.

"If you win, which your chances are slim to none, but if you win, you just call it, tell me what you want." He easily said.

Without any hesitation, she said "A day's work of hard labor. Since you are a 'Pretty Boy Floyd' type of guy, I know you're not normally required to put in a hard day's work."

"It's a bet." He smiled, laughing to himself, all the while contemplating how he was going to sweep up too tight, need to be screwed real good, Ms. Tressa off of her feet.

They hung up and Missy turned the channel onto the game. At Mr. Moccasin wearing Indie's expense, they were going to have some fun. The Wildcats had come back within four points. "Let's call him and rub it in his face."

He answered the phone. "Hello."

"Yeah, your Sooners are soon to lose if we score another touchdown."

He laughed. "This is basketball Sugar, and you ain't out of the woods yet."

"I just thought I'd let you know that we have come back within four, so go ahead and pull the work truck out of the garage because the labor is calling you Boo!"

When Tressa was walking Missy to the door, they continued to get their laugh on about how they had just clowned Indie and this was only the beginning. Once the phone rang, they gave each other high fives and Tressa let Missy out before catching the telephone. It was Indie calling.

"Ok, they scored and won by a touchdown, so what do I have to do to pay off my bet?" Indie said laughing.

"No, no, no city slicker, we won by 3 baskets and a free throw, not a touchdown. Sweetheart, this is basketball." She said in an extra proper speaking voice.

"Well, I need to know when and where I need to report for my hard day's work."

"I'll let you know in a couple of days. I want you to sweat since you tried to take advantage of a sweet innocent girl like me."

"That's cool, but for some reason, I feel like I'm the one that's going to get taken advantage of."

Four days passed and Tressa made the call that Indie had been waiting on. He didn't care what Tressa had planned, help her hang pictures, change her furniture around, etc. Shit, he would have even been willing to plant a garden for her. As long as it meant he could spend time with her, he would do it. He just wanted to get to know her.

She instructed him to meet her at the mall at noon. And he did as he was told. His first thought was she wanted him to take her shopping, but money wasn't an issue. Too bad she didn't know that he was the cash cow, the money bag, the slot machine, the lottery, her voucher to the next level, her way out financially, mentally and physically. The saying, no book can be judged by its cover is a clearly proven fact when one looks at Indie. It was sad to say that he was her Prince Charming and she may not realize it until it is too late.

When they met up, the first thing she looked at was his shoes, *dang, seems like he got all colors of those Timberland moccasin styled shoes. The other day, he had on the brown ones, now today, he got on the blue ones. I told this clown hard labor, not fishing with those dock shoes on.*

Tressa didn't even bother to dress up for him because she didn't think anything of him or consider it a date. She just slipped on some tight Guess Stretch jeans and a 2pac T-shirt with some Air max Nikes on. She had her micro braids in a ponytail resting in the middle of the back of her head. It was obvious she wasn't dressed for a date.

He again caught her off guard, greeting her with a hug when she reached her hand out to shake his hand.

"What kind of hard work at the mall you need me to do? Reaching in my pocket to pull out money to pay for whatever you want doesn't seem hard." He said, shaking his head. "Now I understand, carrying the bags is the hard labor, huh?" He smiled.

She giggled a little, but holding her breath, knowing he may not like the answer. "No sweetie, I need you to entertain some children at my sons' birthday party."

"I can handle that."

"But there are some things that we have to get to assist you in the task. I'll pay for everything."

He liked the fact that she offered to pay and that she wanted him to be a part of her children's party. He was certain that the way to her heart, or any mother's heart, was through her children "There's no need to pay, I can handle that, just show me what I need to get." Indie told her.

So, they strolled off to the party store. She had to control herself with all her might not to laugh, as they approached the aisle that they needed to get the necessary items from. First, they went over to the costume section, and that's when he realized she wanted him to dress like a clown at her boys' party.

He didn't think that was funny. He looked at her with a disappointed look on his face. "You think I am a real live clown don't you?"

"No, I just needed somebody to entertain my sons and their friends. I tried hiring a clown, but they all are booked up." She said, realizing that she had struck a nerve with him, and trying to clean up the joke a little by shifting the weight over on her boys, she said, "and they are so looking forward to having a clown. But don't worry about it, they're only five, they're going to have to understand mommy can't do everything."

"Come on now, you know better, those my lil buddies, you know I'm not going to disappoint them."

They walked around the store, and Indie wasn't really saying anything about how she was playing him. However, he thought to himself, *it's a damn shame, she don't even know who I am. It's all-good though I'm going to let her have her laugh, only because I like her and I gave her my word. Had I not given her my word, I wouldn't do a damn thing. See, she don't understand, I pay people to do stuff like this.*

Tressa saw a red clown nose, placed it on Indie's nose and said, "Perfect!"

He removed the nose and gave her a serious look that could have killed, and all of a sudden, he didn't look like a clown anymore.

194

Seeing how angry he looked, Tressa tried to diffuse any angry outburst by pleading with Indie. "Please do this for me. You said you loved kids, so show me how much."

He didn't have too much more to say to Tressa while she gathered all the things that she thought he would need. He was so angry, but didn't show it when the clerk seemed to be in cahoots with Tressa, making small talk while she rung up the items. "Oh, you picked the perfect nose for this clown outfit!"

Indie wanted to just blow up and cuss both Tressa and the talkative, over helpful sales clerk out, but he didn't. He simply went in his pocket and paid for the hideous things, his makeup, and size 40 clown shoes that were bright green and red two-tone. When Indie looked over at the clown suit, he just shook his head, and thought, *it's bad enough she's making a clown out of me, but she had to pick the most ugly clown suit in the whole store. Then my stupid ass is here reaching in my pocket to pay for this shit. What the hell is wrong with me? A bet is a bet though. But God DAMN!!! She knows how to make a brother feel like a real loser! For Real!!!*

When he walked her over to her car, she handed him a piece of paper. "Here's the address."

"What time is the party?"

"4 p.m. and don't even think about paying someone else to show up either." Tressa slid the last part of the comment in.

"No, I know a bet is a bet. And, most importantly, I gave you my word." He told her, although he was thinking about hiring someone to do his dirty work for him.

Indie went home and gave the situation a lot of thought, as he contemplated his every move in his everyday life. He came up with his own agenda. *Make me into a damn clown, huh. I'll bet one thing, I'm going to get the last laugh, as I always do. I'm going to that party, but I don't think they are going to be ready for me. I got a few tricks of my own up my sleeves that are going to put the icing on the cake.* Indie amused himself with his own idea.

He had only two more days to prepare for the party, and he prepared for the party like his life depended on it. The day before the party, he went to the trick shop on West Broad to purchase additional objects to help execute his plan. He happily rolled his cart through like a kid who had just won a Toys R Us sweepstakes. When he was leaving, he was thinking and laughing both at the same time, "*Turn me into a damn clown!*"

Back in the day when Indie was in middle school, he entered a talent show. He didn't win, but he knew what it took to make the people laugh and sit in amazement in middle school, so little kids shouldn't be any harder.

Indie borrowed somebody's beat up pick up truck. He got them to meet him around the street from Tressa's house. There was no way he was driving that raggedy truck any further than around the corner, that's for sure. To ensure all the children were at the party, he arrived close to a quarter after five. When he arrived, the truck was smoking, making all kinds of loud noises which some of the kids came around from the back yard to the front yard to see what all the commotion was. The one little girl ran back around to the back of the house to alert Tressa that it was the clown, and the kids all ran around the front to greet the clown.

When Tressa went around to the front she was like, "what the hell", while fanning all the smoke. All she could see was Indie getting out of the truck with his polka dot clown outfit, professional clown makeup and the fluorescent striped big bag he toted. However, it was truly the hot pink, big bushy wig that sent her into laughter, but little did she know, the joke would later be on her. When he was closer to the children, the truck made a loud backfire. He had it timed perfect, he pretended the loud noise startled him, which caused him to purposely trip, falling over his own feet. Once he plunged to the ground, out came the rag dolls, baseballs, toy motorcycles, dollar bills, trash candy and anything else he thought would be good gifts for the children, all over the front yard. The kids didn't even help the clown up, instead they were all over the toys and candy. Tressa rushed over to help him up. *Lord, I hope he didn't hurt himself.* She felt a little sorry for him, but never let him know.

After the children picked up all they could, Tressa moved the children to the back. All the children had glitter all over them, it was harmless, and just a part of the act. While she was feeding the children in the back yard, Indie unloaded his truck. He brought in six big boxes, two small boxes and a cart on wheels. He put those things to the side, and as he was walking, he was drying his face with a hanky. As soon as he came close to Tressa, he flicked his wrist and the hanker chief turned into a rose. He handed it to her and didn't even stay around to get a response. He kept moving along to meet the birthday boys again. When they looked closely and realized it was their friend from the barbershop, they were so excited and began to give him hugs and jump all over him.

The show began, he first made the kids faces up like little clowns. Since the children adored him so much for all the fun they were having, he conned the children to get Tressa to get her face made up like a clown too. After the children begged, pleaded and screamed at the top of their lungs in a melody of "Please, Please, Please," trying to be a good sport, she got some red circles painted on her cheeks. Then all of a sudden, Indie went into his pocket and put the bright red nose on Tressa. The kids loved it and then Indie whispered in her ear. "I'm not the only clown, now." She couldn't help but laugh.

"Thank you for coming."

"No, the show ain't over Sugar. As a matter fact, it's just beginning."

Indie went into the house to get his other materials he needed. He brought the cake outside, lit it and it exploded. He ran for cover behind a tree. He was hiding, and it was so funny to the children. Tressa even had to laugh herself. He was taking a minute to come out, waiting for all the dust and smoke to settle. Tressa made brief eye contact with him. He winked at her and didn't let his performance get interrupted by her beautiful smile. He continued all kinds of magic and card tricks. A little girl asked, "Mr. Candy man, can you pull a rabbit out of a hat?"

Indie put one finger up indicating to wait one minute, and went over to the cart with wheels and put his hat on top of it. All the children sat silently, patiently waiting for the rabbit. When Indie was sure he had their attention, he looked at each and every one of them before he pulled the rabbit out of his hat. He started to chant, reciting the words to the old song by the late Sammy Davis, Jr., "The Candy Man".

While he was singing, he started doing a little dance in his clown shoes, which got the kids even more excited. He pointed to the kids and they started singing too. "The candy man can...the candy man can...."

At the moment when he had the children exactly where he wanted them, at the climax of excitement, he pulled out a puppy rottweiler with two rabbit ears on its fat little head. He handed it to Hadji. Lil Ali ran over to play with the dog with his brother. The little girl said, "Do it again." He looked at the little girl and all the boys and girls and said, "You have to sing for me."

The kids began to sing, *"the candy man can...the candy man can...oh, the candy man can!"*

Before they realized, he had pulled another rottweiler out of his hat and gave it to the Lil Ali. He wished them both a "happy birthday." Tressa was amazed and outdone, but little did she know, that he wasn't done with her yet. While the children enjoyed their cake and ice cream, Tressa and Indie talked.

"Look, let me come clean with you, I saw the game earlier that day. I knew you were going to win the bet. So, I never lost the bet. I still was able to spend some time with you."

"How did you know to bring the puppies?"

"Every child needs a dog, especially little boys. I couldn't go and get those little guys of yours a poodle." He said, laughing. "I had to get them something that can give them a run for their money. The dogs are UKC reg, the best breed of rott money can buy."

"Thank you so much! There's nothing I could pay you to compensate you for the good time you showed my boys and their friends today."

"Sugar, that was just a small thing for me to pay for a woman like you."

Tressa was a little embarrassed that she had made a clown out of Indie. The way he played the games with the children, made her decide that maybe she could overlook the moccasins. After all he seemed to be a sweet guy.

They made plans for a date.

He was in!

-22-
Real Recognize Real

It wasn't long after, about six months, before Indie had settled into their life. The transition wasn't hard at all for the boys. They loved Indie, and that is what made Tressa welcome him into their lives. Indie always gave his word to the boys, whatever he said, he did. He did things with them that Lucky had never thought of doing. Indie did a lot of big things for the boys, but it seemed to be the little things that amazed them so much. He took them to pick out their own kites and flew the kites with them. Indie began to show up at every little league game and practice equipped with a video camera. It had gotten to the point where the boys realized that it was more "hip" to have a man watch them from the sideline and cheer them on. With Indie around, Tressa noticed less mischievous behavior out of the boys.

Tressa, on the other hand, was more reluctant to accept Indie into her life. Without a doubt, she knew that Indie was the perfect father figure for her children and was a true lifesaver. She couldn't help but remember, how it seems like every relationship starts out with each person only showing the good face, the acceptable things about them. She kept trying to convince herself that there was more to Indie than he revealed to her. She beat herself up, with every excuse, why she shouldn't give Indie a chance to be a part of her life, not wanting to come face to face with the fact that Indie was her knight in shining armor. The main thing she kept coming up with, was that she didn't want to cause harm to come to Indie once Lucky found out.

One night back in 98, she ran to the store while Indie was over watching the football game with the boys. When she returned, all three were stretched out on the couch, knocked out sleeping. The site was a picture perfect moment. She stared at them for about five minutes, and at that time, is when she decided she would let Indie into her heart.

Tressa shook Indie, "please put the boys in their rooms for me." She walked to her bedroom and shut the door. He did as he was told. He came into her room to say good night and bye to her. When he knocked on the door, she screamed from the half bath off the master suite. "Don't leave, I need to tell you something."

So, Indie just sat on the foot of her bed because she had her work clothes laid on the chaise chair. She walked out of the bathroom wearing nothing, but a red sheer Frederick's of Hollywood nightgown and some stilettos heels. Indie tried not to look at her, but he couldn't help himself. She strutted right over to him and started unbuttoning his shirt.

As astonished as Indie was he had asked her, "What you doing?"

She covered his lips with a long, wet tongue kiss.

"Are you sure you can handle this? Because you know after this, it ain't no turning back?"

She looked into his eyes and told him, "baby don't worry 'bout Tressa, cause I got this! Just sit back and enjoy the damn ride!"

"I ain't talking 'bout the ride, I am talking 'bout the our life together."

"As I said, I got this on my end, you just make sure you can hold your own on this here ride, and be the man I need you to be! I'm tried of wearing the pants."

Indie, shocked as he could be, wondered had *she been drinking or what? I ain't never seen her this bold, or raunchy, but I like this shit. Damn, this shit here, ain't no fucking joke. I see why dude was mad as hell. Shit, if I couldn't get this, I was going to be mad too.*

200

He thoroughly enjoyed the tease as she gave him an intense lap dance. She did it so good, he wondered if she'd been a stripper before. When the lap dance was over, you can best believe the show didn't stop there. Tressa kept her back to Indie and started grinding her hot pussy against his big dick, sliding it up and down with her slit covering it with her juices. She felt his hands stroking her ass as she grinded faster. Low moans escaped his lips as she grinded her clit down on his dick. Indie reached around cupping Tressa's tits. She placed her hands over his, showing him how to handle her tits, first soft strokes then getting firmer as her strokes, became longer. Finally, pulling wildly on her nipples, she bounced up and down on his dick. Throwing her head back with a loud,"uohhhh," she couldn't believe, as long as it had been, she was handling that stallion like she was. In a matter of minutes, both of them were climaxing.

Richmond, being the small town that it is, everybody pretty much knew everybody. There weren't many twins in the town in which one was the quarterback and the other was a tailback, and they both could really play. Everybody was talking about the twins, and even the local newspaper, "The Voice", did an article on the twins. So before long, Lucky got the news that some New York cat was at the football field with his boys. Lucky made it his business to make a trip up to the football field. He couldn't believe his eyes. He was so mad and wanted to kill Indie on the spot, when he looked on as the boys ran over to Indie so Indie could applaud their effort on the field. Lucky was fuming when the twin closest to his heart, Hadji, looked over to Indie for assurance before the play. Lucky, at that moment, realized just exactly what he was missing out on and secretly wished it was him.

Lucky came and sat on the bench right beside Indie. Normally, Lucky would have gotten straight to business, but there was something that stopped him. He could feel the coldness and the same empty heartedness that he had within himself, he felt it in Indie's aura. Upon feeling Indie's vibe, he was spooked for a minute, because he realized that Indie was no lame, he too was a gangsta. Gangster or not, Lucky always welcomed the challenge, and in Lucky's mind, it wasn't who held the most clout, it was who got to their holster the quickest.

Lucky looked him up and down as Indie cheered when Ali made a touchdown. That's when Lucky made his appearance known. "Look shawdy, those twins, they are my boys and I am here to pick them up."

"That's cool you're here to see them I'm happy that you finally made it out, and I am sure the boys will be happy to see you. Much respect on that note, but they came here with me, they are leaving with me unless Tressa, their mother, tells me different." Indie said, holding his own.

"Look, nigga they're mine. I can –"

"Wow, wow, look man." Indie said, in his soft voice, but firm tone, looking Lucky smack dead in the eyes. "I am not here to get into no verbal or gun warfare with you. I told you, I respect that you are here for them. I'll never stand in between a man trying to support his. But, at the same time, respect that I have been here and am here for them."

Lucky was left speechless for the first time in his life.

Indie looked in his eyes for a few more seconds, before directing his attention back to the game.

Once the game was over, both men met the boys halfway. The boys both ran over to get the pat on the back that Indie always gave them, only to see Lucky standing beside him. As soon as Hadji saw Lucky, he pulled out his fingers, pointed like a gun, but before he could shoot, Lucky had already shot Hadji and Hadji fell on the ground playing dead. It was funny how Hadji hadn't seen his father in over two years, but he remembered the gunplay game.

On the other hand, Lil Ali just walked up on Indie's outside leg and gave him a hug. He didn't even speak to Lucky. When Lucky tried to shoot him, he ignored him. "Hey lil man." He said to Lil Ali.

Ali didn't speak a word. Lucky reached out. "You want a lollipop?"

He shook his head, no.

"Why don't you want one?"

"Because suckers are for people who leave their kids. I am not a sucker." Ouch, those words that came from a seven year-old hurt and inflicted the worst kind of

202

pain, more severe than any gunshot or stab wound, and it went straight through his heart.

"I never left you."

"Yes, you did." Ali stood firm, and talked to Lucky unlike any seven old would speak to his father.

"No, I didn't. Your mother took ya'll away and I didn't know where you were."

"Well, Grandma Betty knew and you saw us at Grandma Betty's house." Ali never dropped his head, he gazed in his father's eyes as he ranted on. "My friend, Joshua's momma took him away to another house too but his dad shows up every weekend and takes him places."

Hadji cut in too. "And our friend, Michael's dad do the same thing, and he got a new wife."

Realizing he didn't have an adequate comeback, Lucky said, "Well, I'm going to do better, I promise."

Lucky went in his pocket and gave each boy a five-dollar bill. They took the money, but through their facial expression, the boys showed it wasn't good enough.

The boys grabbed their equipment and got into Indie's Mazda Millennium, and Lucky watched as they drove off.

Lucky knew off the bat that Indie was holding his own and wasn't any kind of slouch. That's the main thing about the whole episode that pissed Lucky off. Now, if Tressa had let a Wack-Jack or poo-putt type guy into her life, he probably wouldn't be bothered as much. When he analyzed the situation, he realized that through all the rage, pain, pranks and disrespect, that Tressa was still standing. She wasn't hurt, she could love again and, most importantly, she had found someone of his status, if not a notch up. When all these things sank in, rage, anger, and fury begin to set in, especially when he realized that this New York cat had entered into the picture and taken his family away. It could have been anybody else, but a New Yorker. Lucky had plans for this dude.

Indie knew and was fully aware of Lucky's capabilities, for he could feel the vibe too. Overall, Indie wasn't shook up or worried, he just drew the conclusion that Lucky was trigger happy, but no real gangster. Real gangster's move with silence and violence, and with that being said, Lucky was too rah-rah, boisterous, and pretty much made his presence known before he arrived. Indie knew, but still studied Lucky's shortcomings, but wouldn't sleep on him.

-23-
Time To Shine

Indie was originally from an Indian reservation in Long Island, New York, hence the nickname Indie. At the age of 14, his father left one day for work and never returned, leaving him as the man of the house, to take care of his sickly mother and younger sister. He wasn't surprised when his father left, because even to this very day, Indie believed that from the time Indie was just a little lad, his father had been preparing him to be the breadwinner. His father taught Indie all kinds of hustles, bad and good, when his mother wasn't looking. He naturally taught Indie to be a fisher and a hunter. But not just any hunting, he taught him how to hunt with shotguns, knives, big and small, cross bows and all kind of other weapons that the average person would not know of. One of the most important things that Indie's father instilled in Indie, was to always have a plan, even under the gun in the worst condition, always map out an escape route.

From the day that Indie's father left, he had never asked anybody for anything, and his mother and sister have never missed a meal. Indie tried several different hustles to feed his family. But what he found out is illegal money is always what gets the most money. So, he met a guy named Ramel, who was from Brooklyn and the two began to hang out together. Everyday he'd go into the city, Ramel would always ask Indie to bring him some cigarettes. After a few days, Indie caught on that cigarettes on the reservation were far cheaper than the ones they sell in the city. First, he started filling his backpack up peddling cigarettes to people on the street everyday, coming home with enough money to pay for the household expenses. Then he sold them to a couple of corner stores. They bought cases of them and word soon traveled. Pretty soon, he started driving 21 feet U-hauls to the city every other day filled with cigarettes, and in no time, he was rich and was only fifteen!

With his riches, he provided his mother and sister with a lavish lifestyle, and everything money could buy, to try and fill the void of his father deserting them. As long as the basic bills were paid, his mother was happy. But his baby sister Reka, there was something he couldn't buy her, and that was, her father's love. Reka, a beautiful petite girl, she too had that bronze exotic looking complexion and those high cheekbones like her brother. Her looks were flawless, and if she desired, she could have been a model on any runway she chose. Instead, she chose to look for the love and acceptance that she longed for and never got from her father.

For a long time, Indie had issues about the men Reka selected. They were always thugged-out, wild, drug dealer guys. Reka felt that, through their on edge lifestyle, they could protect her like her father was suppose. Most of the time, Reka allowed these men to dog her out, they had her carrying drugs, beating on her, etc.

At first, Indie beat up or killed one or two, like any brother would do for his sister, because of the disrespect shown towards his sister. Then he realized that Reka wanted to be involved in the game so she could feel secure, like she could make her own money. He stopped trying to shelter her from the cruel world, and taught her how to play to win in the perfidious world. As messed up as it sounds, he set Reka up with an all girl crew and they got money the illegal way.

When Tressa shared with Indie the infinite love and the deepness of the relationship between her and her brother, Taj, he could truly relate to it, taking into consideration the closeness he and Reka shared. Although Indie had some street ways about him, he never displayed them to Tressa. He was always a perfect gentleman. He owned some real estate and did renovations on houses, which brought a sizeable amount of money, but it didn't compare to the money he was used to getting illegally. But after becoming such a great part of Tressa and the boys lives, he decided that he'd build his real estate empire so they all could live comfortably.

With Indie now an intricate part of Tressa's life, Tressa had a glow all across her face that nobody had ever seen. Tressa dress code even changed. She had once turned into the black widow, wearing everything black or dark colored clothes and everything was conservative, no cleavage showing at all. Outside of work, sweatpants and T-shirts were all she could seem to throw on now. But with Indie now a part of her life, the black was pushed completely out of the closet and replaced with some sexy, but sophisticated clothes. She always wanted to look sexy for her man. Tressa wanted to have such an effect on Indie, so when he saw her, at any given place or time of the day, she turned him on to the point where he wanted to make love to her right then and there.

Tressa started putting effort into their relationship, she'd always come up with some kind of creative ideas to spice up their sex life. With the role of parents, sometimes things were so focused on the kids that, at the end of the day, there wouldn't be anytime for each other. But Tressa always took matters into her own hands.

One day she left a message for Indie to meet her at Fanny's, a restaurant hooked onto the Holiday Inn, and told him when he got there to ask for "Spice". When he arrived, the waitress handed him an envelope, pointed him over to a woman with a long blonde wrap wig, fire red lipstick and reading glasses, in the corner. He opened the envelope, read the note and laughed. There was a note saying:

Hi Sweetheart,

I managed to get Spice to agree to let you take full advantage of her tonight. I could only pay her for three hours, so have fun. If she's good, make sure you tip her.

Love Forever and Ever,
Tressa

PS: Please pick up some orange sherbert ice cream on your way home.

Of course, Spice was Tressa, and the whole time, she made him refer to her as Spice, not Tressa. And when they were on their way back home, in separate cars, Tressa called Indie on his cell phone and asked him, "baby, how long before you'll be home with my sherbert icecream?" This gave her enough time to get home and get into something else sexy. Tressa was very versatile when it came to Indie, she always changed up and became someone else. She also bent the rules for Indie, the things she said she'd never do, she did for Indie. He never asked either, she just did them because she wanted to.

Tressa was totally comfortable with him, she felt like she could reveal all of herself to him. Indie accepted her for who she was, and loved her wholeheartedly, whether she was at her worst or at her best. They laughed and acted silly together. Sometimes, they'd get out of the shower, and just dance buck naked.

Indie's place in Tressa's life consisted of multiple titles, which included best friend, confidant, lover, soul mate, protector, role model for her sons and the love of her life. It was through Indie, that Tressa realized the sayings, "Good things come to those that wait," "No storm lasts forever," and "After every dark cloud is a brighter day," were so true! It was through the relationship that she shared with Indie, and the beautiful experiences she shared, that she came to really recognize and appreciate all the words in her theme song for so many years, "Juicy".

Indie respected how Tressa had held it down for so long without any help from anybody. But at the same time, some massive things were going to have to change since she was Indie's girl, and one day soon, his wife.

First of all, the house she lived in was OK, considering she made the transition from the projects into regular housing. At the same time, it wasn't Indie's idea of where he wanted his boys and soul mate to live. But how would he get her to agree to move? He knew for sure, he couldn't put a stack of money on the table and tell her to find a house she wanted. Although he was sure she trusted him, he knew she still had a few insecurities when it came to men providing her with extraordinary purchases, such as a house. So, therefore, he'd have to come up with an alternative solution.

As Tressa laid in Indie's arms, the alarm went off. She didn't want to get up, but knew she had to go to work.

"Why don't you take the day off." Indie insisted.

"No, I can't. I have to go. I don't want to lose my job, I need my job."

"You might want that job, but you don't need that job. You will always have me."

"Thanks." She said, and gave him a big, long, deep, tongue kiss, morning-mouth and all!

"I am serious. You always have me. I'm yours forever."

"Yeah, until you break my heart." She said, as she got out of the bed, in a joking way, but he knew she was serious. She brushed her teeth and cut the water on for the shower. While she was waiting for it to get hot, she looked in the closet to see what she could pull out to wear to work.

Before she could get into the shower, Indie beat her to the bathroom to take a dump. She sat in the entryway of the door and carried on a conversation with him, while he had his bowel movement. This was confirmation for her that she really loved and cared deeply for Indie. If she could sit at the door, smell his bowels and it simply didn't faze her, now, that indeed was love.

Once she got out of the shower, he was standing over at the cd player.

"No Reggae music this morning?" She asked him.

"Look, baby, I want you to listen to this song, this is exactly how I feel 'bout you. Listen closely to every word, because I need you to know I'm with you."

He pressed play on the cd and the Method Man with Mary J. Blige song came on, "You're All I Need To Get By".

"Shorty, I'm there for you anytime you need me...For real girl, it's me in your world, believe me...Nuttin' make a man feel better than a woman...Queen with a crown that be down for whatever...There are few things that's forever, my lady...We can make war or make babies...Back when I was nothing...You made a brother feel like he was something...That's why I'm with you to this day boo, no frontin'...Even when the skies were gray...You would rub me on my back and say Baby it'll be okay...Now that's real to a brother like me baby...Never ever give my cootie away and keep it tight a'ight...And I'ma walk these dogs so we can live...In a fat ass crib with thousands of kids...Word life, you don't need a ring to be my wife...Just be there for me and I'ma make sure we...Be livin' in the fuckin' lap of luxury...I'm realizing that you didn't have to fuck wit me...But you did, now I'm going all out kid...And I got mad love to give, you my nigga..."

Hearing this song truly made her day. Although Indie didn't speak on the housing situation to Tressa, he had his own plan. Indie was a frequent customer to the guy, Pablo, who owned a convenient store that was located down the street from Tressa's house. Indie befriended Pablo since Pablo was also originally from New York. Pablo agreed to run a contest/sweepstakes, supposedly brought to the community by "The Shed A Rainbow Foundation", at his store. Indie saw to it that Tressa entered into the contest. Little did Tressa know that Indie was the Shed A Rainbow Foundation. Tressa won the money and Indie was certain Tressa wouldn't spend the money foolishly.

A week before Tressa "won" the money, Indie asked her to marry him. He proposed to her with a superior 4.49 carat emerald cut ring with .26 carots of tapered baguettes on the sides. After laying eyes on the ring, without a doubt, she agreed.

After winning the money, $20,000.00, Tressa didn't think twice, she told Indie some of the money would be their down payment towards a new home. He told her that he will put up 10 G's toward the down payment so they will have 20 to put down, and he'd pay for the furniture as well. He then instructed her to go get her a new car, and she did. She went to the dealer the day she closed on her house, traded her old Mazda in for a two-year-old five series BMW, burgundy with tan leather interior, sunroof and fully loaded. She felt that this BMW replaced the BMW that she loved so much, but was forced to give up, so many years ago when she left Lucky.

Tressa was so happy with how her life was going, but there was one thing she felt essential to take care of. First, she prayed and thanked God for the bountiful blessings that had been bestowed upon her. Next, she made the phone call that she had been waiting to make for so many years. She set up an appointment and planned to dress to kill.

Although wearing nothing really too flashy, her outfit was just enough to make her presence known and to let innocent bystanders and the onlookers know that she was on a mission and was not playing. She was wearing some blue Dolce & Gabana jeans, and long sleeve D&G shirt to match the jeans. She wore the D&G black belt with the big D&G on the buckle. The black Charles Jordan sexy, fierce stiletto boots flowed perfectly with the whole ensemble. Tressa threw on her black mink jacket that stopped at her waist, and to top it off, Tressa felt obligated to put the icing on the cake. She wished she had a mink hat to match that particular jacket, but she didn't, so instead, she threw on Indie's black fur Anglo cap and headed off to the beauty parlor, though she vowed so long ago that she would never give Gypsy another dollar of her money. But for some reason she felt the need to just make Gypsy kiss her butt for all the days she had dissed her when she was doing bad.

When she arrived at the beauty parlor, today must have been Tressa's lucky day, because she got a parking spot slam in front of the beauty shop. Whenever someone in a nice whip rolled in front of Gypsy's shop, everyone was alerted, because it was just their nature. All eyes were glued on Tressa when she walked into the shop, and boy did she put the show on for them. She pulled out a stride that she hadn't strutted in a long time, but the walk she gave them was enough to make them vomit with envy and jealousy. Her stroll was always that of a runway model, whether she pushed a stroller, carried her twins when they were babies on her hip, or now, with the mink on her back and a six hundred dollar bag on her shoulder.

Tressa walked into the shop and one of the girls who worked in the shop noticed Tressa and couldn't believe it. She had to ask, "Is that a Kangol coat?"

"What?" Tressa didn't understand what she was saying at first, then the girl asked again.

"Is that a Kangol coat you got on?"

Then it hit Tressa, the girl was insinuating that the coat she wore wasn't mink, that it was the same fur as the Kangol she was wearing. *Oh, shit doesn't ever change around here. But since these broke down chicks wanna talk slick to me, and still don't want give me my respect, I got something for them. It's open field day on these hoes.*

Tressa responded. "No sweetheart, this is mink, baby, sable mink to be precise."

That comment was, without a doubt, a truly low blow.

Gypsy ran over and embraced Tressa with a fake hug pretending like she was so happy to see her. "Girl, I miss you so much. I thought you would never take those micro braids out your hair. Your hair is healthy and long though. Who been doing it?" Gypsy asked, while rolling her fingers through Tressa's hair.

"The Dominicans, you know they do the best roller wraps."

"Yes they do, so what you having today?"

Tressa laughed to herself when Gypsy asked that question. *I know this broad don't think for one minute, that she going to put any chemicals or scissors in my hair. I don't care if she messes up a style, because I can always wash it out,* Tressa thought to herself, but responded to Gypsy, "I just need my hair washed and pin it up some kind of way."

Gypsy could barely pay attention to wash Tressa's hair from staring at the rock that Tressa sported on her left ring finger. She desperately wanted to know "What was really good" with Tressa. *How in the hell this broad go from rags to riches? I'd sure like to know.*

While Gypsy was setting Tressa's hair, Gypsy asked, "So are you going to start coming back to me now?"

"I don't know, but most likely." She knew she wouldn't be coming back, but she didn't want to tell Gypsy that. She had to ensure that Gypsy would do a good job on her hair.

"You know I work on Fridays and every other Saturdays now, and plus, I am pretty much on time now."

"What? What brought on this?"

212

"Girl, I don't get that fat child support check anymore for the baby."

"Oh, for real.

"When Merk got married. I kept taking him back to court and he finally filed for joint custody, and now the $3,000 I used to get a month, I don't get anymore."

"What?" Was Tressa's response, but she thought to herself, *that's what you get for being a greedy bitch!* I had heard that every time Gypsy heard that Merk bought his wife anything new, that she would get mad and take him back to court for a child support increase, and they got tired of her greedy, begging butt and now look, she's stuck with nothing. She's in here practically begging me to come back and get my hair done. Damn, ain't it funny how the tables turn. At first, everybody used to beg her to do their hair. And now, she got the nerve to try be recruiting old clients!

While Tressa was sitting in Gypsy's chair, the lady before Tressa paid Gypsy. Gypsy needed change, she asked every single person in the shop if they had change, except Tressa. She made Tressa the very last person she asked. "Tressa, give me change for a twenty."

With calmness in her voice, but with a little giggle, she said, "no sweetheart, I don't carry anything less than hundreds."

That one comment is what could have sold Gypsy for a penny. *When it comes time for this broad to pay me, she better not pull out no tens or fives because I am going to let her have it.*

There was complete silence between the two of them and Tressa wondered to herself, *why do we put up with people treating us any kind of way? It's so many people waiting to make this money, and yet, even me, I still let this broad abuse me and say what she wants to, and treat me any kind of way. We do it at the restaurant too. Why do we go to places that we know don't want us there? But, yet and still, we still there, not knowing what these people are really doing to our food. Do we do it to prove a point. "Hey, I can afford this?" Or what? I know this is the last time for me. I'm not giving money to anybody who does not appreciate me. I didn't read David Walker's Appeal for nothing.*

And when it was finally time for Tressa to pay Gypsy, she pulled out a hundred dollar bill and Gypsy was again left in silence for a minute. Rest assure, Gypsy was not letting her get out of that shop without a low blow. She looked for something, anything to throw a curve ball at Tressa, only there was nothing. As she watched, in green eyed envy, Tressa was putting on her coat, she said, "Tressa, why would you wear a mink to get your hair done? To me that's crazy. I wouldn't pull my coat out until I was really going out on a night on the town or somewhere special."

Tressa laughed a little to herself, because she knew Gypsy wasn't going to let her get out of the shop without a low blow. Tressa was quick on her feet and was dead serious when she replied, "Darling, I don't need to go anywhere special to wear this coat here. We don't live in Chicago, Illinois, we live in Richmond, VA, and we only get a few real cold days, and every time a cold day rolls around, I'm going to put on one of my mink ensembles, regardless to what or where I have to go. That's what a mink's sole purpose is for, to keep me warm. So, if I'm going to the grocery store or playing carpool to my kids, I am going to wear my this here kick around mink. Besides, this is my casual mink, worn for outings just like today. Best believe, when I have to go to the opera or somewhere like that, I have an array of sables, chinchillas, in the cedar closet to pick from."

That spill shut Gypsy up. A goal that many had set out to try to conquer, but only two would ever leave Gypsy speechless, and Tressa was one of them. On that note, Tressa's mission was complete.

-24-
Surprise! Surprise!
Surprise!

Close to three years back, in 95, when MCI put the long distance collect call block on Tressa's phone, Wiggles agreed to allow Taj to call her house so he could speak to Tressa.   Sometimes, he would call and Tressa wouldn't be at Wiggles, or at home when Wiggles would place a three-way call to Tressa.   In those instances, Taj would just talk to Wiggles.   Taj became intrigued with the woman that Wiggles had become, the addiction that she overcame, and especially the support Wiggles provided to his sister.   All of those things combined, made it possible for Wiggles to be able to squirm her way back into Taj's heart.

They got to know each other all over again, through letters, phone calls and then visits.   Tressa was happy for them both, because Taj needed someone to take away that coldness and emptiness out of his heart.   Besides, Tressa knew for a fact that Wiggles was the only woman her brother had ever loved.

Wiggles was happy for Tressa, as Tressa was happy for Wiggles. Wiggles called Tressa up. "I need to talk to you. It's an emergency."

Tressa rushed over. Tressa used her key to enter into Wiggles' little two-bedroom apartment. Wiggles had sat on her couch bearing a sneaky little smile.

"What's wrong?" Tressa asked, with grave concern written all over her face. This was the first time that she realized that Wiggles must have problems too. Wiggles had spoiled Tressa so much, always being the big sister, and sometimes mother figure, that she needed. So, no matter what, Tressa would be there to be Wiggles' support.

"Nothing bad, I just felt the need to give you a present." Wiggles handed her a gift bag.

Tressa pulled out the white tissue paper, and unwrapped the baby pacifier. Tressa looked at Wiggles with a bewildered look while she smiled with a big Kool Aid smile. "You mean you are having a baby?" Tressa asked confused as she could be.

"Yes." Wiggles said, almost screaming.

"Oh, my God. I am going to be an aunt!" Tressa screamed, although she didn't have the foggiest idea who the father was.

"Tressa you don't understand, no baby, you really are going to be a auntie by blood. It's Taj's baby!"

"What?" Tressa smiled, but looking at Wiggles with a crazy expression on her face.

"Remember the last family day, the boys had their championship football game? And I went by myself."

"Right." Tressa recalled.

"Well, it was packed with wall to wall people, and it was too many people for the three correctional officers they had working the room. And you know I go on a regular basis, and the same old chicks be there seeing their man and we all have become real cool. At first, we just use to talk small talk complaining about all the corruption and bullshit that the prison puts us through to get in to see our men. What at first started out as an alliance, turned into a friendship and we watched each other's back."

"OK." Tressa said, waiting for the juice to come.

216

"Well, we saw an opportunity with a crowded visiting room and we all took turns on lookout while each couple got their chance to go into the restroom and get their groove on.   Girl, and if Taj wasn't your brother, I'd give you the details." Wiggles said with a giggle and continued. "It was quick indeed, but you know that prison sperm is some powerful stuff!"

Tressa hugged Wiggles, feeling so happy that she was going to finally be an aunt. There was one thing Tressa had to remind Wiggles of on a more serious note.

"Wiggles, I know that you don't smoke cigarettes around me or the boys because you know I hate cigarette smoke. But you gotta stop, at least until after you have the baby.

"I will, I know I got to for the sake of this baby.   I won't smoke, trust me."

-25-
All Hell Breaks Loose

News traveled fast that Tressa was on the "come-up" financially. When rumors got to Lucky, he was outraged. Especially, when he saw the engagement announcement in the local newspaper. Lucky was sick of this New Yorker and he had to be dealt with. See, there was an unspoken hostility between a lot of New Yorkers and Richmond guys. The Richmond guys automatically hated New York guys, mostly because New Yorkers in the drug game came down to Richmond and set up shop. They have a cheaper product so they take the Richmond drug dealer's clientele. And, not only do they take the customers, but they take their women too.

In most of these type of cases, there are two kinds of New York guys, the one who foolishly thinks, that since he's from up north, that the people down south are slow and can be taken advantage of. So, they sleep on the Southerners, and most of the time, these are the ones going back to New York in a body bag. Then, there's the New Yorker who knows he's an out-of-towner, and instead of him constantly trying to insult a Southerner's intelligence with that "city slicker" mentality, he thinks long term. Instead of trying to beat them, he joins them. He becomes the supplier with a good quality product with a slightly lower price. So, nobody loses. He gets what he wants, and plenty of it, and so does the Southerner. At the end of the day, everybody is happy and there is peace. These are usually the ones who have longevity in the out of town drug hustling game. This is the type that Indie was.

Indie was well respected throughout the town. He gave respect and played fair with anybody who crossed his path, as long as they didn't bring shadiness to the table. If they did, Indie had no problem dealing with them and nipping it in the bud. Since Indie played the game with the highest morals and principles, he didn't have many problems. In addition, Indie wasn't the limelight, gleam, glitz and glam type of guy. He appeared to look like an ordinary guy, although he was extraordinary. Keeping in mind, that he just wasn't about Indie anymore, he had welcomed three other people in his life now. So, with all of that being taken into consideration, Indie kept his drug transactions to a bare minimum, slowly winging himself from that lifestyle to a family man.

Lucky knew that he had to eliminate Indie from the equation. He was determined to remove anybody that Tressa loved from her life as punishment for leaving him.

Lucky watched from across the street while Indie sat in Gator's barbershop getting his haircut. They all sat in the barbershop laughing and joking on when Wiggles' belly was going to finally protrude out like a normal pregnancy. It was hard for her to accept that her belly had grown so much in the past few months since she stopped getting high, she had faithfully done sit-ups for the past few years to get it down. She was grateful that she wasn't showing a lot, but at the same time, happy that this time her stomach growth would result in the birth of a baby girl in three more months. They all surrounded Wiggles and felt as the baby moved. Wiggles waited for Tressa at the barbershop, they had agreed to meet to go get the things Wiggles needed for her baby shower.

Tressa called to tell Wiggles she was running late. "Hey, big belly."

"Hey Tress, where the heck you at with ya late self?"

"Girl, I'm not late, you're just early, as always. But I'm going to be a lil late. Sorry, but please hold tight."

"I'm good, my brother-in-law and cousin-in-law is over here taking good care of me."

"OK, I'll see you in a little while."

"OK, bye," Wiggles said, as she hung up the phone.

Tressa called the barber shop right back to speak to Wiggles. "Look, are you trying to tell me something?"

"What?" Wiggles asked, not having a clue what Tressa was talking about.

"You said bye to me, and bye means forever."

"No, I didn't." Wiggles raised her voice.

"Oh, OK. Maybe I heard you wrong then, but sister always know I love you regardless of what."

"Same here sister, you know I'd die for you right."

"I know."

"I'll see you later."

Once Wiggles hung up the phone, she walked next door to the Jamaican restaurant and ordered some curry goat. She had just finished eating her food, when Gator glanced at the clock and made the announcement, alerting the patrons of the barbershop that there is no parking between 4 p.m. and 6 p.m.

"It's five till four. Anybody parked on the street, you need to move your car because the tow truck will be through here in a minute."

Indie was in the barber chair getting his hair cut and he threw his keys at Wiggles, "go move my car and make sure you roll the windows all da way up."

Wiggles strolled out to Indie's car, and once she got in, she spotted the cartons of Newport cigarettes that lay across the backseat. Since hustling cigarettes were Indie's first hustle, it never mattered how much money Indie had now, he'd always keep cigarettes in his car. Although most people thought he smoked, since he always had them in his possession, but Indie never smoked anything. For some reason, he kept them for people he came into contact who did. When Wiggles saw all the cigarettes, she felt like a kid in a candy shop, as well as opportunity. Once she pulled away from the barbershop, a light bulb went off in her head when she saw an opened pack of cigarettes laying in between the two seats near the gearshift that rested in the floor. The open pack made her realize that there was a way she could have a cigarette and nobody would ever know. Nobody counted how many cigarettes they had in an opened pack, so this was her chance to finally take a drag.

221

Wiggles, not even thinking twice, took three cigarettes out of the pack and took a long walk around the block and smoked the cigarettes. They tasted a little funny, but she wrote it off as nothing unusual because she hadn't had a cigarette since she found out she was carrying Taj's baby. Before going back into the barbershop, she stopped in the Bath and Body Works store and put some lotion on her arms and sprayed some of the tester body mist on her to cover up the scent of the cigarettes. She knew if Tressa smelled any indication of cigarettes on her, she'd have to deal with her and Taj.

On her way back into the barbershop, she kept losing vision, but she too wrote this off as having the three cigarettes back to back, so she didn't want to mention it to any of the fellas in the shop. Instead, she sat quietly in the back of the shop carrying on general conversation with Indie. Then all of a sudden, diarrhea set in. While Wiggles headed to the bathroom, she began vomiting. No one in the barbershop thought much of it because they ruled it out to be the curry goat she had gobbled down earlier. A few minutes later, Gator walked to the bathroom door to check on Wiggles because he didn't hear any sounds coming from the bathroom.

"You a'ight in there?" Gator asked.

There wasn't any response as he knocked and knocked. So he shook the cheap lock on the door. With a few aggressive shakes, the lock on the door automatically popped undone. Gator opened the door, only to see Wiggles lying on the floor. He felt her pulse, it was weak and thin, rapidly alternating. Wiggles lay there, her muscle power weak, which prevented her from moving, as her muscle strength completely deteriorated. Her sight was gone completely, but her mind remained clear until she took her last breath. Fighting with all her might, while trying to tell them, "tell Tressa I am sorry. I smoked three cigarettes." All she could think about the last minutes of her life was letting Tressa down. As the ambulance arrived, and barged through the door of the barbershop, Wiggles took her last breath. The paramedics pronounced her dead at the scene.

The coroner arrived, but with the sight of the police, he knew they'd want to ask questions. As much as he wanted to, but taking into consideration the police's knowledge of Indie's checkered past, Indie wasn't hanging around. Indie snuck out quietly through the back entrance. Indie called Tressa to try to redirect her route away from the barbershop, this was a scene Tressa did not need to see. However, Indie was too late. As Tressa turned onto the street where the barbershop is located, she saw all the police cars and yellow tape surrounding the barbershop. She didn't even bother to park correctly and sprinted over to the barbershop. Once she approached the scene, one officer reminded her it was a crime scene and that nobody was allowed to go in. She spotted Gator heading over to her, and just then her cell phone rang. Relieved to see Gator, she answered the phone and all she heard was Lucky's voice singing the Boys To Men song, "It's So Hard To Say Goodbye To Yesterday."

Lucky burst into laughter. "This is the song that you better get somebody to sing at your boyfriend's funeral. I told you that anybody you love I'm going to zap them right out of your life, by any means! Sorry, I didn't let you say goodbye to that sucker! Oh, by the way, didn't you always say, tobacco kills!"

When Lucky went into his chant again, *"It's so hard to say goodbye to yesterday,"* for the last time, Tressa just hung up on him before he could finish. She looked across the street only to see Lucky sitting in his car blowing smoke.

Tressa was sure that Lucky didn't know what he was talking about, because she had just talked to Indie only five minutes ago. Gator broke the news to her that it was Wiggles who had died. Tressa broke down screaming, fighting and crying hysterically.

Tressa loved Wiggles like the sister she never had. Wiggles had been her backbone, her support, and her inspiration. Wiggles gave Tressa the will to keep her head up, to keep striving, to keep rising to the top and the person she leaned on most, the woman who would bear her brother's first child was gone! Dead and never to return, she couldn't be brought back. She had survived a severe addiction, but with death, there was no taking back.

Tressa felt like she was having a nervous breakdown, but she held her composure to make it through the funeral, with the support of Missy, Gator and Indie.

She felt she had no choice, but to be strong for her brother, who had lost the love of his life and the unborn child that he had been anticipating. The state allowed Taj to attend the funeral since he had done almost the majority of his time. He was still in shackles and handcuffs, and accompanied by two prison guards with loaded shotguns. It took everything in Tressa to bite her tongue when she observed Wiggles' family members obscene and phony behavior. They were falling out, sobbing, hollering and screaming like they were really sad she was gone. When in reality, Wiggles had been dead to them long before now. None of them had even seen her in years since they disowned her when she started using drugs.

Tressa sat at the burial ground watching Wiggles' family put on a show, and she thought to herself, *I wonder why they are carrying on like that? Is it because they feel guilty within their own selves? So, them coming here with the drama makes them feel better. Well, the motherfuckers need to feel rotten! Now they want to cry when she is in the ground, when they should have been crying tears of pain when she was out there on drugs, or should've been crying tears of joy when she was delivered from her addiction. It's so funny how we all make a big deal when somebody dies. Why do we do that? When people are here on earth with us, we shouldn't spend so much time being negative, bickering back and forth or just taking somebody we truly love for granted. We should always remember that none of us are promised tomorrow.*

224

-26-
From Bad to Worse

Through an autopsy performed on Wiggles' body, the Medical Examiner's Office concluded that she was poisoned with hemlock. Hemlock is a poisonous plant, but the stem and leaves, when dried and ground up, are its deadliest form. Quail are the only living objects that are immune to hemlock, but the flesh of a quail, which has eaten hemlock, can cause death if eaten by someone else.

Putting hemlock in a cigarette is something only a smart, desperate jackass like Lucky will do. Killing with hemlock was a plan that he had indeed put a lot of thought into. As far as Lucky knew, he had succeeded, nobody told him different. There was not even a second thought of regret when he saw the body, covered with a white sheet, come out of the barbershop.

Just in coincidence, the same night that Wiggles was killed, an unidentified man's body was found in the same area of town. These things combined, confirmed that his mission to kill Indie was accomplished. With Indie out of the way, Lucky balled out of control and continued the routine of his everyday life.

Indie knew that the poisonous cigarettes were meant for him and not Wiggles. Indie laid low until he decided when and how he wanted to deal with Lucky. He never made his presence known. Instead, he studied Lucky's

225

every move. The most amusing part was Lucky never realized he was being watched.

Lucky's hangout was the "Red Light Club", which was the only strip club Richmond had for blacks. Mostly all the ballers hung out there, and Lucky was a regular. He had done a lot of his transactions there. This particular night was packed to capacity. The club's owner had brought in some out of town girls. With new faces, and much booty to be viewed, the men flocked in from every section of town, Northside, Southside, West end, Church Hill and Jackson Ward. Lucky made so much money that night, selling his weight like it was no tomorrow. Things were booming for him. There were so many ballers running over to Lucky, coming from the front, the back, left and right. Some only paid admission to get in, to handle business with Lucky. The night was almost over, and all he had was two ounces of heroine on him. He wanted to get rid of them before the night was over, which should not have been too hard, with all the people he was having interactions with.

Lucky was always a big spender, and he and his boys always fought over who would pay for the Moet that night. Moet, at that time, was the most expensive champagne that was sold in the clubs in Richmond.

A light skinned, petite waitress, wearing nothing but some red fur thongs, walked over to Lucky's table and placed the bucket of Moet on the table. "Compliments of the gentleman over there in the black suit."

Lucky smiled and looked over in the direction, and he choked up the champagne, because he thought, no he was certain, he saw a ghost. It was Indie holding his glass up for a toast, and on his face, was a big-pasted Joker smile. Lucky shook his head to make sure he wasn't seeing things. When he realized that it was Indie in the flesh, Lucky drunk his drink, and started snatching his homeboys drinks to gulp down too. Lucky begin to sweat, of all nights, he didn't have his pistol on him. It was a different security guard searching everybody, and he couldn't tip him to let him in with his gun.

Lucky didn't know what to think or how to play his cards at this time. How the hell is this nigga sitting over there? *SHIT, what the fuck I am gonna do? Damn I know how this nigga roll. I know one of us gotta go, and shit it ain't going to be me. This nigga gotta die tonight. To fucking night!!* Lucky took a deep breath, and wiped the balls of sweat off of his face, when one thing dawned on him. *This nigga can't know that hemlock shit was for him. Shit, I know if I knew a nigga was trying to poison me, I wouldn't spend nay dime on no damn champagne. Hell no, so he can't know what time it is. Let me go over here and feel this joker out. I mean ain't neither one of us got no guns, so what the fuck, I got twenty niggas in here deep. What the worst that can happen? Me and this nigga get the rumbling? Twenty to one, this nigga is a dead man. We will stampede his ass in here. Half of these niggas in here can't stand New York niggas either? Please I'm going over here to pop some shit to this joker.*

Lucky went over to Indie's table. "Well, well, well, you the last nigga I expected to be sending me some Mo."

Indie smiled. "I'm sure you're surprised to find out your chemical skull missle missed me, huh?"

Lucky's heart dropped for a minute. "Man what you talking 'bout? I know you ain't beefing with me over no bitch."

Ignoring Lucky's comment, although he wanted to murder Lucky right there on the spot. He knew he couldn't lose his cool, not inside of the club with all the witnesses. "You Sudaam Husseim himself, too bad your missle hit innocent bystanders. You a big ole' man."

"Oh, you talking shit ma'fucka." Lucky said, pointing to Indie.

Indie's smile never left his face. "Just letting you know you've made a war, by missing your target, civilians got killed by friendly fire. You a Big Man, Big Ole' Lucky."

I'm not fucking up my new suit beating the brakes off of this joker ass nigga. We just gonna shoot this shit outside. Shit, the nigga gotta get to his car to get to his gun.

"Ok nigga, since you done declared war, make me know we at war, sucker?"

"Don't worry, I got you. Believe that. I give you my word on that." Indie didn't blink, or show one ounce of emotion, only continued to sip on his drink.

Lucky hopped up from the table, hoping that Indie would follow him outside where they could shoot it out.

227

While Lucky was heading to the door, he was approached by a dude he had dealt with earlier that night. Lucky, without hesitation, reached down in his Versace slung shot briefs under his balls, grabbed the bag, and in a matter of seconds, the exchange was made. Continuing his stride to exit the club he looked back and he saw Indie and the new security guard, walking behind him laughing. He could tell by the body language between them, that the dude wasn't just a bouncer, he was indeed Indie's man.

Lucky continued his stride and bumped into a stripper. "Hey Lucky, one of the girls just got here late and she said the tow truck was towing your car for parking in the lot cross da street. They just put up signs last week, warning people not to park there." Lucky almost shit on himself, as the anger and fear set in every bone in his body, knowing that he had no access to his gun.

Shit! Damn! I can't go out like this! Lucky thought until he saw Motor. *I know that nigga got a gun in his car sho nuff, but damn, I'm gonna have to kill him too because he talk to much, but shit at least this nigga be killed too.*

He walked up on Motor who was talking to two girls and whispered in his ear, "look man, I need ya gun. I got beef wit a nigga in here and I think he strapped."

Motor nodded, he went outside ahead of Lucky, told Lucky to give him a few minutes and he'll be waiting right outside of the door. Motor went outside only to find out his car was towed too. Lucky borrowed one of the stripper's car and knew he had to get the hell up out of dodge and deal with this later. Lucky, with his heart in his drawers, walked out of the door, with Indie not too far behind him.

As soon as Lucky hit the pavement on the sidewalk, out of nowhere, the feds rushed him with warrants for his arrest. This was the last thing Lucky was expecting. With the lifestyle that Lucky lived, just about everyday he heard about someone getting locked up, but for some reason, he never thought it could happen to him. He felt untouchable, but for some reason, he felt relieved. He thought that this was one time the police was on time. They saved his life because he was going to be murdered that night.

Believe it or not, big, bad, prankster, killer, slaughter, drug-dealing Lucky, "cracked up at the pick up". Once he was inside of the Tahoe that the feds placed him in, before they drove away from the club, he was negotiating a deal with the feds.

The first person he sold out was Indie. Other than the vibe he got from Indie, he didn't have any concrete information on him. That didn't stop him, Lucky lied and made up vivid stories, just to get an investigation going on Indie. Lucky was sure that behind closed doors, there were plenty of skeletons waiting to be pulled out of Indie's closet. Why wouldn't there be?   He was a dude from New York, here in Richmond hustling. Most dudes that come down from New York, come down here for one of a few reasons: Either they were no where, had nothing going on and were knocked down from their position up top, so they come to Richmond for a new beginning with a product that's plentiful and dirt cheap on the streets of New York. If street life was the desire, then they'd have a promising future down south.

Then there's the other reason why many New Yorkers hustlers migrate to the South.   They had maximized their hand in New York, got a lot of money, got caught up in a sticky situation, became wanted by the law and decided the law would have to catch him.   So, they come to the south and continue to foolishly live flamboyant lifestyles, merely picking up where they left off.   While others lay back, and enjoy the ride from the background.

Indie tried to play the background and live happily ever after, but Lucky threw salt in the game. Indie knew he had to leave town for a while, and he had to do it tonight. Before he left, he swung by Tressa's house. He knew he was taking a risk, so he arrived in woman's clothing in case the feds were staking out Tressa's house. He didn't know how to explain it to her, but he knew she'd understand.

He held her hand and explained everything to her about what happened that night at the club.

"Look baby, I swear on everything I love, this is the hardest thing I ever had to do."

Tressa looked into Indie's tear filled eyes, which revealed hurt and pain. Although she didn't know what was going on, tears immediately began to roll down her face. He wiped her tears, "listen baby, that bitch ass nigga Lucky, is putting the police on me. I know it's just a matter of time before they come. I love you so much, and as a man, I don't

229

want to put you or the boys in any kind of danger. So, for the time being, I've got to go under."

Tressa tried to be strong, but she couldn't. The tears would not stop, he hugged her and tried to comfort her as she whimpered. He held her tight and continued to wipe the snot away from her nose as she cried. She was angry, mad and hurt. Once she got herself together, she told him, "take us with you then."

"Baby, I can't have you and the boys with me while I'm on the run. I can't have you being an accessory or aiding and abiding a fugitive. I need you here on the home front, taking care of my boys.

"I hate that you have to go, but I understand that you gotta go, I really do understand." She said, shaking her head, while wiping her tears from her eyes.

It was hard for Indie to let go of her hand. "Baby, I promise you, I will hold your hand like this one day. I promise you that."

Tressa shook her head in agreement. "Baby, I love you so much. Please just get all this straightened, out. I will be here waiting on you, I promise."

After giving her some money to hold her over for the next few months, his last words to her were, "look baby, I promise I will be back. And for every tear you cry, I'll replace them with diamonds. I love you so much."

He hopped on I-95 and headed south in his "Plain-Jane" Mustang convertible. Before he was quite outside of Richmond, he realized that he needed to give the boys something to remind them of him. He turned around, and when he approached Tressa's street, the feds were all over Tressa's house. He knew she was safe. He was certain that they were looking for him, he wasn't there and neither was anything illegal.

-27-
The High Speed Chase

Indie, reflecting on a saying that his mother told him as a child, he could hear her voice just as plain as day. "Boy, what you do in the dark will come to light. Keep on keeping all those skeletons in the closet, they're sure going to come falling out when you least expect it." His mother's warnings were all flashing through his head, especially when he heard his name and saw his picture plastered all over the television on "America's Most Wanted". Though shocked, but not surprised, he knew this day would come. He just anticipated that he'd be out of the country before this day arrived.

I'm not tripping because I only have about a hundred miles before I reach the Florida Keys, and I'll be home free. Shoot, I hope Reka don't mess this up. She ain't never slipped before, so I don't even know why I am tripping thinking she'll leave me for dead.

Just then his pager went off, he looked at it and all he saw was "800", which when the pager was held upside down, it looked like "BOO". He smiled and knew it was Tressa sending him a message, letting him know that she was thinking of him. He put the pager down in the console of the car, and as soon as he did, it went off again. He swerved a little and boy, was that little mistake blown out of proportion.

A Florida State Trooper, trying to make his ticket quota saw him, and automatically put the blue lights on Indie. Indie knew he wasn't getting caught. He had come

231

too far to just turn himself in. He pulled over to the side of the highway, and as soon as the police got out of the car and came up beside and approached the car, Indie sped off giving himself a two-minute head start on the police.

As he pulled off laughing, he got excited when the thought sunk in that he'd be able to try out his new toy, as well as get his money's worth out of his $50,000 investment, his black Mustang 5.0. While the other guys were busy installing televisions, DVD players, 24-inch rims and a booming system, Indie was thinking for the future. He took the basic 5.0 Ford Mustang, brand new off the showroom floor, and tricked it out for predicaments, especially like these. He went to an old country boy, Secret. Secret wanted to be called "Secret" because his whole identity was a Secret. Secret lived like a hermit back in the deep woods of North Carolina, and he too, was on the run and knew every in and out about a getaway vehicle. His whole existence was to beat the police. All he did all day was gather info on the newest street vehicles and used that information to enhance his own. Secret was forever indebted to Indie, and owed Indie his life, so the limited times that Indie ever needed anything, Secret came to his aid. So, the first thing Secret did, was lower the suspension to the ground to keep it steady on the street, while the oversized tires made it stick to the road, making them both go hand and hand. The turbo charger boosted the horsepower from 290 to 490. Indie didn't feel it was enough, because he was well aware of the technology of some of the modern police cruisers, so to be on the safe side, he added 150 shot of NOS to add another 150-horse power.

For Indie's protection, Secret installed a flip license tag to flip-flop the license tags from Maryland to Texas with just the hit of a button. It was Indie's idea to get Secret to mount a spotlight behind the license plate. This enabled Indie to hit a code on the radio, when the tag folded down and the spotlight would blind everyone behind him preventing them from seeing him.

The trooper called in for back up. In a matter of minutes, there was about 30 police cars chasing him and this really got his adrenaline flowing. He was most intrigued, because not one of his of illegal devices failed him. Right when he thought he had lost one of them, here comes another one trailing him. With this being the first time Indie ever used the tricked out devices, he crashed three different times, but was able to maintain the control over the car to keep it moving.

The chase finally ended in the Florida Everglades. The Everglades is a national park in the southern region of Florida. It is mostly known for the swampy land and hungry alligators. Taking into consideration, its clumps of tall grass, numerous branching waterways, quicksand and maneating gators, this is no place for a city boy and especially not a New Yorker. But what the troopers didn't know, is Indie wasn't the average city slicker. He was off the Indian reservation, and though his dad left him at a young age, he had unusual survivor and wilderness skills.

The state troopers were furious that Indie had made them the laughing stock of the media coverage, so they had no choice but to form a manhunt. The manhunt for Indie included plenty of bloodhounds, boats and helicopters circling the swamp, and they were closing in from all directions, the north, south, east and west. All of a sudden the search came to an end when the cops heard about twenty gunshots, Pow! Pow! Pow! Pow! Pow! Pow! Pow! Pow! Pow! Pow! Pow! Pow! Pow! Pow! Pow! Pow! Pow! They zeroed in on the location. When they get there, all they found was a bloody crime scene. There were two alligators, one dead and the other badly wounded. Then there were other gators in the swamp voraciously devouring what was left of Indie.

None of them would dare to try to stop the gators, by any means, from devouring Indie's body. The troopers saw his body surface twice, before rolling under the water. By the time they blocked off the crime scene, hoping to preserve what evidence wasn't contaminated, all they found was Indie's DNA all over the dead gator's nose and all across the ground where they observed that he had been dragged. About six feet away, was his chrome 9mm with his fingerprints all over it, some swatches of his jeans and his wallet baring his ID and three credit cards.

Even though a couple of cops went on record saying they saw Indie's body being taken under by the alligators, it still took Indie's loved ones twenty months to finally receive a death certificate. Therefore, no one could collect any money from insurance policies in which they were the named beneficiary.

-28-
Empty Hearted

Once word reached back to Tressa, she was heartbroken, but she was not surprised. *Why would I expect to live happily ever after? My luck has never been that good. It's just never been in the cards for me. I believe there is a bad spell over me. I hate that damn Lucky, he meant it when he said, he was going to take everybody out of my life. Shit, might as well say he killed Indie too, because had Lucky not ran his mouth to the Feds, Indie would still be here with me. Now, Lucky is a shoot em' up, bang-bang type of guy, and as soon as he got put under pressure, he sung like a canary. And all that weight they caught on Lucky, he got nerve to be out already walking the same streets. I really try to look on the bright side of things. They say when God takes one thing out of your life, he replaces it with something else. When Taj was taken away, I was given Wiggles. My mother was removed out of my life so many years ago, and then eventually, I lost her permanently, but now I have been blessed with Indie's mother, Beulah, who has embraced me, as one of her own. Although, she can never replace my mother or Indie, her being here with me makes me feel close to both of them.*

Tressa really took Indie's death hard. The pain for her was escheating. Not only was she experiencing being hurt mentally, but she hurt psychically. The chest pains would never stop, not to mention the constant pain in her heart, it was like a knife stabbing through it. She started getting puffy eyes from crying too much, then the puffy eyes turned to bags under her eyes, because of her lack of sleep. Falling to sleep was hard for her because she often dreamed about Indie, and the dreams would be so true that when she woke up, looked on his side of the bed, and saw he wasn't there. She'd tell herself that he must have gotten up to use the bathroom or maybe was in the kitchen. It was taking him to long to come back to bed, so she would get up and search the house. Then reality sinks in, and she realizes Indie is dead and never coming back. So she start sleeping in short spurts, so she wouldn't or couldn't dream but sometimes from being so fatigued, she'd fall off into a deep sleep and feel like she's hugging him, but it's just the pillow. So, she stopped sleeping with any pillows at all.

Tressa began wondering should she move out of the house and start over. Then she couldn't, because the memories of him are very much there and an important part of her life.

Anything could trigger her depression. Every little thing reminded her of Indie, she'd hear one of the raggae songs, or any song for that matter, that Indie listened to. Sometimes when it was 7:00, usually the time Indie got home, she'd keep looking out of the window, hoping he'd come. He never came and it was always a constant disappointment when he didn't. She'd feel the wind blowing a certain way, she wondered if it was him coming to visit. When his birthday came, she'd wondered what he would've looked like, and what they would have done.

Tressa even contemplated suicide. *Will this pain ever go away? Maybe I should take my own life, but will I go to heaven or hell? If I go to hell, then I won't be there with him. What would my children do? Am I even any good to them right now? I can't take my life, because I have them to live for.*

Tressa started questioning her religious beliefs, *God, why did you take him,* was always a question that she seemed to ask God everyday. Then it came to the point where she was bargaining with God. *God, please I will give up everything for you to bring him back. God, I will give up this house and move to the projects. Just anything, just bring him back God. God, why can't I be happy? God, why did*

236

you even bring him into my life, if you were going to take him away? God, if this is your will, please send me some answers why?

Then there was Missy, Tressa's only friend, she tried to be there for Tressa, but there was no way she could possibly understand the heartache Tressa was going through. She became withdrawn from Missy. At times, she got angry with Missy because she had a man.

Everybody told her she had to let go, so she started keeping it a secret when she would visit Indie's gravesite. Truthfully, the grave was the only place she felt close to Indie. She'd feel guilty when she had to leave.

Every decision that had to be made, she second guessed herself, and the questions that she always asked herself was, "what would Indie do if he was here? What would he want me to do? Am I doing the right thing?"

Tressa still had the kids to think about, what would she tell them. She had to be strong for them, of course they didn't understand what death meant. She had never experienced anything, like this, so she didn't know what to say, and she didn't want to say the wrong thing to get to the children all upset too.

To try to lift herself up, she'd try to focus on everything, but herself. For a few hours it would work, but then in the middle of the day and the phone would ring, and it wasn't Indie. The pain would start all over again. She'd run into the bathroom and burst into tears. Once she was all cried out, she'd pat water on her face to try to pull herself together.

Then there was the hate for Lucky, she wished every type of accident could happen to him. It actually scared her when she thought of the things she'd do to him, and would not have one ounce of remorse for him, if she ever got the opportunity. There was not a day that went by when she thought about simply turning in the evidence to the police that she had in the safe deposit box from the murders of Peako and the girl. The only thing that kept her from turning it in is that she didn't want to betray her brother and go against the grain, but a few things she came to grips with. He will have to understand my position. She knew it was no turning back at this point, she didn't want any of the money that crime stoppers paid, she just wanted the satisfaction of getting Lucky out of her life so he wouldn't hurt anyone else she dearly loved.

Tressa got a letter from her brother telling her that he was going to be released. Although she considered it good news, she knew that all hell was about to break loose. Anticipating his immediate release kind of lifted her out of her depression a little. Tressa had been looking forward to this day she had been saving, preparing for his arrival. Although she gave her brother five hundred dollars so he could buy himself a couple of things and hoped the money would hold him over until he was able to get himself a job. It wasn't good enough, he simply told her, "If you have been out here ten years and all you got is $500.00 to give me, then you need it more than me."

This hurt her like a sharp knife because her brother wasn't even the brother that she knew. He had become so bitter, acting as if the world owed him for the ten years he was locked away from society. The same day he was released, she found out her brother was on the same corner he got busted on slinging drugs. When she heard the rumor, she went to look for Taj, she had to see it with her own eyes. Tressa found out the rumors couldn't be any more true, she had hoped they were false. He was selling drugs, which was a hard pill to swallow, because she knew that he too would be snatched away from her again and thrown back into jail. Regardless of the fact that he was selling drugs, he was still her brother and practically her only family. She vowed that she'd be there for him, but at the same time, she couldn't get used to the idea of him being on the street.

It didn't take Taj long to get his money and was right back. Once his money was right, Taj had become so flamboyant with trying to play "catch-up", after being gone for so long, he didn't realize that times had changed.

He had girls lined up from coast to coast. Women had never been a problem for him. The saying, "the blacker the berry the sweeter the juice", must have been made especially for Taj. Taj was a fine, downtown brown complexioned brother with full lips. His hair had permanent waves in it, which were embedded by a prison wave cap. His physique was something to write home about, the 500 sit-ups and pushups had paid off. The reaction from the women went straight to his head. It's sad to say, he didn't realize the things he could do in the late 1980's, he couldn't do in 2001. He had to learn the hard way, when he had to call upon his sister to do his dirty work.

"Hey Sugar, I need you to go to the pharmacy to pick up my prescription."

"What's wrong with you?"

"Some chick got me, my dick is dripping like running water. It's killing me. I got a prescription at CVS, but I'm too embarrassed to show my face in there to go get it. I'll pay you to go get it." He said, pleading.

"What is wrong with you sticking your damn dick in any and everything?" Tressa asked, while hitting him on the arm like a mother scolding her son.

"Look, I'm just trying to make me some babies, that's all. You know I want kids more than anything." Taj told Tressa and she understood totally.

"Damn, can you find you a nice girlfriend or a wife first? Shoot, I shouldn't go get nothing. You better be lucky I have to get some personal items." She said, snatching the money for Taj's prescription.

She went to get his prescription, but then her depression started back up, on the way over to the pharmacy. She thought about how this time, it was just something that could be healed with some penicillin, but next time, would it be AIDS. Would her brother to be taken away from her too?

239

-29-
Momma's Baby, Papa's Maybe

Taj was out of control spending his money. His famous motto was "Ball until you fall". News had traveled all around town that Taj was "the man" and he was getting money out of control. Taj was so consumed with counting and spending his money, that he sidetracked and missed his appointment with his probation officer. Today was the third appointment that she had rescheduled for him. He knew he had to be there in an hour, but he had just gotten the strangest phone call from a chick he used to mess with back in the day, requesting to see him. She was a straight skeezer back then, scheming on his money. He screwed her when Wiggles was on her period. He was pretty sure that she only wanted to get back on the bandwagon again and rekindle the old flame. He told her his location and she stopped by.

At first, they talked a little small talk, until Taj wanted to cut to the chase. "Look, what you need to holler at me about? I got somewhere I got to be and, straight up, if you ain't trying to give up no ass, you are wasting my damn time. Now, you dropping them drawers or what?"

At that very moment is when she dumped some mind-blowing news in his lap.

"Look Taj, I know this may come as a shock to you, but we have a son together."

"What?" Taj said laughing, but was all ears.

"No, Taj I am serious, dead serious."

"And how is that? I remember you had kids by the Old Head, the dead dude and then the professional football player. So where do I fit in?"

"Look, if you remember correctly, we was together like a week before you got locked up. When I found I was pregnant, I heard you were going to be gone for a long time. I had met Merk and he had just got a million dollar deal, so he automatically assumed it was his."

Taj was silent as a lamb and left speechless. He listened attentively as she continued. "Taj, believe me, Merk has taken care of Lil Merk so good for so many years and..."

Taj interrupted, "You mean to tell me, that for twelve years, you kept my son from me?"

"Yes. I thought it was the best thing for the baby."

"You thought lying to me about my son for twelve years was the best thing." Taj raised his voice, as he asked Gypsy. She was too afraid to utter a word to answer Taj.

"You mean to fucking tell me, all this time, I've been wanting a child and I had one."

"Well, you got one now." Gypsy spoke up, and said with no shame.

"Bitch, you are acting like you are giving me a pair of shoes or something, we are talking about a person here!" Taj screamed, almost spitting on Gypsy, he was so close to her face. "So all this time, I have missed twelve years of this boy's life, because you felt it was best, or is it, because you are greedy as hell?"

Gypsy didn't answer him. "Answer me!" He continued to holler at her. He was furious and so close to loosing it.

Gypsy said with tears in her eyes, "You can catch up from now on. As a matter of fact, you should be glad I found a father for him. Had you stayed out here, you would have known, but instead you left me for dead. You left all the money with that junkie ass bitch Wiggles."

"Clap!" Was the loud noise that sounded when he smacked the cowboy shit out of Gypsy. He hit her so hard she stumbled and hit the floor. Taj went into a trance out of the hurt and frustration. A child was all he desired, and this low-life gold digging chicken head concealed his son from him. It was bad enough that she named his son after another dude knowing that he wasn't the father. Then she had the nerve to insult his soul mate, Wiggles, God Bless the dead! Now, she brought it all on herself and she was about to get it.

Before he knew it, he was stomping her in between her legs, and he knew God was the only person who had that type of control over him to make him stop, because Lord knows he didn't have it. Gypsy lay on the floor, almost lifeless, with her teeth laying a few inches away from her. Although she had just gotten the worst beaten in her life, it wasn't even the beating that was so detrimental. It was the truth of the words that proceeded out of Taj's mouth.

"You trifling, no good bitch! I ain't ever knock your hustle of a gold digger or sac chaser, but ya ass ain't shit, using your kids as a fucking pawn. Auctioning them off to the highest bidder."

"Using your kids as a fucking pawn, using your kids as a fucking pawn." Was all that she kept hearing, over and over again, as the room was spinning around and around. She tried to block out the truth of those words, but couldn't, because this was the first time she ever evaluated what she had been doing for so many years. Those were the words that played over and over again, even though the words that came out after that, were powerful and she knew it came from the heart.

"I hope you get AIDS and die in three days, you trifling bitch! I hope you die sucking a double jointed dick because you gonna die soon and very soon."

Taj missed his appointment with the probation officer, so he was sure he had violated his parole. Gypsy had recovered from her fractured pelvic bone and scammed some other guy, she perceived as a sucker, to give her money to have her teeth replaced and in exchange, she'd put his car in her name since he didn't have a license. She pushed the fact out of her head, that she did indeed, pawn her children in exchange for her extravagant lifestyle. Gypsy figured after she had given Taj a few weeks to get used to the idea of having Lil Merk for his son, he would be pouring money her way. She had nothing to lose, since she wasn't getting anymore of those healthy child support checks, because of Big Merk and her shared joint custody.

When she went into her shop after recovering from her beating, Taj's name was ringing around town about how he was getting money like Donald Trump. Gypsy's car had just been repossessed because times had truly gotten hard for her. She was a burnt out gold digger in this town now. People had no mercy for her when it came to providing her with rides. Her little sucker boyfriend, not answering his cell phone only pissed her off. Frustrated because her whole world was crumbling in front of her, she decided to show Taj and Mr. Lucky, her sucker boyfriend, a lesson.

Since Lucky didn't answer his phone, she felt he was ducking her. She went over to his house and had the police to meet her there. Now, Lucky who had been playing low key since Taj was home, vowed to kill Gypsy for bringing the police to his house. She showed the police the title to the car and they gladly made Lucky turn over the keys to her. Now, she had wheels to carry out the rest of her plan.

Since she was off her heels and now on wheels, she went to pick up Lil Merk, and drove him over to the drug spot where Taj was known to hang at and make his money. She rolled up and told Lil Merk, "go knock on the door and ask for Taj, and when he comes, tell him you are Lil Merk and ya momma said to watch you."

With one foot on the gas and the other one on the brake, Gypsy waited until somebody came to the door and sped off, putting the pedal to the metal, laughing and driving like a bat out of hell. *This nigga thinks he ain't going to be a father to my damn child. I guess I showed him. I wish I could have seen the expression on his face when all he saw was the car brake lights.*

Gypsy laughed until tears came to her eyes. *Now, he got to be responsible for Lil Merk, buy his clothes, and feed him, everything. I'm going to make sure he keep him for about a month, so Lil Merk can have some new clothes. That's right.*

Gypsy was so fascinated with the disgraceful, cruddy stunt she had just pulled, she didn't pay any attention to the stop sign and a dump truck hit her going 55 miles an hour. The truck dragged her car two blocks down the street. Nobody could believe that Gypsy didn't die. Some felt like she was better off dead, taking into consideration that the car accident made her a quadriplegic. With her whole body paralyzed, she could only move her eyeballs and mouth, which had to be hooked up to a respirator. She took air through a straw, which controlled pretty much everything. According to how much air she blew into the straw, controlled the movement of the wheelchair.

It was so sad that Gypsy never realized how truly rotten she was until she was paralyzed. Out of all her family and laundry list of friends she thought she had, the only person that even stepped up to the plate to take care of helpless Gypsy was, Ms. Ethel, her middle child, Pee's grandmother. It wasn't until this time, when Gypsy really regretted being a poor mother, she understood just how much her own son, Pee hated her.

Pee would push her out of the wheelchair on purpose, and leave her on the floor for hours. Pee was so mean to her. On a regular basis, he would let the air out of the tires on the wheelchair, and when his grandmother was gone, he'd urinate on her. There was not a day that went by that she wished she would have known how to be a better mother to her children.

In spite of all the dirt throwing that Gypsy had thrown over the years, Tressa went to see Gypsy at Ms. Ethel's house and got the shock of her life when she saw, Mr Ethel's dead son's pictures displayed throughout the living room. She was in shock to find out that Ms. Ethel's son was Peako. Tressa looked into Gypsy's eyes as she thought, *it's so funny how this no good bitch is connected to me in all kinds of ways. First, she has a baby by my brother, which makes her my nephew's mother. Not to mention she was messing with Lucky and Lucky was the same person that killed her other baby's daddy. And Peako, died because he was helping me out. Richmond is really too small. The saying, everybody knows everybody here, couldn't be any truer.*

Tressa wanted to express one thing to Gypsy. "Look, I want to get custody of my nephew when, and if, the police ever catches up with Taj."

Gypsy just blew into the straw to agree.

-30-
Joy Comes in the Morning

"**H**ey Reka, I don't mean to call you so much, but girl I just miss your brother so much! And I ain't gay or nothing, but talking to you makes me feel a little closer to him." Tressa stressed to Indie's sister while they were on the phone.

"Girl, I understand, my brother loved you so much."

Ding, Ding, Dong, Ding, Ding, Dong, Tressa's doorbell sounded. "Hold on girl, let me get my door." Tressa looked out the window, before going to the door.

"It's Airborne Express." A person said, from the opposite side of the door.

"Girl, I wonder what they want?" Reka asked inquisitively. Probably a special notice that one of my bills is late." They both laughed, as Tressa opened the door and took the package from the man.

She read the letter; it was from the "Shed A Rainbow Foundation."

Dear Ms. Shawsdale,

We are proud to announce that you and sixty other single, devoted mothers were put into a drawing for a relaxing vacation at one of the most exclusive spas in the world, and you happen to be the winner. Enclosed you will find your tickets to an all expense paid spa getaway vacation! We will need you to confirm within the next 48 hours. Please call 1-800-444-5555.

Tressa had doubts that this was all too good to be true. Reka convinced her to go. Missy agreed to watch the boys while Tressa was away on the trip.

Tressa's flight to St. Barts was long and tiring. All she wanted to do when she got into her exquisite suite, was to take a long candlelight bubble bath and go to sleep. Her pampering would start in the morning.

Laying in the tub with bubbles all around her, she let the warmth of the water soothe her body, candles burning, soft music playing. She didn't hear him open the bathroom door, but sensed his presence. She slowly opened her eyes and there he was. She couldn't believe her eyes, was this a dream come true? Although some of his physical appearances had been altered, it was Indie back from the dead. He had some light brown contact lenses to change the color in his eyes, and it was apparent that he had some cosmetic surgery. He just stood there looking into her eyes, and damn he was so fine, so sexy, her bronze God.

She wanted to get out of the tub and rush to embrace him. There weren't any words to be exchanged, at least, not right now. Letting a soft moan escape her lips, she beckoned him to join her. She watched him remove every stitch of clothing, licking her lips and wanting to devour every inch of him.

He eased down in the tub facing Tressa, as tears of joy rolled down her face. Indie opened his lips to speak, but she silenced him by putting her finger against his lips. Soaping the luffa sponge, she began rubbing it across his shoulders, down his chest, letting her fingers gently scrape across his nipples, never letting her eyes leave his. Tressa could hear the sharp intake of his breath, as her hands slid down his muscular stomach, knowing if she went a little further down, she would find his magic stick! Moving closer, she wrapped her legs around his waist, her arms around his neck and looked deeply in his big brown eyes. Tressa's breast pressed tightly against his chest, hearing him whisper in her ear, "baby, I missed you so much. I love you, need you and want you."

Tressa begin whispering back, "Oh baby, I'm going to give it to you so good."

Tressa took control, stepping out of the tub and extending her hand to help him. She proceeded to dry him off slowly with her tongue, making a trail down his stomach, kissing, licking and feeling his body tremble. Looking up at him, she took his hardness in her hands. Indie really had it going on in that department!

When I'm done with him, I am going to make sure he'll never leave me again.

She began slowly stroking his cock from the base and gently squeezing his tip, feeling the drops of his nectar oozing out. Licking her lips, kneeling slowly, making the tip of her tongue hard to catch the drops of his pre-cum, she felt him buckle trying to balance himself.

She slowly opened her mouth, sucking him deeper and pausing. Tressa surprised herself as she was arched her neck preparing to bring the brotha home. Tressa's hands were caressing his ass, pulling, urging him to make love to her mouth, picking up good rhythm up and down, back and forth, dipping down caressing his balls with her tongue, slowly taking turns sucking one, then the other, in her mouth humming, kissing and licking the length of his cock, taking the tip between her lips and letting her tongue dance across the head of it. She felt like she had conquered him when could hear him pleading, "Sugar pleaseeeeeeeeeee!" Releasing him from her lips, Tressa lead him to the bedroom, motioning for him to lie down. She slowly climbed on top of him rubbing her body against his, feeling his strong hands squeezing her ass, motioning for her, urging her. She was fully aware of what he wanted, but her intent was for him to watch and learn what he had been missing. Keeping complete body contact, by giving him a sensual massage, her hands circling his shoulders, his chest, and a tap on each of his nipples with long firm strokes, with teasing circles, kissing and nibbling at his chest, Indie could not resist. He was mesmerized.

Straddling his legs, her hair falling around her face, her hands slowly caressing his body, mouthing the words, "baby, I missed you". She cupped his cock with her hand, putting his cock between her pussy lips, letting his cock massage her wetness. He stroked himself the entire length of her cock, gently rising just a bit, slowly easing his cock in her pussy feeling her body tense, squeezing his cock tightly with her pussy muscles. He wanted more, but she teased him, taking his cock out, smiling, and again, resuming her firm strokes. She slid the head in deeper until she could squeeze farther down his cock, feeling him so deep. Neither couldn't hold back any longer, and they both knew it. She began moving my her slowly, in a circular motion, closing her eyes her hips began moving as if they had a mind of they're own.

Hair wildly falling around Tressa's face, her breast bouncing up and down, at any moment they were both going to reach limits neither had ever explored. He began grabbing her full hips and pulling her deeper, harder onto his big hard cock Knowing their moment was near, she opened her eyes to stare into his, her body tensing, the grimace on his face telling her he's ready to fill her love nest. His hands spanking her butt. "Oh, my God." She screamed

"Baby, I missed you so much, I love you."

"I love you too." She said while working her pussy harder, faster over his cock, and then, he lets out this deep growl, holding her so tight. Her coochie was squeezing his dick milking, wanting and needing every last drop of his sweet love juice.

After the sex they lay there, with tears in her eyes, happy tears and tears of intense sex with the man she loved.

Once the shock of the passionate lovemaking and him actually being there in her arms wore off, the questions started to roll in, she sat up in the bed. "Indie where have you been? I thought you were dead? How did you get away? I'm glad you're here. I love you so much. I miss you. How did you do it? Please tell me everything. Why didn't you call? I can't believe you had me grieving like I was, and the whole time, you chillin' on a damn island, living it up.

"No, baby, I was counting down the days that I could be with you. See, I never loved anyone like I loved you, and to be away from you and the boys, it almost killed me. But

I knew what I had to do, to make it so I could be with you and the boys."

"OK, fill me in on everything. How did you get away in the swamp? I saw all those gators on TV and nobody could survive it. Plus, officers said they saw your body go under the water."

"Well, when I was running, I purposely dropped my ID because, if I was going to die, I wanted to be able to be identified either way it went down. But when I got a few feet away from where they actually thought I was killed, it was another man there in one of the Everglade boats, in an area that was supposed to had been a restricted area. Dude on the boat agreed to give me a ride. And you know, it's always a motherfucker, that wanna experiment and do what he wanna do. So, he decided he wanted to fuck with the gators and baby, he should known better. This is real life, it ain't no Crocodile Dundee movie. It ain't no way in the world that a man can beat no gator. I told him not to fuck wit the gator, but he didn't listen. So, I saw the gator trying to kill him, so I shot one of the gators, but I couldn't stop the other gator from taking bits out of him. I even got a flesh wound from one of the gators right here in my arm." He pointed to the bite.

He could see the terror on her face. "It's looks worst then it is, but that's how the DNA probably got on the ground or whatever." He continued with the story.

"But once the police heard the gunshots, that's how they zeroed in on me. Then I hid in a log in the woods until the police left. They saw parts of his body, and since they weren't looking for anybody else or aware anybody was out there, they automatically assumed it was me, which was cool by me. It took me like almost two days to find my way out. Shit, a nigga is grateful for the survival skills my no good ass father gave me. On my way back out, I actually got bit by a snake, but I was able to take the venium out tho."

"Oh, my God." She hugged him. "Well, what did you do after you got out of there?"

"Well, I had some money in an off shore bank account here in St. Barts for an emergency and Secret had supplied me with a plastic surgeon, and a passport. I just kinda kicked back, thought alot about you and the boys. I had to make sure they gave me a death certificate before I

251

could come back, because I didn't want to have to go and face all the charges in New York and be separated from you and the boys ever again. See, I could have got out of doing the time one of two ways, the sucka way or the gangsta way. And for me, the sucka way that won't happenin'. I'd die, do life in prison before I betray the oath I took. So, I had to do the only thing a real gangsta would have done it if he had the opportunity presented to him."

"Well, are you going to go back with me?"

"Yes, but I am going to have to lay low. I don't want anybody to get any ideas.   I need you to tie up all your loose ends. Tell everybody that you can't take it there in that town, and you're moving. I bought us a house on the Florida keys."

"Well, what else did you do to pass time while you were gone?"

"Like I told you, I mostly thought about you and the boys, mapped out everything so we could be together, I read a lot. I read this book called, "A Hustler's Wife", by Nikki Turner. That book is off the hook. One of the best books I ever read, a tourist recommended it to me. I want you to read it on your way home."

"OK, somebody else was telling me about that book to, but I was so caught up in grief that I couldn't read anything."

He took her hand. "Didn't I promise you that I would be able to hold your hand again."

They cuddled, talked and made plans until day break. Indie also explained how he got away.   Tressa filled Indie in on everything, and they agreed, if and when, Taj gets caught for being on the run from his probation violation, they'd get custody of Lil Merk and let him live with them. Once they finally awoke, Indie placed a black velvet box on the pillow for Tressa. Tressa opened the box. It was a bag of diamonds. "I promised you a diamond for every tear I caused you to shed."

-31-
When the Dust Settles......

Sad to say, the paradise rendezvous was interrupted when Missy called, informing Tressa that Lucky had gotten the twins from school and she had no idea what to do. They both returned back to Richmond. Tressa was so out of her mind, that Taj gave her a valium to make her sleep. Although Taj hated Indie simply because he was a New Yorker, they both agreed to come together and join forces for the sake of the boys. They both knew with Lucky around, life was going to be a living hell. In both of their eyes, Lucky had violated their lives, one too many times, and had he to be dealt with.

Since word was out that Taj had been in hiding, Lucky came out of hiding. But this time, he had taken his pranks a little too far. They knew exactly where to look for Lucky, at the Red Light Strip Club.

After Lucky left the club, Reka followed Lucky in her car. It appeared as if she was following him too closely, because she ran into him from the back and caused a slight fender builder. She motioned for him to pull over to the side of the road off the main strip. Once he looked into his rear view mirror and saw just how attractive the lady getting out of her car was, he cut his engine off and got out of his car, not only to exchange information with her, but to flirt as well. As soon he was out, a van pulled up and snatched him away. It was Taj and Indie, and when he saw Indie, he damn near shit his drawers.

Taj only muttered one set of words to him. "I brought you into my sister's life and I will take you out!"

Taj pimp smacked Lucky. "You stupid ass nigga. How you going to fall for the oldest trick in the book. Of all the games you play, this is the one you fall for, your favorite one, and you fell victim to it."

Taj smacked Lucky again. "You made me lose $500, I bet ya ass wouldn't fall for it."

"But I knew you would." Indie said, and when Lucky heard Indie's voice, he pissed on himself. "Nigga, how many lives you got? Got Damn. Nigga, your ass is a damn black cat fo real."

"Shut da fuck up, told you that this was a war nigga, and you slept thinkin it was a Peace Treaty."

They drove him down into the boondocks near where Secret lived. Secret already had a hole dug and a wooden box for Lucky. When Lucky saw the box, he begged, "please man whatever ya'll do, please don't put me in that box. I know ya'll gonna kill me just shoot me."

"Naw, mafucka you gone suffer, just like you made my sister suffer, putting her through all that unnecessary bullshit all them years." Taj said, as he spit on Lucky.

"Man, just not this way, please!" They could see the fright all over Lucky's face.

"I know Big Ole Lucky ain't scared."

Lucky was so terrified, screaming like a little girl, of being thrown into the box, he pissed on himself. Taj and Indie looked on without any remorse as Secret took care of everything, including dropping a big fat rat down in the box with Lucky. Lucky was already claustrophobic, and the fact that a rat was in the box with him, made it even worse. He struggled and tried to kill the rat with his naked hands but it was almost impossible, for it being so dark and so limited amount of space in the box.

On the way back to Richmond, the ride was mostly silent until Indie spoke out to Taj. "Look man, I never had ill feelings about putting anybody away, but this is different. I never loved a woman as much as I love Tressa and I don't want one thing to hurt her."

"Fuck that nigga, he done enough fucked up shit." Taj said with no emotion.

"Look, I ain't worried about that cat. I just don't want to hurt your sister in any kind of way. This just ain't any nigga, she bore children for him. I'm not worried about the boys, cause they are mine anyway, but if taking his life is gonna hurt her..."

Taj cut him off. "Look, my sister is thorough and we going to let her decide. It's as simple as that. As much as she loved Lucky, if she saves him, then we know she still got feelings. If she leaves him where he is, then I'll accept you as my brother-in-law."

Once they arrived back to Tressa's house, she was up, but feeling groggy. They began explaining to Tressa the situation. They told her that Lucky had about eight hours to live and the ball was in her court. Taj called Lucky, evidently Taj had placed an untraceable blow out cell to only receive incoming calls phone in the box with Lucky. He gave the phone to Tressa.

This was the moment of truth, this was the way Indie would find out how deep her love really went for Lucky.

"Looks like you got your self boxed in." Tressa said coldly to Lucky.

Taj and Indie looked at each other, stunned at how bitter Tressa was towards Lucky.

"Look, I need you to look out for me."

"I told you, you were going to need me one day when you were all boxed in huh?" She said, eating a Snicker's candy bar.

Taj and Indie couldn't believe how much Tressa really didn't have an ounce of emotion for Lucky and how she was making jokes.

"Yeah, you did. And you were right, I do need you right now to come through for me." He said as humble as he knew how.

"I know you don't need me, not broke ass Tressa!"

Lucky nervously laughed with her as she had her moment, talking all the junk that she had desired to spit at him so long. "OOOOUCCHH, shit, the damn rat just bit me. I thought I had killed the damn rat!"

255

"You always said you'd go out fighting, well don't forget to throw an uppercut and a straight right for me. This time next year, you'll be a one-year-old ghost. Don't worry; I'll pour a little bit of beer out for you." Tressa was making jokes big time!

"You know I am going crazy locked in this box, I can't take it.

"Oh, they forgot to give you a window huh? Shame on them!" She said in a whining voice.

"Damn Tressa, how could you be so cold?"

"Because you made me this way! Had you shown an iota of compassion towards me when I was living in the projects, having to walk past crackheads and drunks, ducking and dodging bullets all day long, barely making enough money to feed YOUR kids, maybe I would be compelled to take pity on your sorry ass!"

"What you gonna tell my sons?"

"You don't have any sons. Damn, your ass wasn't no good to them when you were alive, shoot, you better off dead to them anyway."

"Always remember I made you, you were nothing without me. You was my project, I molded you."

"The worms should be arriving shortly too, I hope the worms eat all the evil out of you and crawl up in your ass."

"You mean like I used to be in your ass?" Lucky knew there was no hope at all now, so he just felt the need to hurt Tressa's feelings. "Oh, that nigga got you brainwashed huh? Do you be sucking his dick like you used suck mine?"

"Better than you could ever know. So there's no need to be jealous."

"Tressa, all jokes aside, please give me one more chance. I am going crazy in this box."

"Scram! NIGGA get out the best way you can." She screamed, and then hung up the phone in his face.

Lucky in his last hours reflected on every horrific act he'd done. He began crying asking God to get him out of this jam, but he never asked God for forgiveness not one time.

The last breaths Lucky took, he was laughing because he couldn't believe how he slept on Tressa for so many years. This time the joke was really on him. He might as well die laughing than crying, because he realized that he had burnt the bridge down concerning Tressa and she was the one who won the game that he felt he had invented. She was the one who got the life insurance policy, the one who had his balls in her hand. She had the power, she could give life or she can give death. At the end of the day, there was only one saying that kept playing in his head that Tressa said to him years ago, **"When the dust settles, Tressa gonna to be the last one standing!"**

And she was!

Afterthought

Tressa begin having second thoughts and started feeling guilty about letting Lucky die. In spite of everything Lucky had done to her to make her life a living hell, she still wasn't God, she had no right to take Lucky's life.

The phone rung and it was Betty, apologizing to Tressa about scaring her. She was shocked when the police showed up at her door to get the boys. She had no idea that Tressa was in such a panic over the boys being missing. Lucky had told me, "you were strung out on drugs and didn't want the boys anymore and they were coming to live with me, so I can get a second chance to be a mother."

Tressa was pissed off at this story, but it was the confirmation she did the right thing by leaving Lucky in the box.

ORDER FORM

Triple Crown Publications
4449 Easton Way, 2nd Floor
Columbus, Ohio 43219

Name: _____

Address: _____

City/State: _____

Zip: _____

TITLES	PRICES
Dime Piece	$15.00
Gangsta	$15.00
Let That Be The Reason	$15.00
A Hustler's Wife	$15.00
The Game	$15.00
Black	$15.00
Dollar Bill	$15.00
A Project Chick	$15.00
Road Dawgz	$15.00
Blinded	$15.00
Diva	$15.00
Sheisty	$15.00
Grimey	$15.00
Me & My Boyfriend	$15.00
Larceny	$15.00
Rage Times Fury	$15.00
A Hood Legend	$15.00
Flipside of The Game	$15.00
Menage's Way	$15.00

SHIPPING/HANDLING (Via U.S. Media Mail)   **$3.95**

TOTAL $_____

FORMS OF ACCEPTED PAYMENTS:
Postage Stamps, Institutional Checks & Money Orders, all mail in orders take 5-7
Business days to be delivered.

ORDER FORM

Triple Crown Publications
4449 Easton Way, 2nd Floor
Columbus, Ohio 43219

Name: _____

Address: _____

City/State: _____

Zip: _____

	TITLES	PRICES
	Still Sheisty	$15.00
	Chyna Black	$15.00
	Game Over	$15.00
	Cash Money	$15.00
	Crack Head	$15.00
	For The Strength of You	$15.00
	Down Chick	$15.00
	Dirty South	$15.00
	Cream	$15.00
	Hoodwinked	$15.00
	Bitch	$15.00
	Stacy	$15.00
	Life	$15.00
	Keisha	$15.00
	Mina's Joint	$15.00
	How To Succeed in The Publishing Game	$20.00
	Love & Loyalty	$15.00
	Whore	$15.00
	A Hustler's Son	$15.00

SHIPPING/HANDLING (Via U.S. Media Mail)   **$3.95**

TOTAL $_____

FORMS OF ACCEPTED PAYMENTS:

Postage Stamps, Institutional Checks & Money Orders, all mail in orders take 5-7 Business days to be delivered.

ORDER FORM

Triple Crown Publications
4449 Easton Way, 2nd Floor
Columbus, Ohio 43219

Name: _____

Address: _____

City/State: _____

Zip: _____

		TITLES	PRICES
		Chances	$15.00
		Contagious	$15.00
		Circumstances	$15.00
		Black and Ugly	$15.00

SHIPPING/HANDLING (Via U.S. Media Mail)   **$3.95**

TOTAL $_____

FORMS OF ACCEPTED PAYMENTS:
Postage Stamps, Institutional Checks & Money Orders, all mail in orders take 5-7
Business days to be delivered.